I0764359

The Angel Chronicles ... The Road to Damascus

By J.K. Johnson

Edited by Ina Hillebrandt

The Angel Chronicles ... The Road to Damascus
By J.K. Johnson

Edited by: Ina Hillebrandt
Cover by: Carolyn Allen, www.SunshineByDesign.com
Interior book design by: Ina Hillebrandt
Sword graphic by Carolyn Allen

Published by Angel Fire Publications

Printed in the United States of America.

Library of Congress Control Number: 2008935434

ISBN 978-0-9819193-0-0

For information on group sales, reprints, author appearances or other questions, please contact the publisher at:
info@www.AngelFirePublications.com

Dedication

In loving memory of my best friend and mother, Darlene. The final and greatest gift of love is letting go.

J.K. Johnson

The Angel Chronicles … The Road to Damascus

By J.K. Johnson

The Angel Chronicles...
The Road to Damascus

A cool ocean breeze gently blew the curtains as it entered Morgan Deveraux's kitchen window. The sun was just peeking over the horizon, giving the ocean a golden shimmer. Gulls sang out, diving, dipping into the water, scooping up their morning meal. Morgan's large, beautiful blue eyes stared across the rim of a coffee cup as the sunlight danced off her radiant blond hair. Her thoughts were of Laura, her lover who had been murdered two years ago to the day. She glanced at the clock; panic rose in her chest as she realized how much time had passed while she daydreamed. As she stood up and walked over to the sink, she smiled. She thought about the call she had received from her best friend James the morning before at the gallery.

"Hello, Deveraux's. How can I help you?"

"I'll tell you how," said the voice at the other end. "You can help by calling now and then to let me know you're still among the living." It was James. His attempt to sound stern was feeble at best.

"James, how goes it?" she said lightly, always glad to hear from him.

"Huh!" he spat. "Besides the fact that I'm about to come and kick your little lesbian ass, everything is fabulous."

"Threaten me with a good time," Morgan bantered.

"Hey, Doll, the reason I'm calling is to invite you to have dinner with me. I'll open one of my special bottles of Merlot." James' voice was giving way to his more familiar tone.

Morgan expelled an involuntary breath. "I'm sorry James, but I don't think I can. This week is so...busy."

"Screw that!" James said, cutting short her words. "Look, Morgan, I don't know what's so special about *this* week. Week after week you've been busy, busy, busy." He gave a heavy sigh.

"Look it's the eve of Laura's anniversary, so this time I'm not taking no for an answer. See you at six-ish, OK?"

The phone line went abruptly dead. Morgan stood with the dial tone in her ear, then lowered the handset into the cradle and laughed out loud. She loved James. Walking through the gallery she began to switch off lights, closing for the day. Reaching the back of the gallery, she heard the heavy glass entry doors announce someone's arrival. "The shop is closed!" she shouted to the front of the building. No answer. Making her way back to the main showroom floor, she found a beautiful Hispanic woman standing in front of her latest sculpture. She was petite, with exquisite bone structure covered by dark, sensual skin. Her hair was pushed back tightly in a pony tail, which gave her the dramatic look of a classical beauty. Her clothes, a navy gabardine suit over a white blouse, were smartly tailored.

Morgan quickly ran her fingers through her blond hair, making herself presentable. "Hello," she said as she approached the woman. "Can I help you?"

The stranger looked up, not failing to notice how striking Morgan was. Electricity coursed through her body as Morgan stood beside her. After a moment, the stranger pulled her eyes away from Morgan and back to the sculpture. "What do you call this piece?" she asked, hoping her voice was steady.

Morgan noticed a light in the stranger's whiskey-colored eyes that intrigued her. "Fallen Angel," Morgan replied in a soft voice.

The two women quietly admired the statue for a moment. The sculpture was a female angel with broken wings, pulling herself from the sea, tattered feathers dragging behind her as she crawled along the sand. The angel's hair was strewn across her face. The detail into which the clay had been manipulated was magnificent; it made the stranger feel a swell of emotion. She turned to Morgan, reached in her jacket and retrieved her wallet. "My name is Detective Ryan Delgato," she said, exposing the badge inside the billfold.

Morgan wondered why a detective would be in her gallery; it made her very uneasy. “I'm Morgan Deveraux. How can I help you, Detective?”

Seeing that the badge had upset Morgan, Ryan slipped it back into her jacket. “I am investigating a recent homicide in the area, and I'd like to ask you a few questions, if I may.”

Morgan felt even more nervous and raised her eyebrows. “Homicide?”

“I'm afraid so,” Ryan replied.

Morgan walked over to her desk and began shuffling papers around. She was shocked. Nothing like this had ever happened in the art district since she had been there.

“Miss Deveraux, have you seen or heard anything suspicious in the past few days?”

Morgan sat in her large upholstered chair and crossed her leather-clad legs. “Nothing that I can think of.” She glanced up at the detective and found her scanning the desktop with her eyes. “May I ask,” Morgan said as she slid forward in her chair, “who was murdered?”

Ryan pulled her eyes from the desk and fixed them on Morgan. “Actually, it's not who was murdered, it's who's *being* murdered. There have been a number of killings in the area, and the violence seems to be directed toward the gay community.”

Morgan felt a shockwave run through her at the thought of someone stalking her neighborhood. She propped her elbows on the desk. “Are you saying that *all* the murders are here in the art district?” Morgan asked nervously.

Ryan had a thoughtful look on her face as she pulled out her notepad. “Yes, I'm afraid so. My partner and I wanted to alert the locals and have a look around.” The detective jerked her head toward the glass doors. Outside, a tall slender figure stood in the shadows.

Morgan's eyes dropped back down to her desk; she felt a sudden sadness pierce her heart. “Why would anyone kill because of someone's sexual preference?” She knew the question was rhetorical, but she felt the need to ask it out loud.

Ryan scribbled on the notepad. “I don't think its sexual preference, as much as it is that gay men are easy targets. They get into cars often with strangers.” Ryan pulled a card from her well worn wallet and handed it to Morgan. “If you see, or hear, anything, don't hesitate to call day or night.” She gave Morgan a brief smile, walked to the doors and stopped just short of them. “Be careful and be aware of your surroundings.” she said. “And I meant what I said about calling.” Ryan left the building.

Morgan stood for a moment and stared where the smile had been. The situation had unnerved her, and not simply because a killer might be stalking the art district. Her mind was on the detective's face. Morgan thought Ryan looked like a young Sophia Loren. She returned to closing up the gallery, and her thoughts moved to visiting James. She was looking forward to seeing him.

When she stepped outside Morgan was thankful it was still light out. After the conversation with the detective she would think twice about being alone at night. She could not help but feel a fleeting sense of insecurity as she walked up Jackson Street to her car.

Her unease did not leave her until she reached Half Moon Bay.

Half Moon Bay

When Morgan had pulled up to the curb in front of James' cottage, the front door swung open and James' face poked out. He stepped out on the porch. Black slacks and a black turtle neck sweater adorned his thin frame. He wore Birkenstocks on his feet. His bright red hair glowed as he stood smiling his infectious smile. Dimples gave his face the prepubescent look of a very young man.

Morgan got out of the car and began to walk toward the house, James went running to her and they wrapped their arms about one another in a tight embrace. He quickly pulled her into the house.

"How was the drive, Love?" He took the jacket that his friend had pulled free of.

"It was beautiful, as always," she said as she watched James throw the jacket over the arm of the sofa.

James took her by her hand. "You sure are a sight for sore eyes," he said, coaxing her toward the back deck.

"You don't look too bad yourself," she told James as she walked to the edge of the deck. Leaning on the railing, Morgan looked out at the bay. She could hear James in the background talking about cocktails. "It's so great to see you and the bay again." She couldn't help but smile; it felt good to be back. She and Laura had spent a lot of time here with James.

As soon as she had got the words past her lips, James came with two gin and tonics. He stood beside her grinning. "So, Cupcake, what's new in the big city? It's been forever since I've seen you." His eyes narrowed, trying to tell her that he was not happy about the distance between them. "In fact," he continued, "I thought the earth had swallowed you up." He handed her a cocktail with one eyebrow raised.

In reality, they both were partially at fault. Morgan had turned down numerous invitations to dinners, shows and parties. Feeling a little guilty, Morgan took a long, slow drink. She licked her bottom lip, trying to look as though she were thinking. "I guess I just got wrapped up in the Angel sculptures and didn't realize how long it had been." She smiled at him sheepishly. "Ever since Laura died...I..." Morgan's expression grew tight; she looked into her glass.

James knew she was still having trouble dealing with the death of Laura, and, always sympathetic, put his hand on hers, not saying a word. They finished their drinks in silence. Then Morgan leaned over and kissed James' cheek.

San Francisco Police Department

After leaving Morgan Deveraux's gallery, Detective Delgato returned to the precinct. She sat with her head in her hands. A lack of sleep and countless hours of sorting through reports made her head pound. She tried to recall the last time she had eaten or opened her own apartment door. Her office was small, the air stale with the smell of cigarette smoke. Every inch of space was filled with stacks of files.

She leaned back in her chair, throwing her legs up on the desk. She fixed her eyes on the evidence board. *What's your next move you sick son of a bitch?* Lighting a cigarette, she took a long pull and contemplated the situation. As she exhaled Detective Delani burst through the door.

"A 911 call Delgato. Came from the art district. It sounds like your perp."

Suddenly energized, Ryan sprang from her chair. “Who called it in?” she asked as she grabbed her jacket from the back of her seat.

“Some broad.” he said. “From what I could gather, she knew the victim. She's pretty hysterical. I guess she found the body.”

Detective Delgato pushed past Delani, leaving him with the sounds of her footsteps.

When Ryan arrived on the scene, two squad cars were there. A uniformed officer approached her as she got out of her car. “Detective Delgato?” the young rookie asked.

Ryan nodded and closed the door. “What have we got here, Officer?” The rookie looked down at his notepad nervously and then back to Ryan. “There is a dead male on the third floor,” he said, pointing. “There is also a very upset woman who found him in his apartment. Two officers are up there with her.”

Ryan walked up the stairs. As she grew nearer, she could see the door to the apartment was open. Inside, sitting on a sofa, was the woman the rookie had told her about. Beside her crouched an officer. Ducking under the yellow crime tape, Ryan entered the room. She flipped open her wallet, exposing her badge. “Detective Delgato, San Francisco Police Department, ma'am. I understand you found the body?”

The woman looked up at Ryan and shook her head. “Why would anyone want to kill Jimmy?” Her eyes were bloodshot, mascara running down her face from crying.

Ryan could see the woman was distraught with grief; she tried to speak gently. “What's your name, ma'am?”

“Eleanor Himes.” she said

“Ok, Mrs. Himes, I need you to answer a few questions, but right now you need to relax. Do you think you can do that for me?” The woman nodded.

Ryan made eye contact with the officer crouched next to Eleanor. He said, “Don't worry, Detective, I'll take good care of her.”

Ryan swept the room with her eyes, as she slowly walked around the apartment trying to assess the situation. She saw what appeared to be the master bedroom. A second policeman stood guard at the doorway. She looked at him inquisitively. "Anyone touch anything?"

"No ma'am, you're the first one on the scene...besides us."

When Ryan entered the room, she noticed it smelled sweet, sickeningly sweet. She pulled out a handkerchief and covered her nose and mouth. She looked at the back sliding glass door; there did not seem to be any forced entry. As she neared the bed, she recoiled at the sight. *Keep calm, professional detachment. Caucasian male approximately 5'-11" tall, arms and legs bound, apparent strangulation. Human bite marks, eyes...missing.*

She pulled a pen from her jacket pocket, being sure to keep the cloth against her mouth. Ryan examined the leather strap around the victim's neck with the tip of the pen. She turned away from the bed and walked out of the room. *Violence escalating.*

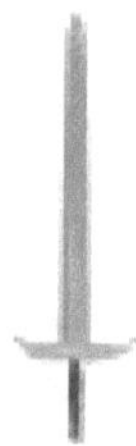

Half Moon Bay

James' kitchen had an open and airy feel to it, with its cathedral ceilings and large picture windows. In the center of the room sat a cook-top island; above it hung stainless steel pots and pans. Expansive counters flanked both sides of the kitchen. To the left of the island, the counter was accessible from both the living room and kitchen. This enabled James to entertain while he prepared his dinners. James was dubbed "The Cuisinart Queen" by many of his friends. He was a Food Network junkie, having ordered Emeril's pots and pans (hanging above the island), Paula Dean's mixer, Rachael Ray's knives and every appliance known to man (or woman).

In the living room several bar stools lined the pass-through, and Morgan's boot rested on one of the rungs, her elbow leaning on the counter as she watched James move busily about the kitchen. He raised his glass and asked with his eyes. Her smile answered. He mixed two more drinks, wiped his hands on his apron and slid his friend her cocktail.

Morgan looked in the glass and sighed. "I still miss her, I see Laura everywhere and in every thing." Lines formed across her forehead. "When she died, a part of me died with her, almost as if a piece of my soul was torn from me." There was a tremor in her voice. "I feel so alone sometimes...lost like I can't find my way home, no matter how I try...I..." She gave up trying to speak, her jaw tightened, she felt pain clawing up her chest. A lone tear ran down her cheek.

James was touched by her words. His eyes welled with emotion; he hated to see his buddy hurting. He reached over and took her hands in his.

"Morgan, I know how much you loved Laura, and still do, but sweetheart, you can't keep grieving for her. It's holding her spirit back." He gave her hands a squeeze. "She needs to move on and do what she's meant to do, but she can't until you let go. This is the final act of love that you can give to her." James gently cupped her face in his hands and looked her in the eyes. "To wake to the truth too late is a terrible thing," he whispered.

Morgan's expression made it clear that she had heard her friend's words.

* * *

San Francisco

While Morgan and James spoke in Half Moon Bay, Detective Delgato was securing the crime scene. She had taken the witness statement, Forensics had been called and the Coroner was en route, every conceivable agency either on the scene or on the way.

Ryan sat quietly in her car with equal measures of disgust and disbelief.

She was in need of sustenance and sleep, and her mind had begun to betray her. Her mind returned to the crime scene. How much further will the killer go next time? Clearly, the crimes were getting much more brutal. Overwhelming doubts had surfaced, causing her to question her ability to catch the murderer. Trying to maintain an objective outlook on the way home was difficult.

* * *

Half Moon Bay

Morgan and James had cleared the dinner dishes. They sat in the living room enjoying a vintage bottle of wine James had discovered on one of his many trips abroad. "This Merlot brings back such memories," he said, holding up the glass and swirling its contents. "I picked it up in a charming little village in southern Italy when Stan and I were still together." He set the glass down and looked at Morgan. "Why I stayed with him so long I'll never know. He was a complete asshole."

Morgan laughed at the comment. "I believe," she said, "that you stayed because you loved the sex."

James gave a silly grin. "I guess you're right. Hell, at one time I thought he was all that and a bag of chips. What doesn't kill you makes you stronger."

They swapped smiles. Morgan sat back on the couch and crossed her legs. A stillness lingered between them. She cleared her throat. "Thank you for dinner, James. It's been lovely." She took a sip of wine. "By the way I forgot to tell you what happened today." James sat forward in his seat. "Today when I was closing the gallery, someone came in...a woman. Actually, a female detective."

James raised his eyebrows. "A detective?"

Morgan's expression suddenly changed. "Yes, she was investigating a murder in the District."

"Murder?" James stood up, fear sweeping across his face.

"I couldn't believe it either," Morgan said. Her finger played with the rim of the wine glass.

James walked over and sat next to her. "Go on, tell me what happened," he said in a sharp breath.

She poured a bit more wine into their glasses. "I was in the back, shutting off lights, when I heard the entry doors open. I shouted that the gallery was closed, but there was no answer, so I went to the main showroom." Morgan handed James his glass. "Standing in front of the Fallen Angel sculpture was this woman." She took a drink. "I went over to introduce myself and out came the badge. It was the last thing I expected. She told me that there had been several murders in the area, targeted against the gay community, all men."

Morgan stole a look at James. He was peering inside his wine glass. He raised his eyebrows again. "My God, Morgan! A serial killer...is that what you're telling me?" His words came out almost strangled.

Morgan rested her elbows on her knees and looked at James. "This sort of thing happens all the time, but usually we aren't involved. We don't think that it can happen to us, or our neighborhood. At first I was freaked, but I'm not going to let some sicko affect my life. I have to leave it to the cops to get him." Morgan gave a thin smile. James gave a look that made his feelings obvious...*Bullshit.*

Silence took over the conversation. Morgan knew that James would worry himself to death over this, so she decided to lighten the situation.

"Ryan Delgato," she said.

"Huh?" James' look asked.

"The detective's name was Ryan Delgato. She was really quite beaut..." Morgan slapped her hand over her mouth, but it was too late. The can of worms was open. Of all the things she could have said to lighten the conversation...why that?

Her head dropped between her shrugged shoulders.

Please, oh please...don't say anything.

"You say that she was...b-e-a-u-t-i-f-u-l? Hmmm?" James was smirking at her. She tried to ignore his comment, especially the spelling part.

"What I meant was that she had great bone structure, high cheek bones and wonderful jaw line...that's all." She was trying to backpedal as fast as she could, but it wasn't working.

"Ah, I'm sure that your observation was strictly on a professional level," James snorted. "Hey, maybe she'll come sit for you so that you can sculpt her." James was laughing.

Morgan rolled her eyes at him. “I'm sure that Ryan doesn't have that kind of time. I mean Detective Delgato...”

James raised his hand to her. “Oh, Puh-leese, girlfriend!” He stood and put his hand on his hip, looking very flamboyant. Morgan laughed at the way his hip was thrown sideways, one hand resting on it and the other limp in front of him.

After the teasing had died down, James sat next to Morgan. He smiled coyly. “You're attracted to her, aren't you?”

Morgan sat back into the couch and crossed her legs Indian style.

“I really haven't given it much thought.” *Liar,* her mind said.

“Uh-huh,” James parried, tongue in cheek. He was not going to let this go. “Hey Doll,” he said, “even if you are, it doesn't mean that it has to be sexual.” He patted her leg. “So...are you attracted to her?” he asked again.

Morgan blushed, heat beginning to crawl up her face. “Define attracted,” she bantered.

“I knew it!” he chimed. “I think it's fabulous!” James had been so worried about Morgan and her grieving for Laura. He wondered if the conversation that they had this evening was about guilt Morgan might feel over being attracted to another woman. James knew how much in love Laura and Morgan had been. He had introduced them to one another, at his cottage.

Laura was gorgeous — tall and slender with lots of beautiful copper-colored hair strewn about wildly, sometimes covering her piercing green eyes. She had a kind and gentle face and a smile that lit up a room. He remembered that Laura would tell Morgan *that their kind of love only came once in a lifetime.* They were soul mates and would be bound through time. Morgan was about to find out that not even death could break their bond.

Ryan Delgato's Apartment

Ryan fumbled for the alarm clock on the bedside table to see what time it was. Her night had been spent running from a phantom killer who had been chasing her through her dreams. Exhausted, she finally succumbed to the frustration and the restlessness, deciding she could no longer battle the night.

Sitting at the edge of her bed, Ryan lit a cigarette. As she watched the smoke play with the light spilling in from the hallway, her mind went over the report she had taken from Eleanor Himes. Eleanor knew Jimmy Monroe for over a year, and was aware that he worked at The Wild Side Club (a sex bar) as a stage man. She had told Ryan that the night of Jimmy's murder they'd been planning to go out. Eleanor said that she came home at her usual time and began some household chores. When she was done she went to the lobby to check her mailbox. Passing Monroe's apartment, she'd heard voices. She recognized Jimmy's but the other was not familiar. Thinking nothing of it, she continued on about her day. After nightfall, she thought it odd there was no music coming from Monroe's apartment. He had always played music at night.

She finished getting dressed and went over to get her friend. She knocked on the door. No answer. As she later told Ryan, she'd thought maybe he was in the shower and went back to her own place. An hour later she decided to call Jimmy on the phone, but again received no answer. She went back to his apartment and knocked. Again, without getting any response. Then she remembered the spare key. She slid her fingertips along the trim above the door until she located it. Eleanor opened the door, calling several times before entering. She stood for a moment and listened to the silence. She told Ryan the apartment was eerie, sending shivers down her spine. She forced herself to enter the living room and began to search the rooms one by one. Finally she came to the door of the master bedroom. Horrified when she found Jimmy staring at the ceiling with two empty eye sockets, filled only with pooled blood. His lifeless body ignored her as she stood in a frozen fog of cold hard emptiness. Slowly the layers of shock peeled away, and were replaced by a rising, deep-seated fear.

Ryan stubbed out her cigarette in the ashtray. There was little to go on, but Eleanor said something that hit home, *the quiet.* Ryan had felt it on every crime scene. It made her skin crawl; not only could she hear it, she felt it. The quiet seemed to be filled with expectation. It made her nervous, as if the energy were waiting to take some monstrous form. Two words ran through her head as she sat on the bed...*Impending doom.*

Present Day San Francisco

Dark: The absence of light.
Angel: An immortal being attendant upon God.

Damascus stood before a full length mirror, his brilliant venomous smile reflecting pure admiration of the new reflection he saw. A 6'2" structure was crowned by a mane of long ebony hair, luxuriously framing an olive-toned face. Dark hypnotic eyes contemplated the muscular body and beautiful pianist's hands. Damascus' persona exuded charisma, yet around him an aura of malevolence loomed. To his right against the wall sat a vanity table with a wide array of handsome brushes, combs and mirrors. He chose one of the ornate brushes and slowly groomed the hair back from his chiseled face, binding it back in a single ponytail that fell between his shoulder blades. Satisfied, he turned away and walked to the bed, picking up a black silk robe. Slipping into it, he drew a long deep breath and closed his eyes. He knew that once again his nemesis drew near; he could always sense it. Like flames of a fire, tendrils licked at him deep within.

"This time," he said, "it will be different. I am stronger, more aware of who and what I am." He turned once again to the mirror and smiled, his lips contorting into a bizarre grimace.

Morgan Deveraux's Kitchen

Morgan snapped back to the present and rinsed her coffee cup, setting it on the drain board. After the conversation with James the night before, she wondered if she could finally let Laura go. Could grieving for her have caused repercussions that she didn't understand? It was weighing heavily on her mind. She and James had discussed how perhaps the pain she felt over the loss of physical contact with Laura was clouding her ability to comprehend the damage she could be doing to Laura's soul. If she could stand outside herself, she would see that Laura deserved to move on.

Morgan left the house, locking the door behind her. She was anxious to get to the gallery. The downstairs had just been remodeled, which gave her room for her clay studio and all her kilns. She had dreamed of this day for years, her favorite part of the studio was the huge butcher block workbench that ran the entire length of the space. She was looking forward to the free-standing work area near the kilns; it would be warm on those frigid San Francisco nights.

As she drove her Jag into the city, she thought about the sculpture she'd been working on. It came to her in a dream. Many of her sculptures came to her in that way, but this one was different. It came over and over again, almost as a nightly ritual. She was frustrated by it because there were no lucid features that she could see. It was as if it were purposely tormenting her. Morgan slowed the car as she passed The Wild Side Club, where a crowd had gathered outside the building. She thought this odd, for she knew the club was geared for a strictly nighttime clientele.

What are all these people doing outside the club at this hour? She wondered. Suddenly she saw Ryan Delgato standing on the sidewalk talking to people, a couple of uniformed officers beside her. She quickly pulled the Jag over to the side of the road. She rummaged around in her briefcase to locate the card the detective had given her the night before. Finding it, she dialed the number.

"Delgato."

As she watched Ryan answer the phone, she felt strangely like a voyeur. "Detective?" Morgan asked.

"Yes, this is Detective Delgato. How can I help you?"

"This is Morgan Deveraux. We met last night at my gallery..."

Ryan stepped away from the crowd. "Yes Miss Deveraux, what can I do for you?"

"Please call me Morgan. Listen, I was going to work and saw the people outside the club. Has there...been..."

Ryan interrupted her. "No, nothing like that. I have all the employees out here to take statements. We were having some problems getting them organized inside, so we decided to take statements here on the sidewalk."

Morgan watched as Ryan pointed to one of the officers to stop an employee that was trying to leave.

"Thank you, Detective, I appreciate you telling me. I should let you go, I'm sure you are very busy." Morgan saw that Ryan had her hands full trying to keep everyone together. She hadn't realized how many people worked at the club.

"Wait, Miss Deveraux...I mean Morgan." The detective shuffled her feet.

Morgan watched, smiling.

Ryan cleared her throat. “Maybe we could go out for coffee?”

“When?” Morgan asked.

“When I'm done here. Maybe a couple of hours?”

“I should be able to break away for awhile,” Morgan said.

“Great, how about Starbucks around the corner from your gallery?” Ryan felt funny in her stomach.

“Sounds good.” Morgan replied. “See you then.”

Ryan slipped her cell phone back into the case she wore on her hip. Morgan continued to watch her for a few minutes more. She had met many women over the past two years. Why was she attracted to this woman? Why now?

Starbucks Coffee House

The two women sat at a corner table. Morgan listened to Ryan talk about the case in more detail. She was taken aback by how genuinely concerned this detective was for each victim. She had heard how officers had hardened with time. This was not the case with Ryan Delgato. “How did you get involved in police work, Ryan?” Morgan sipped her coffee, waiting for the answer.

“My grandfather was an officer and my dad followed his footsteps. It seemed natural for me to do the same.” Ryan looked at the table, then looked up and continued her story. “When I was first accepted into the academy there was a lot of animosity. With time I earned the respect of some of the guys, but I don't know which is worse, their treating me like crap or their being overprotective.” She picked up her cup and looked at Morgan and then changed the subject. She had always felt uncomfortable talking about herself. “It must be rewarding, being an artist,” Ryan said.

“I can't imagine doing anything else with my life. My mom use to tease me saying I came out of the womb sculpting,” Morgan replied.

Ryan laughed. “Morgan, do you have a significant other?”

“No,” she said, her expression changed.

“I'm sorry, Morgan, you don't have to answer. It's the cop in me that makes me ask personal questions.” Ryan felt bad. She knew that she had crossed a line.

“You don't have to apologize. It's a normal question people ask,” Morgan said, holding her cup with both hands. “There was someone in my life, but she died two years ago.”

“Jesus, I'm so sorry.” Ryan said, suddenly feeling worse. Morgan felt an unwelcome sadness settle inside her. She looked around the coffee shop, then back to her coffee.

“My lover's name was Laura Saubert. She worked at the San Francisco Chronicle,” Morgan's world seemed to shrink to the size of the cup she stared into.

“*The* Laura Saubert?”

Morgan lifted her eyes from the cup. “You've heard of her?” Morgan asked with surprise.

“Who hasn't? She wrote some incredible articles.” Ryan fiddled with the napkin on the table. “I remember there was controversy surrounding her death.” Looking at Morgan to see if it was safe to continue, she decided it was. “My father was still Chief of Police when she died.”

Morgan listened, holding back tears. “She didn't die...she was *murdered*,” Morgan said with a tremor in her voice.

Ryan shot a look at her. “Do you really believe that?” she asked, sitting forward in her chair.

“No doubt in my mind. She was working on a story, and I had asked her to tell me about it. When Laura said that it was too dangerous, I pleaded with her not to continue with it, but she felt she had a duty to the city to expose the people involved.” Morgan gave a heavy sigh, drumming the side of her coffee cup with her fingers. “Laura hadn't been feeling well, we had a makeshift office in the bedroom and she, as sick as she was, kept working on that damn story." Morgan shook her head. "I tried to get her to eat, nothing would stay in. Finally I put my foot down and took her to the hospital. She protested, saying it was probably just the flu."

Ryan lit a cigarette, listening sympathetically.

"I was in the waiting room for hours, I kept asking the nurses how she was, and they said the doctor would let me know. I tried to get through the emergency doors and a couple of big orderlies stopped me." Anger consumed Morgan's face.

"They stopped you physically?"

Morgan nodded. "I started raising some hell and finally the doctor showed up. He told me that Laura had died. She'd been poisoned." Morgan's head dropped to her chest.

"My God, Morgan, how awful."

" I don't remember how long I sat at the hospital with her body," Morgan said, "but by the time I got home, the house had been ransacked...the briefcase, tape recorder, and all her papers were gone."

"Did you call the police?" Ryan asked, stubbing out her cigarette.

"Of course, but they were not much help. Understaffed, overworked. They did do an autopsy and found that she had strychnine in her system."

Ryan felt a stab of guilt; she knew all to well the case loads. "I'm sorry, Morgan." Ryan felt the silence weighing in on them. There was nothing she could do or say to bring Laura back. Her destiny was beginning to unfold. She was going to solve the murder of Laura Saubert, but as right as it felt, a small trickle of excitement was slowly turning into a sinking feeling. Detective Ryan Delgato was about to embark on a clandestine journey.

The Outskirts of San Francisco

Ed and Marion Delgato sat with their coffee reading the morning paper on their newly constructed deck. It had taken six weeks for the retired Police Chief to build with the help of some of his friends from the precinct. Ed snapped the paper in half, folded it and began to read an article. It was about the murders in the District. “I'm worried about our little girl, Marion.”

She looked over the top of her paper. “She's not little anymore, Ed.”

Ed tossed the article down in front of him and pushed away from the table. He shoved his muscular hands in the pockets of his robe and walked along the railing of the deck. He watched the mist slip through the trees that crowded up to the shoreline. Distant fog horns from the lighthouse drifted on the air. He took a long, deep breath and looked over the bay.

Marion went to her husband, gently took his elbow and laid her head on his broad shoulder. “She's a good officer Ed.”

“I know,” he said softly. “It's not her that I worry so much about, it's the damn press. They overstep their bounds and give information that puts the men and women in the Department in jeopardy.” Ed put his hand on Marion's. “I just don't like the idea of Ryan chasing some sick bastard around the city.” The gruffness of his voice turned to remorse. “I should've never allowed her to apply to the academy.” He looked down at the deck.

Marion pulled her hand free of his and wrapped her arms around him. “Ed, we've been through this a thousand times. She's doing what she was destined to do.” Her tone was slightly exasperated.

“Do you really think you could have stopped her from becoming an officer?” She placed her hands on Ed's chest and looked him squarely in the eye. “Ryan is what she is, and nothing is going to change that." Ed pulled his wife tightly against him. She always knew what to say to calm him. "Come and sit with me," Marion said. She pulled him back to the table and they sat back down. Marion picked up the coffee pot.

"There was another murder last night," Ed said.

Marion filled their cups. "What is it that you want to do, Ed? Do you want to help her? Protect her? This is a delicate situation; you're retired and she's a detective, and you know as well as I that you have to use discretion. Ryan has worked too hard to get where she is."

Ed picked up his cup but halfway to his lips he stopped and set it back down. "Maybe I am overprotective. Maybe I do want to help her, and I don't want to embarrass her, but I'm still her damn father." This time the cup made it to his mouth.

Marion knew Ed would never be able to sit on the sidelines in retirement. It was just a matter of time before he would figure out a way to swing back in the saddle of service. She looked at Ed, his elbows on the table, his chin in his hands, a full grown little boy. As she watched him, an idea suddenly came to her that might solve the restlessness in her family. A grin crossed her face, but it took a minute for Ed to notice.

"What?" he asked. "You look like you swallowed the canary...what gives, Mare?"

"Why didn't I think of this before?" she asked out loud. "It makes perfect sense." Her voice resonated with excitement.

"What makes perfect sense?" There was less patience in Ed's tone this time.

Marion grinned. "Hold on to your boxers, Ed."

"Dammit, Marion, will you tell me what makes perfect sense?"

Laughing at the sight of him squirming in his chair, she leaned across the table. "Why don't you ask Ryan to go into private investigating with you? You can open your own firm and make her a partner." She sat back in her chair and smiled. She knew it was a great idea.

Ed looked dumbfounded. Mouth agape, he stared at his wife in silence.

"Well, what do you think?" she asked.

"What do I think? I think you're a freaking genius!"

Ed bolted from his chair, grabbed his wife by the shoulders and kissed her forehead. "That's a terrific idea, Mare. You're the best!"

The back of Ed's robe was all Marion saw as she reached up to feel the moisture where he had kissed her.

Somewhere on the Bay

Tucked along the waterfront stood a stately bi-level villa with majestic, sprawling green lawns that ended at the edge of the bay. Beautifully manicured Chinese oak sequoia groves led to a private dock. Gently rocking, nestled against the slip, was a lavish thirty-foot cabin cruiser named "The Brotherhood." From the pier, a stone footpath ribboned its way back through a fragrant rose garden, up over the greens to the grand entryway of the house. Several stone columns supported the second story balcony that extended off the master bedroom. Past the colonnade on the lower floor, two mammoth hand carved oak doors opened into the marble foyer. A handsome spiral staircase snaked its way to the second story, which was totally devoted to the master suite. The room was filled with art and grand antiques from all corners of the world. In the center of the room was a bed where Damascus lay, putting himself in a deep trance. He was about to travel to the other realm, *his realm*...Limboshia. His blood was hammering through his veins. A feeling of vertigo overtook him. He focused harder on his target. The faint sound of a voice was becoming clearer now.

"Damascus! Damascus!" it said. He opened his eyes to find his young companion leaning over him.

"Calm down, Cameron. I am here," he said sternly. He slowly sat up, swinging his legs off the edge of the bed. "Why must you get so excited?" he asked the young boy. "I told you that I would return from Earth in a few days, did I not?"

Cameron shuffled his feet and looked pleadingly at the large man.

"I hate when you leave. Why can't I go with you?"

Damascus cut through the boy's words. "How many times must we speak of this? Why can't you get it through that thick skull of yours that you cannot travel until you are older?"

Cameron hung his thick yellow head of hair and groaned. His bright blue eyes had become narrow slits on his tanned face. He was only fourteen when he arrived and was having a hard time understanding matters of this nature. On Earth, boys his age were dealing with the latest trendy clothes and girls. Damascus could see that the boy was hurt and angry. This did not itself bother him, but he needed Cameron and could not afford to alienate him.

"Perhaps one day you will journey with me, but until that time comes you must have patience." He stood, placed a firm hand on the boy's shoulder and gave a squeeze. Cameron looked up with many questions on his lips, but thought better of asking.

"Have you located the Saubert woman?" Damascus folded his arms across his massive chest and waited for the boy to answer. Pride washed over Cameron's face.

"Yes, I did; she lives across the mountains, in the valley of the Elders. There is always someone with her. They watch her very closely."

Damascus smiled. "As it should be. She does not know it yet, but she comes from a long lineage of Elders. She is very powerful." He reached down and ruffled the boy's hair. "You have done very well, little man. Come, let us go outside and smell the sweet air."

* * *

About Limboshia

Limboshia, on Earth, is known as Purgatory, a place where souls go to await their destiny. Coma victims also arrive to await the decision on whether they live or die. In the case of people who pass on and arrive in Limboshia, they remain until their loved ones stop mourning them. Sometimes this takes many years.

Once the grieving is over, the souls move on what is known as the Monolith, a marble building that holds all the records of past lives. Here they view their entire history from the beginning of life itself. After the viewing has taken place, their future lives are revealed to them and they must choose one. At this point the soul has full memory of all its loved ones from past lives.

In the beginning of time, souls retained this knowledge as they started a new life, but many problems arose. Most souls in their new bodies would go in search of their past loved ones, including daughters, sons, husbands and wives. This caused mayhem, and so the law was rewritten.

Now after returning to Earth, souls are spared the emotional strife that this would cause. Their minds are cleared so they may concentrate on the current life they chose.

* * *

The History of Damascus

During the Angelic Reign, when Earth was first being created, all was new, fresh, unsullied on the planet. Damascus, one of the Winged Ones bearing witness to the marvels unfolding, wanted to be Overseer. But this was not in the Higher Power's plan. Damascus, infuriated at this rebuff, tried to start a rebellion among the other Winged Ones. Thus was he cast down from the heavens.

After being thrown to Earth, as a mere mortal, Damascus used his considerable charisma to start a cult of men, who like him, shared the weakness of pride. Unlike him, his followers had another weakness – the need to have a leader so that they could follow, and not have to be original thinkers. Damascus and his men wreaked havoc across the continents, burning villages, raping women and stealing anything of value.

But at last his very lust for power damned Damascus. When he died, his loyal followers clung to his memory. They founded an organization, little more than a cult in reality, called The Brotherhood, and mourned Damascus for thousands of years. Tethered in this way to people still living on Earth, Damascus was unable to move on to another life on the planet. He became trapped in Limboshia. Bitter and angry, Damascus damned the human race and all of creation. Over the thousands of years that passed, his spirit was slowly eaten away, leaving a cold and empty void that knew nothing of hope or love. He had become one of the lost souls of Limboshia. He watched as other souls came and went and learned many powerful things about the universe. He mastered the art of Shape Shifting and, finding that comatose victims were easy prey, he would take their bodies and live on Earth. Many of them were wealthy, and he became accustomed to living well. He would visit hospitals and find out which patients were in a coma and had money. If he liked the patient's lifestyle better than the one he had, he would simply discard the old body and slip into the new one.

Damascous had become what is known in the occult world as a *Souljourn,* a feared creature in Limboshia. On Earth, however, outside the occult world, he was but a mystical being, an entity of which fairy tales were made.

Limboshia

Damascus stood with Cameron, looking over the land. This was *his* territory. He had proclaimed himself ruler of the region and would enslave souls that arrived.

Many of the Limboshian people had escaped, forming their own tribes, and it was through these small bands that they remained free from his grip.

Limboshia was a beautiful realm, much like Earth during the era when dinosaurs roamed. Huge trees covered the lands, some of them hundreds of feet tall. Boston ferns grew next to banana trees, and fruit and nut trees were abundant. Flowers as large as dinner plates sent up an aroma that could be smelled miles away. The air was special, allowing a person to see far beyond normal distance. Everything appeared different, surreal. Lakes, mountains, rivers and clouds were clean, free from garbage and pollution.

* * *

The Valley of the Elders

Across the Limboshian mountains lay the Valley of the Elders, where all the small bands of tribes joined together and lived. Well-crafted huts and buildings made of indigenous materials dotted the landscape. In the center of the village a large gathering place had been constructed; this was where any problems were brought for discussion among the villagers. A Council of seven Elders made all final decisions.

On the outskirts of the village lived Tom Landry and Marti Jackson, who were constructing a new hut. Marti was tying the last porch post with a strip of rawhide. Her face had lines of concern on it.

"I'm worried about Laura," she said. "She's hardly said a word all morning."

Tom came alongside her and shook the post she had tied to make sure it was secured. "She'll be all right," he said, wiping his brow with the back of his gloved hand. He helped Marti down from the stump she was perched on. "She's got a lot on her mind," he went on. "The Council told her that Deveraux and Delgato are in danger on Earth."

Marti stood back and admired their work as she listened. "It's hard knowing and seeing our loved ones in danger or hurting," she said. Tom nodded his head. He knew the frustration all too well. In fact, all of them had experienced it at one time or another. He had been in Limboshia for three years. His wife had let go, but his son could not, and until he did Tom would remain. He sat in the grass and leaned against the new structure.

Marti joined him, giving a slight grunt when she made contact with the ground. "Is there any way we can call on the Council and maybe warn Deveraux?" she asked.

Tom readjusted the cowboy hat he was always wearing. "All we can do is try. I know Laura would feel better." He laid his head against the hut and closed his eyes. "It's settled then," he declared. "We'll request a meeting."

Marti felt better. She closed her eyes, along with Tom, and fell asleep.

Starbucks Coffee House

Morgan and Ryan were finishing their coffee when a cell phone rang."I think it's mine," Ryan said, picking it up. "Delgato," she answered.

"Hey, Sweet Pea."

"Hey dad, what's going on?" Ryan's eyes always lit up when she talked to, or was around, her father.

"I was wondering," he said, "if you could come over to the house tonight after work. Your mother and I have called a family meeting." Ed tried not to sound excited in any way.

"A family meeting? Sure Dad, I don't have any other plans. I'll see you tonight then?"

"Great, your mother will be happy you're coming. 'Bye, Hon."

"'Bye, Dad." Morgan smiled. She had just witnessed a full grown woman turn into a little girl in a matter of seconds. Fathers seemed to do that to their daughters. They had a way of making them feel protected.

"That was my father," Ryan said, looking at Morgan.

"I figured that out," Morgan said, smiling.

Ryan looked embarrassed. "Sorry, I guess it was obvious."

"Let's just say that it didn't take a detective to figure it out." They couldn't help but laugh, and Morgan was happy to lighten the mood after their discussion.

"So, what's it like, being a detective?" Morgan asked.

"Well, let me tell you," Ryan said, playing with her pack of cigarettes.
"I am overworked, underpaid, and when I ask questions half the punks are blowing smoke up my ass."

"Hope you've got a good proctologist," Morgan quipped.

Ryan laughed at Morgan, finding her adorable and funny. "Most of my days are like walking through jello; the rest of the time I feel as insignificant as a speck on a gnat's ass." Ryan smiled sarcastically.

"And on top of that they pay you?" Morgan asked

"Try not to be jealous," Ryan replied, smiling broadly.

Morgan picked up a napkin and wiped an imaginary spot from the table. She was feeling a little nervous because it was so easy to be with Ryan.

Sensing a chemistry between them, and not wanting to rush it, Ryan thought this would be a good place to end their date together. She cleared her throat and stood up. "Morgan, I've had a great time, and I hope we can do this again sometime." Ryan straightened her jacket and was about to wipe a piece of lint, but stopped herself, thinking it was perhaps just as invisible as Morgan's spot on the table.

Morgan stood up. "I had a good time too," she said. "I'm glad we were able to meet under better circumstances." Both women smiled in agreement.

Beneath the Streets of San Francisco

Following the fires of 1906, The Brotherhood began to build a secret domain out of old twisted buildings and infrastructures that lay below the city. Over the course of many years, they constructed elaborate tunnels, rooms, and passageways up into the city. At a moment's notice they could surface anywhere on the streets of San Francisco.

* * *

In a large meeting hall in The Brotherhood's underground world, several dozen men gathered in hooded robes. The air was heavy and dank. Their voices reverberated off the concrete walls, and through the passageways, creating a frightening sound. The *Book of Shadows* lay open on the altar. Robert Pontis stood before it, alongside five other men. "The Council has been asked to tell you that another offering must be made."

The many men gathered in the room dropped to their knees and began to chant. From under his heavy hood Pontis looked at his friend standing next to him, and with a movement of his head signaled for him to meet in the hall. Robert quietly opened the door and stepped out of the room, his friend following close behind. After securing the door, Robert removed the garment from his head. His friend was William Reese. They had been friends since grade school and had served in the Viet Nam War together. During their tour overseas, they had gotten in the habit of calling one another by their last names.

"Reese, what the hell are we doing?" Pontis asked.

Reese removed his hood. His eyes were vacant, and it was clear by his expression that he didn't have an answer.

"We are lawyers, for God's sake." Pontis said.

Reese stood rubbing the back of his neck. Finally he spoke. "All I know, Pontis, is that we're up to our fucking balls in this cult shit."

"I don't remember it being like this in the beginning...how did we get talked into joining these idiots?" Pontis asked.

"What do you mean, talked into? We were threatened with our lives!" Reese slapped his hand over his mouth, looking up and down the hall to make sure no one had heard his outburst.

Pontis leveled a finger at his friend. "I told you this would come back to bite our asses."

"Bullshit, Pontis, you took the money right along with me. You could have walked away."

Pontis knew his friend spoke the truth. "Who would have known it would go this far?" Pontis sighed.

"Let's not play stupid, Pontis. We should have gone to the police at the first sign of trouble." Reese watched Pontis nervously move a rock around on the concrete floor with his shoe.

"I know," Pontis whispered. "I guess we're up the proverbial creek."

Reese put his hand on Pontis' shoulder. "Looks that way, my friend."

Pontis sent the rock ricocheting down the dark hall. "Damascus is a mother fucker. If he heard us talking like this he'd have our heads...or should I say our eyes." Reese added in a trembling voice.

"Jesus, Reese, how can you make jokes at a time like this?" Pontis hadn't meant to yell at his friend. He knew that he made jokes when he was frightened or nervous.

In the war, one of the men they had fought with on the fronts lines had gotten his hand and a part of his arm blown off. Reese had stood staring at him. When finally he had bent down beside the wounded soldier, he asked if he could give him a hand. "I'm sorry, Reese. I didn't mean to snap at you. I just don't know what to do about our situation."

Pontis put his hand over his face and moaned.

Reese paced the hall trying to figure out what their next move should be. He was sweltering in the robe they had to wear. Feeling sick, he sat down and leaned against the wall. "We made it through the war, Pontis, so we should be able to make it through this." Reese felt bile bubbling in his throat.

Pontis took his robe off and threw it on the floor. "I'm getting the hell out of here. It's getting out of hand."

Reese shot a look at his friend and swallowed hard, trying not to vomit. "*Getting* out of hand?"

The two men went suddenly silent. A strange energy seemed to descend upon them. Pontis walked over to his friend and crouched next to him. "Do you feel that?" he whispered. Reese shook his head, his eyes as large and round as saucers. They sat for a long time looking down the hall…waiting for someone or *something* to come, but nothing did.

Pontis stood up, pulling his friend with him. His voice was a shuddered whisper. "C'mon, we've got to get the fuck out of here."

Reese pulled off his robe. His clothes beneath were soaked with sweat. He let his garment fall to the floor. They began to walk slowly, the sound of their shoes echoing down the dark passageway ahead. Every so often Pontis grabbed Reese's arm, and they would stop to listen.

Afraid that Damascus would be waiting at every turn, Reese jumped at imaginary footsteps and half-shadowed figures. Like blind men, they felt their way along the tunnel walls, when finally a small beam of light shown down a few feet in front of them. As they drew nearer, a rusted ladder appeared, bolted into the concrete pipe that led up to the street.

"Where do you think we are?" Reese asked softly.

"I don't know," Pontis said, looking around for a sign or a symbol. "There's no way to tell as far as I can see." He and Reese had never used the tunnels beyond the one that led to the meeting hall. Pontis grabbed the ladder with both hands and gave it a tug. The last thing he needed was to fall on the way up. He looked at Reese. "I'm going to have a look. Maybe I can figure out where we are."

Reese's heart pounded inside his chest. He could hardly bear another minute underground.

"You O.K?" Pontis asked.

"I think so," Reese rasped, his mouth dry.

Pontis climbed the ladder, and at the top was a manhole cover. With both hands he pushed it open a crack.

"What do you see?" Reese asked anxiously.

"It looks like an alley." Pontis slid the cover aside and poked his head into the alley. It was deserted. He didn't recognize the area, but he could smell the bay, and that was enough for him. He glanced down at Reese. "Let's go," Pontis said, already standing on the street. He reached for his friend's hand and pulled him up.

"Thank God!" Reese exclaimed, brushing off his clothes with his hands.

Pontis replaced the cover and looked around.

"Any idea where we are?" He asked Reese.

"Not a clue," Reese answered as he looked down the alley. "But then, I don't spend a lot of time in alleys."

Pontis swallowed down the retort, "*How about tunnels?*" He knew his friend was still nervous. The two men started walking toward the smell of the bay.

The Delgato Family Meeting

After work Ryan drove to her parents' house, she thought about what Morgan had said.
Who was Laura investigating? Once she found that out, it would be relatively easy to find the killer. She was anxious to talk to her father and see if he remembered the Saubert case. She also was curious about the family meeting. She hoped she would have the chance to talk to her father about Laura.

Ryan was trying to pry information from her mother while they waited for Ed.

"Come on, Mom, tell me what's going on. It's not like you're betraying Dad."

Marion went to the freezer and took out trays of ice cubes. She shook her head. "You're as bad as your father!"

Ryan rolled her eyes playfully.

"He can't stand to wait, either," she said, cracking the ice into a bowl.

"What am I waiting for?" Ryan asked coyly.

"Ryan Marie Delgato, if you don't stop pestering me, I…"

"What?" Ryan said, cutting her off. "You going to send me to my room?"

Ryan and Marion starting laughing. Just then Ed walked in.

"What are my two favorite girls in the world doing?" He asked entering the kitchen.

"Dad!" Ryan ran to her father and wrapped her arms around him.

"Hey, Sweet Pea, how's my girl?" Ed asked with a twinkle in his eye.

"I'm well, but..."

"But what?" Ed asked, eyes fixed on Ryan.

Ryan pointed a finger at her mother. "I have a hostile witness over there, withholding crucial information."

Marion smiled at the leveled finger. "Ed, she's been nagging me for thirty minutes!"

"Will someone ***please*** tell me what is going on around here?" Ryan's eyes darted back and forth between her parents. Ed walked around the counter where his wife stood behind a bowl of ice and gave her a hug.

"So did you get *it* done?" Marion asked, looking up at Ed.

"Sure did," he said, pulling a card out of his shirt pocket. He handed it to Marion. "Nice job," she said, stealing a look at her daughter. Ryan reached across the counter and snatched the card.

Delgato and Delgato Private Investigators
101 S. Winston Ave., Suite 200
San Francisco, CA 94133
(415) 555-5550

Ryan read the card several times. "You and me?" she asked. She looked back at the card. "This is Grandpa's old building isn't it?" Wonderful memories washed over her. When her grandfather retired he had bought the building and opened a bar. It was a typical neighborhood gathering place, including all the officers from the precinct. Ryan would run home from school, change her clothes and make a beeline for the bar. Her grandfather would let her pick up dirty glasses and sweep the floor for extra money. All the officers loved her and would tip her nickels, sometimes quarters. She wore a cute little apron that her mother had made, which had a long pocket in the front near the hem where she'd put her tips.

"Well, what do you say?" Ed asked. His voice snapped her back to the present. Ryan walked around the counter. Ed felt nervous. His daughter had a distant look in her eyes. He didn't know that Ryan had been sweeping and clearing glasses at the old bar. He tried again. "So what do you say?"

Ryan looked at the card, then at him. "I say I love you, Partner." Ryan buried her face into his freshly laundered shirt.

The Wild Side Club

The clientele of the Wild Side Club was from the higher echelon of society. This elite group of people enjoyed perverse sexual desires, and the club catered to these fantasies. Stage men would perform the fantasy with other Stage men, or with the client. Regardless of what they wanted, they were willing to pay the price.

Security had been bolstered because of the recent murders. Violence had gripped the District and fear had become prevalent. The owner, Bill Cameron, sat alone under a light with an adding machine and a smoldering cigarette.

His nicotine-stained hands held his head as he stared at the stack of receipts from the night before. Lifting his worn face, he looked across the room with emotionless eyes. He had become a stranger to himself; guilt slowly ate at him with each passing day.

Bill pushed his fingers through a full head of gray hair. Up until the death of his son Billie, his hair had been jet black. He was haunted by the day that he had found his fourteen-year-old boy in the house. Billie was lying on his side with his knees drawn to his chest. His beautiful blond hair lay across his face, revealing two blue eyes staring through a milky fog.

Two weeks earlier, a customer had broken down the door to his house, located behind the club. He and Billie were eating popcorn and watching movies. John Malcolm was drunk and angry when he kicked the door in. He wanted the money that Bill owed him for cocaine. Bill's habit had spiraled out of control; though he'd tried to quit, he couldn't. John Malcolm was beyond reason when he broke through the door. He ordered two of his thugs to restrain Bill against the wall while he sodomized his son. Billie was unable to deal with the rape. Feeling that it was his fault, he had committed suicide.

After finding his son's body, Bill called the police. He was stunned to learn the officer in charge was none other than John Malcolm.

Bill stubbed his cigarette in the ashtray. Although it had been two and a half years, he still couldn't believe that Billie was gone. His life felt empty without him. He thought about the reporter that had left several business cards on his door after the suicide. At the time he was unable to deal with anything or anyone, let alone a reporter. Now he wondered if she could help him prove his son's rape and convict John Malcolm. He got up from the table in front of the stage and walked to the office. Bill opened the top drawer to his desk and shuffled through the business cards. Finally he found the one he was looking for. He sat in the chair and dialed the number.

"San Francisco Chronicle, how can I help you?" The voice was pleasant.

"I would like to speak with Laura Saubert, please," Bill said.

"I'm sorry sir, did you say Laura Saubert?" The voice suddenly sounded strained.

"Yes, Laura Saubert."

"I'm sorry, sir, but Laura died two years ago. I…" Bill terminated the call. He opened the file drawer and pulled out a bottle of bourbon. *Dead. How did she die?* He opened the bottle and took a long drink. *John Malcolm.*

The San Francisco Chronicle

"Hey, Sam!" Jennifer Collins' high heels chased the pink shirt that Chief Editor Sam Mansfield wore. Sam slowed his pace when he heard her call out. He continued to read the paper in his hand as Jennifer came alongside him. "Hey Jennifer, what's going on?"

She smiled at his newly shaved head. "New haircut?" she asked.

"No, just a buff and wax," he said, running his hand over the smooth surface.

"Sam, I wanted you to look at this lead story." Jennifer handed him the papers she held.

"Let's see what you've got here," Sam quickly read across the page.

"Stephane Damitree...Romanian...pianist...complained of headache...rushed to hospital...family and friends...coma..."

"Here's the strange part," Jennifer said, pointing at the paper. "The day before yesterday, the guy gets up and walks out of the hospital. His family's there, they try to talk to him, he says he doesn't know who they are and tells them to leave him alone." Jennifer looked at Sam.

"Amnesia is not uncommon when coming out of a coma," Sam said, unimpressed. He started to hand the papers back to her but she pushed them gently back.

"Wait there's more." she said. "This guy is pure Romanian, always brings an interpreter when he tours," Jennifer said, noticing Sam's growing impatience.

"When he tells his family to leave him alone, there is no accent. He speaks perfect English." Sam raised an eyebrow and looked down at the paper again. This was not the usual type of story that he ran. He thought for a moment. What could it hurt to let her pursue it. If things didn't work out she'd at least be gaining more experience. He and Jennifer where close, like father and daughter. Sam had taken her under his wing, not because she was a tall, gorgeous, leggy redhead, but because he had lost his daughter, who had been Jennifer's age. Sam looked at Jennifer. "I think maybe we should give this to Bob over at the National Enquirer.

It's starting to sound like a bad episode of the *Twilight Zone.*" He handed her the papers.

"Come on, Sam, at least let me check it out."

"I don't know..." he said, walking toward the elevators. He tried to protect her from anything dangerous. After the death of his daughter, and of Laura, he didn't want to take a chance of losing someone else close to him.

"Please Sam, give me a chance. I want to go out and report the news, but how can I if you never let me? I know you worry about me out there, but do you really think I'm happy behind a desk?" Jennifer's face was taut with frustration.

Sam rubbed the back of his neck. He knew she was right. He sighed. "All right, go check it out."

"Really?" She thought it would take days to convince him. The elevator doors opened and Sam stepped inside. "Before you write anything, I want to see a hard copy, capice?" he asked.

Jennifer nodded her head. The doors closed. Sam hoped he hadn't made a mistake.

Deveraux's Gallery

After returning from the coffee shop, Morgan went to the studio below to sculpt. She sat at her workbench for hours trying to capture the features of the phantom angel that visited her dreams. She cradled her chin in her arms on the bench top and looked at the sculpture. The warmth of the kilns lulled her to sleep. The terracotta-stained smock she wore hung loosely around her as she began to dream of Laura.

They were holding hands walking along the beach, as they had done many times before. The sand beneath their feet was cool and moist. Morgan could feel the electricity around them; it was like music. Laura stopped, pulled Morgan to her and kissed her. She could smell the clean scent of Laura's hair. Her kiss was sensual, wet and deep, and Morgan's body melted into unadulterated bliss. From the back of her mind she could hear the waves crashing rhythmically against the shore. Suddenly a scream came from further down the beach, but as soon as she turned to look, Laura had vanished.

Morgan saw a woman stretched across the sand. She started to run toward her, but as she drew near she stopped. Her heart thumped against her chest, then slowly the pounding crawled to her temples. She saw....wings. It was Laura's face. *Oh my God, the fallen angel...How can it be?* She felt her mind teeter. Fear swept through her. Shaking uncontrollably, she tried to call out to Laura, but the words died in her throat.

Morgan began to run toward the woman-angel, but her legs were heavy, and it took all the strength she could muster to make them move. The sand tugged at her, beckoning for her to give in to it. She reached out to the angel, but the sand turned into a quagmire, pulling her down, crushing her. She clawed at the ground trying to dig her way back up to the surface.

Morgan jolted awake, arms thrown out in front of her, her lungs gasping for air. Her eyes darted around the room frantically. She sat up and grabbed the workbench.

Breathe.

Eyes closed, she concentrated on breathing. She could smell the clay being fired in the kilns; could hear the traffic as it passed outside her studio window.

Just a dream.

Her heart slowed to a normal beat and she re-opened her eyes. Sitting in front of her was the phantom sculpture. She recoiled at the sight of it. It was ... finished.

The figure was crouched low to the ground, prowling. His right arm extended high above his shoulder, in his hand a torn-out heart, dripping with blood. With lips peeled back over his teeth, the clay face looked at her with hatred. Behind him, sinister bat-like wings were folded tight against his muscular body.

Define crazy, her mind said.

Limboshia

It was nightfall. Damascus and Cameron were sitting together in their spacious cabin. The large man was telling the boy a tale from one of his many journeys. Cameron was spellbound as Damascus stood acting out the story.

"The great serpent swooped down on me," Damascus said. "His giant claws coming at my face. I grabbed his foot and held on for dear life!" He pretended he was wrapped around the leg of the dragon. "The flying demon took me up into the sky. His monstrous wings swooshed past me again and again until I could no longer hold on. I lost my grip and plummeted to Earth." Cameron let out a gasp.

"Then the ugly winged snake of a beast came at me once more, soaring low to the ground, trying to snatch me up. I held my ground, steady, with sword held high. He came at me....I cut his heart out!"

"Wow!" Cameron exclaimed. His eyes were wide with excitement. "Were you a knight, like in King Arthur days?" He was sitting cross-legged, leaning back on his hands, looking up at Damascus.

"I was the most famous of the knights, and the most handsome," he said, crouching to the boy's level. "I killed many of the King's enemies." He stood tall as if in armor, flipping open as imaginary face mask. Cameron laughed with glee.

"I slew many fire-breathers that dared challenge me." He stepped out on one leg and plunged his sword victoriously. The boy sat up and started clapping as Damascus took a deep and regal bow. As he stood, a knock sounded at the door. "Who is it?" he bellowed. Cameron jumped at the thunderous volume of his voice.

Damascus walked heavy-footed to the door and jerked it open. In the doorway stood a slender, dark-haired woman. Two men were with her, one on each arm. Damascus gave her an appraising look. She was wearing a short dress fashioned from animal skins, gathered at the waist with a leather thong. She glared back at Damascus with a defiant expression. The two men that held her pushed her through the doorway and left without a word.

Damascus shut the door. "Cameron, leave me. I have business to attend to." The boy knew what that meant. He had this sort of *business* often. Cameron exited the room quickly and quietly.

"So we meet again, Starling," Damascus said, walking around her.

"Why have you kidnapped me? What do you want?" she asked, showing no fear.

Damascus' lustful eyes on her made her cringe. He reached over and put his hand on her breast.

"Don't touch me, you pathetic bastard!" she yelled, slapping his hand away.

Damascus grabbed a handful of hair, pulling her face to his. "You are here for my pleasure," he hissed. "If you do not do as I command, I will let my men have their way with you for as long as I see fit." He released her. She touched her head were he had pulled some of her hair out of her scalp. Damascus picked up a log and threw it on the fire, then walked across the room and eased himself into a large willow arm chair. Starling watched silently.

"Take off your clothing," he said sternly. She reluctantly untied the thong and let the dress fall to the floor.

Damascus smiled. He liked what he saw.

Starling had voluptuous, firm breasts with hard pink nipples. Her waist was tiny, then curved to a full hip and buttock. With his eyes he studied the delicate pubic hair between her legs. This excited him. His penis grew hard. He unbuttoned his trousers and began to rub himself. She was sickened by the sight and turned away. "Look at me, Starling," he demanded. She did as she was told.

Damascus continued to pleasure himself while she watched. His excitement escalated. He suddenly stopped, stood and walked over to the table where he and Cameron ate their meals.

"Come over here," he motioned with his hand. Starling clenched her teeth behind her lips. She knew what was about to happen.

"Lie over the table...here," he said, pulling his belt from the loops of his pants. He bound her wrists, then tied them to the table leg. "I am going to show you something that a *man* could never do." He grabbed his swollen penis and thrust it in her.

Cameron was in the dark, looking through a crack in his bedroom door. He knew what Starling was feeling. Because of John Malcolm, he, too had been through it. Unable to watch any longer, he ran to his bed and buried himself under the blankets and animal hides.

They did little to stifle Starling's screams.

Across the Limboshia Mountains

Marti, Tom and Laura were having their first meal in their new hut. The feast consisted of fresh-baked bread, coral mushrooms, wild onions and grouse. The night was special. It was Laura's second anniversary in Limboshia. It was also the first night that the three were going to spend together in the new structure as roommates. In Limboshia, if a choice is made to live together sharing a common dwelling, the existing hut would be torn down and a new one erected in its place. New materials and old would be utilized. Marti and Tom were already living together, so they tore down their old hut and built a new one for the three of them.

Laura gazed across the table at her friends. She was grateful to have a family in Limboshia. It had made her time there much easier.

"Today is an emotional day for you, Laura?" Marti asked.

"Not as hard as last year," Laura replied. "This place is so beautiful in most respects. But I don't understand how an entity like Damascus can be here, in a place so picturesque and spiritual." Laura finished her last bite of grouse, wiped her mouth, tossed the napkin on the plate.

"I know it's hard to understand," Marti said, clearing the table. "You have to remember that Limboshia is like a waiting room, all types of souls are here — good, bad and in-between. This is not Heaven," she laughed, "it's far from it." She took the plates to the kitchen and set them in the sink. Laura looked at Marti, giving her words thoughtful consideration.

"Tom, can you bring the pot of water from the fire, please?" Marti asked.

Tom pulled on his gloves. "I'll tell you one thing, Laura," he said walking over to the fireplace. "You're sure handling your second anniversary better than I did."

"That's because you're not as *old* as Laura." Marti teased.

"Hey! What do you mean, old?" Laura asked smiling, one eyebrow raised.

Tom grabbed the pot off its hook with a grunt. Laura watched him while she waited for Marti to back-peddle.

"What I meant to say was, his soul isn't as old as yours," Marti said. She stole a quick look at Laura, saw the brow was still arched.

"So how old do you think I am?" Laura inquired.

Marti watched Tom pour the steaming water into the sink and playfully pushed his cowboy hat over his eyes when he was done. She smiled at Laura. "You're really, really old!" Marti snorted. Tom, having cleared up his sight by putting his hat on straight, now threw a gloved hand over his mouth to hide his amusement.

"So this is how you treat your new roommate, huh?" Laura bantered.

"Wait until you see the chore list for tomorrow." Tom tossed back at her.

After Marti finished the dinner dishes, she wiped her hands on the kitchen towel. "Tom," she said, "Will you bring the you-know-what from you-know-where?" He sprang up from the table and quickly went into Marti's bedroom. A few minutes later, Tom returned with a package wrapped in brown paper. He sat it on the table.

"What's this?" Laura asked. Tom and Marti sat across from Laura. They wanted to see the look on her face when she opened their gift to her. They had spent untold hours making an outfit from animal skins. Marti designed it and Tom had hunted and skinned the animals.

Limboshia dress was primarily handcrafted skins and furs and, much like the style of Native American clothing design, each tribe had its own distinctive style and markings. Marti designed a dress with a thong that cinched at the waist. The thong was hand-beaded in bright colors; the length of the dress hit just above the knee. She also made a pair of pants that could be worn under the dress, in case Laura wanted to climb or go hunting.

"We made you a gift," said Marti, "Not only for your anniversary, but to welcome you as our roommate." Tom was squirming in his chair.

"I'd better open it," Laura said, jerking her head at Tom, "before our friend has a heart attack." She tore off the brown wrapping. She couldn't believe her eyes. It was beautiful. She held up the dress. It was the finest craftsmanship she had ever seen.

"There's more!" Tom blurted out.

Laura pulled out the pants, which were just as wonderful as the dress. She touched the matching bead work that ran down the side of each leg. "They are marvelous!" she cried out. "I have never seen anything so stunning in all my life." Her face was that of a child at Christmas. She ran to her room to try them on.

"I don't think she likes them." Marti said, tongue-in-cheek.

"I got that impression, too," Tom said, laughing.

Laura came running out, twirling around the wooden floor of the living room. Her copper hair lay abundantly over her shoulders, her eyes like two green emeralds against the buckskin. She looked like a Tribal Princess. Running to the table, she said, "Thank you both," kissed them on the cheek, gave another spin, and then sat down.

"So, you like them?" Marti laughed. Laura wiped joyful tears.

"I'll take that as a yes." Marti replied. Tom walked into the living room to tend to the fire. "Come in here-it's really cozy," he said, motioning with his hand. The living room was open and spacious, with two chairs, a love seat, several small tables, a bookshelf and many throw rugs and pillows made of hide. Tom worked with some of the men and women in a large carpentry shop located against the foothills of the Elders' village. They built things, including furnishings for all the huts and cabins. The wooden furniture had stretched skins, tied with rawhide to the frames of the chairs, making them very comfortable.

Laura and Marti followed Tom into the living room. The glow of the fireplace and candles cast shadows that danced across the walls and ceiling.

"You two did a great job building this cabin," Laura said, sitting in one of the skin chairs. She ran her hand over the smooth wooden arms.

In the building of the cabin and furniture, Laura's job was to peel all the bark from the trees that were cut. She and several other villagers formed an assembly line, and each day would chip the bark from the trees using pulling knives and crudely fashioned axes.

Across the mountains in the region of Damascus, they had many modern tools and conveniences. When a person died on Earth, whatever they were wearing, or touching (up to their physical size) came to Limboshia with them. Damascus and his men hunted souls as they arrived. He employed full time scouts, whose primary function was to patrol all the Territories. When they found a soul, they would receive twenty percent of all possessions that the soul had. Damascus had no need to be concerned with thievery; it would be obvious if a man or woman had any Earthly item not accounted for by the Talley. The Talley was a detailed list of all persons who lived in the Territories, specifying what each one had earned. Perhaps a knife, pan, pot, hammer, even guns for hunting animals. If Damascus was in need of something, he would simply make sure that the person on Earth had the item on him or her at the time of death. He had arranged parts for a distillery to arrive in Limboshia, so he could produce his own wine and hard liquor.

"It's customary," Tom said, clearing his throat, "on the second anniversary, to share the story of how you arrived here." He and Marti both looked at Laura.

"How I died?" Laura asked. She studied the shadows on the wall, not knowing where to begin. "I...didn't feel good for about a week," she began. "Morgan finally took me to the hospital...well, let me back up." She slid forward in her chair. "I was working on a story for the newspaper, and uncovered some things that I shouldn't have. Of course I was not about to ignore the facts, and a lot of people were very upset. I was threatened. If I didn't leave the story alone, *they* would make my life...not worth living." Tom filled their cups with fresh coffee as he listened.

"I became paranoid at work. Not knowing who to trust, I started taking every bit of information and paperwork home with me. One day I woke up feeling nauseous. I thought I had a touch of the flu. A week later, Morgan took me to the hospital."

Laura took a sip from her cup, then resumed her story. "I remember being in the emergency lobby. They took me to a room right away." Laura lifted a hand, then let it drop in futility. "I could hardly move. It was awful. Morgan tried to go with me when they took me to the room, but they said she had to calm down before they would allow her to. I could hear her yelling at them as they took me down the hall. Then a doctor came in, and another man. By this time I could barely keep my eyes open."

She readjusted herself in the chair. "I could hear things around me. The doctor's name was Lang. I didn't know the other man. Then a nurse came in. They were talking about me." Laura set her coffee cup on the table. She looked at Marti, then Tom. "The doctor asked if someone had gotten rid of the cup in my office. The nurse said that she thought John Malcolm had taken care of it. The doctor grew angry, saying it had better be taken care of. He was not going down for my death." Laura's voice had a desperate edge to it. "They talked about me as if I were already dead."

She shook her head, looking down at her lap. "They had people in my office poisoning my coffee every day, people that followed me, listened to my conversations." A primal anger stirred inside Laura. She felt hatred, but managed to keep it off her face. Mentally she had been betrayed by people she did not know, by people she did. Her mind became filled with dark thoughts. She swallowed hard and put herself in check. Gently she stroked the new outfit she wore, then glanced at her friends. "If I had it to do over again, I would still pursue those bastards." Her mouth turned up slightly at the corners, showing a small grin of defiance. She picked up her cup and took another sip, looking across the rim at the fire.

Tom stretched his legs out in front of him, releasing a breath. He crossed his arms over his chest. "Man, that's tough," he said, "All those people running around behind your back, trying to shut your story down." He shook his head.

"Is it customary to tell *your* stories on my second anniversary?" Laura asked smiling. Marti propped herself up on a pillow on the love seat.

"Sure, we can tell our stories, if you want to hear them." Tom said. He pulled himself up from the chair and walked over to the fireplace. "I don't know if I told you or not, but I was from Colorado. My story begins when I was camping with my son Richie and his Cub Scout troupe. We had planned a two-day outing — fishing, hiking, teaching the boys about nature. There were fourteen boys and four other fathers." He picked up a log a tossed it on the flames.

"It was close to sundown when one of the fathers repeated a news flash he had heard on the radio. He said a couple inmates had escaped from the Colorado State Prison, last seen headed our direction. Of course my first thought was that nothing could happen to us...things happened to other people. The other fathers and I discussed the situation, and decided to pack up and play it safe. The kids were heartbroken." Tom sat back in his chair steepling his fingers.

"By the time we got everything packed up, it was dark. We had lanterns hanging in the trees for light. I was putting a tent into the back of my suburban when I saw a shadow come from behind me, passing between the light and myself. At first I didn't think anything of it. Suddenly, I got an eerie feeling; the hair on the back of my neck was standing up." Tom mentally groaned.

"I turned around, and standing right behind me was this huge black dude." He wrapped his arms around himself, leaning forward in his chair.

"The guy was so tall I was eye to eye with the pocket of his denim shirt. *Inmate,* that's what it said." Tom stopped and took a shaky breath. "I could smell the sweat on the guy. He didn't say anything, he just stood there, silent with brown-eyed rage." Tom rubbed his face with both hands.

"Then the barrels of a shotgun were aimed at my face. I could hear yelling in the background, but I couldn't make out what was being said. He pulled the trigger, and it was all in slow motion. I could see behind thc inmate. One of the fathers was leaping at him. I saw the shell coming at my face. I could hear my son screaming, 'Daddy! Daddy!'"

Tom took a drink of his coffee. Laura held her hand to her throat, much like a person who had received bad news.

"The next thing I knew, I woke up in Limboshia...In Damascus' territory."

Laura sat in shock, silent, not knowing what to say. Finally she spoke. "How awful, to see a shotgun shell coming at your face." She stood up, trying to shake of the emotion that clung to her.

Silence wrapped around the three of them, all with their own thoughts. Laura was thinking that compared to Tom, her death was nothing. She walked over to Marti, who moved her legs to make room for Laura to sit.

"How old is your son, Tom?" Laura's questioned, her green eyes focused on his face.

"He's eight years old now," he said, tracing the rawhide straps on the chair with his finger. "He's still having a hard time with my death. I suppose he will for the rest of his life." He looked up at Laura, then to Marti. "I'm not sad. Once you know the 'Big Picture,' you can overcome the grief. I just worry that his life will not be as happy as it could have been."

Laura and Marti understood his feelings.

"I guess it's my turn," Marti said, sitting slightly forward on the love seat. "I lived in Arizona, with my husband Joe." She smiled thinking of him, how kind and gentle he was.

"We owned a tour guide company in the Grand Canyon area. I had been on him to expand the packages we offered." Marti dropped her head, thinking how she was never satisfied with things as they were.

"I had been doing a lot of rappelling on the cliffs in our area, and wanted to include that in some of the outings we put together." She walked to the fireplace and leaned on the mantel.

"Joe wasn't too thrilled about it, said it was too dangerous." She sighed, looking at the flames. "I kept on him until he let me have my way." *God, how I wish he wouldn't have.* She thought.

"Anyway, one day I talked him into going up to the site I had picked out and do a trial run. I knew if he saw how easy it was, he would feel better about it." Marti turned to stoke the fire, and then propped herself against the mantel again.

"It was early, we had just finished breakfast — bacon, eggs and toast cooked on the grill outside." She expelled a long breath. "The morning was absolutely beautiful. I'll never forget it. It was a sunrise...to die for." Her words trailed off and then she began to laugh nervously. Tom started to chuckle as well. The statement was so innocent. Suddenly everyone in the room started laughing, louder and louder until it reached frenzied heights. Marti tried to catch her breath and wiped tears from her eyes, as did Tom and Laura.

"Oh, my gosh," Marti said, trying to compose herself, still wiping away tears with the back of her hand. "Joe and I packed up all the gear and headed for the cliffs. When we arrived the sun was just coming over the tops of the mountains, casting a shadow on the side where I was going to rappel down into the canyon." Marti raised her hands, palms up, offering a little smile. "It was so perfect. I thought after we took people out all day, either four-wheeling, or rafting, we could rappel down the cliffs to the canyon floor. The location was a great place to set up camp for the night. In the morning, have some breakfast and take them back to the lodge." She held her head in her hands. "I had it all figured out. Yup, I sure did."

Marti began to pace the living room floor, throwing a hand or an arm up every so often as she continued. "I had Joe convinced about the whole thing, so...anyway, I had him help me with the harness. He checked the anchor in the cliff wall. I stepped out on the ledge, he clipped me in and I slowly leaned back. As soon as all my weight was tethered, the anchor pulled loose. The last thing I remember was the look on my husband's face. Surprise at first, then he realized that I was free-falling. His mouth opened, nothing came out, then I heard a scream. To this day I don't know if it was me or him that was screaming." Marti gave a macabre chuckle and slipped her thumbs into the waistband of her buckskin pants. "I, like Tom, and you Laura, woke up on Damascus' side of the territory, only I've been here six years."

Laura knew that they had brought her to the Elders' village before she woke up on her arrival. "So tell me again how it works...the Territories, I mean." Laura was told when she first arrived, but things did not make sense to her for quite some time. She had felt disconnected for the first six months.

Marti sat down next to her, crossing her legs. "As far as we can tell," she said, "Arizona, New Mexico, Texas, California and parts of Colorado coincide with Damascus' territory. The Midwestern states are in the First Territory, and from what we can gather the Eastern states are in the second territory. Other countries are the third territory."

Laura knew that they all had escaped the "Dark Territory" as the local tribes called it, but what of the fourth, she wondered.

Before she could ask the question, Tom's face broke out in a ridiculous grin. "Laura, I still say you had the most incredible entry ever!"

Laura had heard the story of what Marti and Tom had done when she arrived before, on her first anniversary. She knew she was about to hear it again. "Marti and I were told by the Elders where to find you." Tom's voice was filled with excitement. *Here we go.* Laura thought.

"So," Tom went on, "it wasn't more than maybe ten minutes after we got to the location, when...wham!" He jumped up from his chair. "I says to Marti, hey, do you think that's her?" Marti starts laughing at the story. Tom shot a look at her. "Well damn, man, Laura should have heard it...Bang!...Pow!...That's what the air sounded like just before you came." Laura was giggling at him. He was just like a little kid acting out the entire story.

"Then Marti says, what the hell is that?" Tom snaps his head as if he were there. "What? I say to her, looking to where she pointed." Tom cupped his eyes as if looking in the sky. Laura and Marti snorted.

"I see this bending, I get scared. How can the sky bend?" By this time Tom had a manic grin across his face. "I'm telling you, the whole horizon was bending, then a huge rainbow of color."

Tom stopped to catch his breath. Marti began to look a little manic herself. "The chimes, Marti...do you remember?"

She nodded her head, sure she was about to break out in hysteria at any moment from the way he looked telling the story. She slapped her hand over her mouth.

"The music they made, wonderful, as if there were thousands of wind chimes." Both women did not dare interrupt him. He was hardly ever childlike; he carried so much responsibility for the village.

"Wondrous chimes," he babbled. "So then, we grab you, right at the second you hit the ground. Marti and I throw you over a horse and run for the border." He shook his head, as if he were having a conversation with himself.

"That's what we did..." His words broke off and he sat down. Laura and Marti looked at him with grins plastered to their faces. Marti nudged Laura. They looked at Tom, who sat with a big smile, staring at the fire...content.

San Francisco Police Department

Ryan Delgato had always dreamed of the day she would be a private investigator. She still was in shock over her father's offer. Cleaning out her desk at the precinct, her thoughts were on Morgan. Ryan couldn't help but see her handsome face, strong hands, artist's hands. Deep blue eyes, with a seductive depth to them, something she couldn't explain. Being a detective, she noticed every detail about people. She wished she could keep her mind off Morgan, if only for a minute.

"So, you're cutting bait and running huh?" A voice said from the doorway, and Ryan jumped.

"Didn't mean to scare you." It was Delani. She smiled.

"As fast as I can find a knife," she said, laughing, and motioned with her hand for him to come in. Delani sat on the edge of Ryan's desk. It was clear that he was upset. He cared for her, like a big brother. He was in his late fifties, his head balding slightly on top. He wore a pair of slacks and a white shirt with a maroon v-neck sweater. Delani always had beautifully manicured nails and carried a pipe.

"You and your father are going into business, I hear," he said with a flickering smile. He looked at the box that Ryan was closing.

"For once you heard right," she replied, walking around the desk to retrieve another. Delani picked up a paperweight from the desk, turning it gently in his hand. He put the unlit pipe in his mouth, holding it between his teeth.

"There is some talk around the Department..." Delani began.

Ryan shot a look at him. "What kind of talk?" She stopped packing and leaned against the desk. He looked down at his shoes.

"Some of the guys," he said, bringing his gaze back to her, "they're jealous...or...mad, I don't know." Delani took himself and the paperweight to the window and stared out at the city. "I just heard some shit...that's all."

Ryan slapped the top of the desk. "Why, dammit? My father is trying to make a better life for me. Can't they understand that?" She felt the blood drain from her face.

Delani turned and raised a hand in protest. "I'm on your side, kid. Always have been." He took the pipe from his lips and pointed the stem at Ryan. "I just want you to be careful out there. OK?" His face was stern. Ryan nodded. "Look, Ryan," he went on, clenching his jaw, "who knows why these assholes act the way they do? I just thought you should know what's being said."

*Assholes and opinions...*she thought. She stood next to Delani and put a hand on his arm. "I appreciate your coming to tell me," she said, "You've been a good friend."

Delani placed a hand on hers. "If it means anything to you, I'm happy for you, and so are a lot of the guys," he said with a sad smile.

Ryan was going to miss him, and from his expression it was obvious he would miss her as well. Ryan cleared her throat. "Don't you have anything better to do than bug me?" She quickly turned her attention back to the box.She didn't want Delani to see her eyes welling.

"Don't be a stranger." he said softly.

"I'm going to miss you, Eric," Ryan whispered. She turned around and he was gone.

"Hey!" she yelled down the hall. "You have my paperweight!" Delani kept walking. Ryan was touched that he wanted a memento of her. *Sweet bastard.* She threw the remaining items in the box and closed it. She took a look around the small depressing office. She would not miss the peeling paint on the walls, nor the cramped environment. She grabbed a box under each arm and pushed the door shut with her foot.

Ryan walked down the stairs, and when reaching the bottom she turned and took a final look at the building. She was unaware that she was being watched from a window on the second floor by John Malcolm, Chief of Detectives. She loaded the boxes into the car, and slid behind the wheel.

"That bitch is going to be a thorn in our asses," Malcolm said. He took the cigar out of his mouth and set it in the ashtray. Two men sat silent across the room.

"I wish her fuck of a father wouldn't have offered her a job. At least I knew what she was up to when she was here." He wiped the sweat from his forehead with his meaty hand. "I know she's going to stir up trouble," he said, watching Ryan pull away. John Malcolm turned and faced the two men sitting on the couch.

"It all started when we gave women the right to vote. Now the bitches think they're our equals." John barked out a laugh, grabbing his cigar from the ashtray. "We should've kept 'em barefoot and pregnant, that's what I say." He placed the chewed cigar back between his lips. "Every time you turn around these days, you got yourself a damn sexual harassment suit." He searched his pockets for a match.

"And another thing. You seen the TV Lately? Nothin' but feminine hygiene commercials." Malcolm struck a match, lighting the cigar. "My old man use to tell me that, anything that bleeds for seven days and lives can't be trusted." John Malcolm laughed behind large plumes of smoke and waved a hand to clear a visual path to the silently sitting men.

He stepped closer to them, assumed a wide stance and grabbed between his legs. "I think little Miss High and Mighty needs to be taught a lesson...if you know what I mean." Another bark of laughter. "First things first," he said releasing his crotch, then looking to the men. "We've been ordered to take care of that guy in Half Moon Bay."

Damascus owned most of the Police Department, including John Malcolm, who had been promoted to Chief two years earlier. He had told John to bring him James Peterson. Laura Saubert was James' best friend, and Damascus was concerned that Laura had confided in James about the article she had been writing. For the past two years he had had Morgan and James under close surveillance, but with the detective quizzing Morgan about Laura, it was only a matter of time before she and James would put things together.

"We're going to take a little trip, boys, and if you don't like the idea you talk to Damascus about it." John ashed his cigar and grinned. Pontis and Reese looked at one another. They knew their situation had just gotten worse.

San Francisco Chronicle

Jennifer Collins had been on the phone all morning, checking out leads for her story. She put a call into the police station to set up an interview with the officer who had taken a statement from Stephane Damitree's mother, Anusca Damitree, and from Stephane's fellow musicians. One of the violinists told her where Anusca Damitree was staying, and gave her some information about Stephane.

Considering he was a famous pianist, Stephane Damitree, up until the coma, had led a very low-key life. Jennifer learned that he was close to his family, calling his mother in the evenings after each concert. She was surprised, when she reached Mrs. Damitree at the Hilton, at how pleasant and cooperative she was. She didn't expect the mother of someone so famous to be so accessible.

Jennifer was excited to get out in the field to do investigative work and eagerly arranged a meeting at the hotel. She collected her tape recorder, notepad and pens, threw them into her briefcase and headed for Sam Mansfield's office. She smoothed her hair with her free hand as she quickly made her way to his office. Peeking in the widow, she saw Sam, head down, typing on the keyboard to his computer. Never looking up, he motioned her in with his hand gesture. She had a list of questions in her mind as she entered.

"Your high heels," Sam said.

"Excuse me?" Jennifer asked.

He finally looked up at her, smiling. "How I knew you were at the door. Your high heels."

She looked down at her stilettos, smiled , then got serious again. "I got an interview with the Romanian's mother over at the Hilton," she said, laying her briefcase on the desk.

Sam leaned back in his chair, running his hand over his scalp. "What's your angle for questioning?"

Jennifer looked over the top of his head and put a finger to her lips. "I thought I would start about Stephane, the son." She glanced at Sam. "Then get his background as a child; you know...follow his career and lead into what happened the night of the 911 call." Jennifer hoped he approved of her tactics. He slid forward in his chair, resting his elbows on the desk.

"Well," he said, looking down at his blotter, "I think it sounds pretty good." He fixed his eyes on her. "I want you to check in after you're done. Let's get at least a blurb in tonight's edition." Sam pulled a cigarette out of the pack lying on his desk.

"O.K," Jennifer said, nodding.

Sam cleared his throat. "You be careful out there, capice?" Jennifer had to fight to keep from laughing; Sam was so predictable...*capice?*

The Hilton, Penthouse Suite

A small dark-haired woman answered the door, greeting Jennifer Collins. "Hello Miss Collins, my name is Anusca Damitree...please come in, won't you?" Her accent was thick but articulate. Jennifer towered above her, bending over slightly to shake her hand. Anusca swept her hand inviting Jennifer to enter. She followed the tiny figure into the living room.

"This is gorgeous," Jennifer said, amazed. She had never seen such a room, nor such a view of the ocean. The entire west wall facing the ocean was plate glass; a stunning panoramic view of the bay lay before her.

Anusca clasped her hands in front of her. “Beautiful...yes?” she asked, looking at the ocean. Then she looked at the tall redhead standing next to her, whose mouth was agape.

“Absolutely,” Jennifer murmured.

Anusca took the young woman by the arm and led her to the seating area, where pastries and tea awaited them. Putting her briefcase on the ottoman, Jennifer smoothed her skirt over her long legs before sitting down. She noticed the platter where the pastries sat was made of silver with white dollies under each one. The tea service looked hand-painted, perhaps antique china. It reminded her of her grandmother, and how she made everything so special.

Jennifer looked at Anusca, who was staring at her with a twinkle in her eye. “Are you all right my child?” she asked.

“Yes...yes, of course,” Jennifer replied. “I was admiring the china.”

Anusca nodded. “I thought we might...have some tea, before we...how do you say...get down to it?” She looked at Jennifer with eyebrows raised.

“Yes, that would be nice,” Jennifer said, smiling. Mrs. Damitree poured tea into their cups, gingerly handing one to Jennifer. “This smells wonderful, Mrs. Damitree.”

Anusca made a hand gesture, like shooing an insect.

“Please, call me Anusca. There is no need for such formalities.” Jennifer commented again about the tea.

“Ah, yes...the tea is from my homeland,” Anusca said. “It is called Nostrial, the translation...in your language, would be...nostal...how do you say...” Anusca looked at Jennifer, frustrated.

“Nostalgic?” Jennifer queried.

“Yes, this is correct,” she smiled. “To remember...we drink to remember our loved ones...nost...ala...gick.” Anusca shook her head repeating the word. Jennifer grinned at her continuous attempt to pronounce the word. Anusca sat her cup and saucer on her lap, gently holding it with the tips of her fingers. Jennifer admired her gauze dress. It had a delicate red floral brocade belt, showing her trim waistline. Damitree's hair was pulled back in a French braid, her temples salt-and-pepper gray. Jennifer watched her looking into her cup as if it spoke to her. “I do not know where to begin,” Anusca said, almost in a whisper.

Jennifer sat the tea on the coffee table, pulling her briefcase on her lap. “Mrs...Anusca, do you mind if I record this? It's so I have the whole conversation, and don't misquote you, or leave important facts out.”

Damitree nodded. “I suppose I should start the day when Stephane told to me that he wishes to go to United States.” She shook her head. “I did not like this thing in his head. I try to tell to him that it not good idea.” Anusca raised a hand, palm up with a shrug of her small shoulders. “But, you know how those young peoples are, they get one thing in the mind, nothing else matters,” she said, looking at the tape recorder in Jennifer's lap. “I tell to him, Stephane...I say, I do not wish for you to go. If you do, I am thinking that I never see you again.” She put her cup on the table next to Jennifer's.

“Why did you feel that way, that you wouldn't see him again?” Jennifer picked up her cup and sipped, eyeing the woman over the rim.

Anusca smiled. “I had premonition.” Jennifer's eyebrow went up. Mother's intuition, she wrote on her notepad.

Anusca smoothed her dress, setting the cup and saucer back in her lap. “My mother,” she began, “was a Gypsy, from Gypsy blood...very many years.” Damitree squinted her eyes, fixing them on Jennifer. “Women in my family tell fortunes...see things before they are there.”

Outer Limits, Jennifer thought, trying not to grin.

Anusca could see the expression was one of disbelief, but continued. “When my son reaches your city of San Francisco, he not call. Me, I worry...I am mother.” Damitree's eyes clouded. “He is good son, he call from every city he goes.” She dropped her head to her chest. “Not this city...no call.” Jennifer looked at the recorder to make sure it was still running.

“I get call, not from my son, from man he plays instruments with.” Anusca's hands began to shake. “This man say that Stephane is hurting in hospital.” Jennifer reached over and put a hand on Anusca's to calm her. “I take air-o-plane to here, with my husband and my daughter." She pulled a lace handkerchief from the sleeve of her black dress and dabbed her eyes. Jennifer was aware of how much anguish this woman felt.

"Would you like to take a break, Anusca?" she asked the teary-eyed woman.

"No...I am fine." She tucked the hanky back into her sleeve. "I walk into room where my son is..." Anusca looked at Jennifer with sad, old eyes. "He has things coming from him. The doctors say that this is to help him to breathe." Jennifer made an occasional note on her pad as Anusca's story unfolded.

"When I see my son, I want to hold him, like when he was little boy." She smiled, thinking of Stephane running and playing as a child. "He was always good boy to his mother and father, he loves every person." Damitree put the cup back down on the table and walked, hands clasped behind her, to the window. She stood for a few quiet moments looking at the ocean.

"We sit for three days, next to bed in hospital, my husband he has to go back to our home. My daughter...we stay for him to wake up." The old woman paced in front of the large window. "One day, in morning...he wake...he sit up. Rada, my daughter, she runs to Stephane. They are close and she loves him. She goes to him and puts arms around him. He tears things out that help him breathe and he push Rada from him."

Jennifer looked up from the notepad and focused on Anusca. "Pushed her?" Damitree nodded. "Why?"

Anusca held a hand up and turned to Jennifer. "He say, 'Get away from me!'" She sat back down in her chair and took a sip of tea. "He has no accent...none, he speaks in your language. He knows not this American." Anusca nodded as if she were having a conversation with herself.

"I know that this person not my son. His body...yes, but what is inside...is not."

Jennifer ran her hand across the grin that was about to surface. *The Exorcist,* she wrote on the notepad. "Mrs. Damitree...I mean Anusca, are you suggesting that your son is possessed?"

"This is what I am saying," Anusca said in a serious tone. Jennifer's smile froze on her face. Trying to escape the stare from Damitree, she watched her pencil tap on the notepad.

"O.K, then" Jennifer said lapsing again into silence. Anusca sighed and looked back in her tea cup.

"So...Anusca, where is your daughter?"

The small woman's face showed even more concern. "She follows her brother...I tell her..." The words trailed off.

"You told her what?" Jennifer leaned toward Anusca, whose lips grew tighter.

"She would not let her brother be...she loves him too much." Anusca rubbed her forehead. "She follow him to a villa, on ocean, to see what he does, I tell her he is not brother that…she must not put herself in danger."

Jennifer sat straight in her chair. "What do you mean, danger?"

Anusca let out another sigh. "He pushes her hard at hospital, he makes face of anger. My son would not do this thing."

Jennifer jotted down a series of notes. "Rada is at the villa this minute?" Another nod. "When will she be back?"

Damitree closed her eyes. "She has been two days. She calls me on telephone, She say that he go in and no see him since."

"Your daughter has a mind of her own" Jennifer gave a faint grin.

"Yes, this she has. My husband and myself, we send her to the States to get education. She also has American ideas,"

Jennifer readjusted herself in the chair and again checked the tape recorder. Glancing back over her notes, she said, "So, you think that your son has been taken over by an evil spirit?" Jennifer gave a nervous snort and held a hand up quickly, surprised it had escaped. "Please don't misunderstand my reservations, Anusca, but I am having some trouble believing all of this evil...spirit..."

The old woman raised a hand. "My dear child, when you have lived as long as I have lived, anything is possible. All my life as a child, my mother, she has spirits around her. I grow up with these things." Anusca stood, smoothed her dress, and walked slowly back and forth in front of the coffee table, hands behind her.

Jennifer watched her face as she searched for the correct words.

"These things," Anusca began, "that I speak of, there are these spirits, they take over a people's body. The Indians call this shape-shifting, the Eastern peoples call it another name, and Western peoples call it possession." She flicked a glance at Jennifer. "Your culture, they tell to you as child there is no magic, to grow up."

Jennifer felt her heart skip a beat; she had experienced this in her upbringing. She had wonderful parents who wanted the best for her, but they had told her time and again to be realistic, to grow up. Not to live in a fantasy. Jennifer returned her attention to Anusca.

"You see, Miss Collins, in this room, now...there are spirits." She motioned between them. "They walk in our open spaces, as we walk in their open spaces." As crazy as it sounded to Jennifer, somewhere deep inside...it felt possible. She tried to clear her head. Was she being hypnotized by this woman? she wondered.

Anusca smiled at Jennifer looking around the room as if to catch a glimpse of movement. "That is right, child. They are here, right now between us. The Catholic church does this thing...called...exorcism...no? How is it then, if there is no such thing as this...that they have name for it?" Anusca knew she had Jennifer where she wanted her. She smiled coyly at the redhead.

"This religion, they say, 'Be good or go to hell.' They have clothes, they are black and white...good and evil, yes? I say no, the spirits are not black or white, they live in gray area."

Anusca returned to her chair. "Once peoples can grasp this, then they live. You see that evil cannot live without good and good cannot live without evil." She wove her fingers together and held them up.

"One cannot exist without the other." Jennifer repeated, looking at Anusca. The older woman nodded. She could see the reporter was beginning to understand. Perhaps she had a young ally on her side.

Half Moon Bay

James had been trying to reach Morgan all morning, but her cell phone had been busy. He knew that today was the anniversary of Laura's death, and was concerned. He wanted to be there for Morgan. James had a new client coming to his office, and after the meeting with him he would go to the city to see his good friend. Knowing he would see her soon, he felt better.

James poured a cup of coffee and went to sit on the deck that projected from his office. As he looked through the trees into the parking lot, he noticed a car parked next to his. Was his client early, he wondered. Just as the thought went through his mind, he heard something behind him. Between himself and the building stood a heavy-set man.

James recoiled as if he'd been slapped. “I didn't hear you knock,” he said, knowing the man did not even entertain the idea of the gesture.

“Didn't mean to scare you, friend,” The man said with a detached smile. Two more men entered the doorway.

Oh shit. His mind was racing. James knew this was trouble. The possibility of all these men showing up for a session was not probable. James' heart sank in his chest.

“My name is John Malcolm, Mr. Peterson. I'm your new client. We have an appointment.”

“Yes, John, we spoke on the phone yesterday.” *Client my ass.*

John Malcolm stepped toward James and his heart plummeted even further. James swallowed hard. “What's this about, Mr. Malcolm?”

“My client would like to have a few words with you, James, that's all.” John Malcolm's smile turned suddenly dangerous. He poked James in the chest with his thick finger, knocking the small body off balance.

Malcolm pretended to have a surprised look on his face. "What's the matter fag-boy? I thought your kind liked a good poke." Malcolm reared his head in laughter. James clung to the railing. Malcolm stepped forward, cocking his arm, and struck the side of James' head. The blow was powerful enough to jar him loose from the rail. Malcolm grabbed James by the back of the neck and threw him into the sliding glass door. James' face pressed against the glass, and he wondered, absurdly, what he might look like from the other side. As the thought went through his head, he felt the warm sensation of his own blood running down his face and neck into his shirt.

James knew he was hurt, but all his mind would do is worry about Malcolm ruining his new shirt. John smashed James into the glass again, this time with all his might. James' body crumpled like a piece of paper. He lay face up on the deck, his red hair looking oddly apricot against the crimson of his bloodstained shirt.

Malcolm hovered over the slender body and gave it a slight kick. He looked disappointed when there was no movement. Standing erect, he snapped his attention to the two men standing in the doorway. "Pontis, Reese, tie this butt-fucker up, gag him, and throw him in the trunk of my car!" Neither man moved. They stared at the pool of blood forming around James. "Did you hear me, assholes?" He tucked his shirt tail back in, and looked at them.

"Is he dead?" Reese asked, flushed.

"Would I tell you to gag a fucking dead man?" Malcolm hissed sarcastically.

"I don't know what you would do anymore!" yelled Pontis, looking at James' motionless body.

"For fuck's sake," Malcolm said, "You two are as worthless as tits on a bull." He bent over James, straddling him and pulled a bandanna out of his back pocket. "You both make me sick," he said, grabbing a handful of James' hair and yanking his head off the deck. A semi-coagulated web of blood stretched between the wood plank and the side of James' swollen face.

Malcolm tied the cloth around James' mouth and dropped his head with a dull, wet thud.

Pontis and Reese slapped their hands over their mouths in an effort to keep their breakfast down. Malcolm shook his head in disgust at the two men. "Do you think you could get this fuck down to the car, or do I have to do that myself?"

Pontis grabbed his friend by the arm and pulled him down the stairs and out to the car. Both men leaned on the hood, trying to compose themselves. Pontis saw that Reese had his fists clenched. "Hey Reese, you've got to take it easy." He knew if Reese blew it would mean trouble.

Malcolm came out of the building with James slung over his shoulder. He pulled the keys out of his pocket and unlocked the trunk. Malcolm's scowl deepened as he looked at Pontis and Reese. He dropped the body into the trunk. James was unaware of his temporary tomb. Malcolm drove, Pontis sat in the passenger seat and Reese in the back. Malcolm stared at Reese in the rearview mirror. "Ain't much for bloodshed, huh, Reese?" Malcolm's eyes narrowed at Reese's reflection.

"Why don't you leave him alone, Malcolm?" Pontis asked. He turned to his friend in the back seat. "Are you all right, buddy?" Reese nodded, but it was obvious that he was far from it.

Malcolm made a noise in his throat and rolled his eyes. "Are you his fucking mother or what, Pontis?"

Reese could take it no longer and leaned forward, white knuckling the front seat behind Malcolm. "Maybe you enjoy beating people half to death…I don't. I'm a lawyer, and all I ever wanted was to put thugs like you behind bars." Reese shot the words through tight lips. Pontis put his hand on his friend's chest, giving him an appraising look. Reese reluctantly slid back in the seat.

Malcolm smiled, enjoying the confrontation. "What a sweet little story, sissy boy. Pontis, will you open the glove box and hand me some tissues?"

Pontis' eyes became narrow slits on his face. "You are really a bastard…do you know that?" He clenched his teeth,

Having pushed his passengers as far as he dared, John remained quiet the remainder of the trip, letting Pontis and Reese off at their law office. Once out of the car, Reese spewed obscenities at the taillights as Malcolm drove away.

"I hate that bastard!" Reese screamed over and over.

Pontis waited for his friend to calm down and said, "You should really learn to get your anger out, and not hold that shit in."

Reese started laughing and Pontis grinned. "Let's call it a day and go over to Ray's Bar, grab a cold one, what do you say?" Reese nodded.

The two men began to walk to Ray's. Pontis was thinking back to when he and Reese just finished graduate school. They had planned for years to open their own law firm after they finished school. He remembered that Reese had just proposed marriage to his soon-to-be-wife, Ruth. He smiled as he walked. Ruth's best friend Rita was single and, seeing an opportunity, she had thrown Pontis and Rita together. As it happened, the four ended up having a double ceremony.

Pontis and Reese took nighttime security jobs on the dock to support their wives until the law firm was established. The first month on the job, they were confronted by a well dressed Italian man coming off a yacht. He has asked them several questions about the city, claiming he was new in the area. One thing led to another and soon the gentleman was aware of the new law firm. He had taken a business card from them and, several weeks later showed up at their office. At the time, they knew him as Mario Galliano. The first six months went smoothly. Pontis and Reese drew up large contracts for boats, Reebok footwear, many other clients. They were thrilled with the money they were making. It afforded them new houses and cars.

But then they began to question some of the things that Galliano started asking them to do. One night in particular came to mind. Pontis and Reese were sent to a location to pick up a man and deliver him to the docks. They had tried to make small talk with him, but he spoke not one word. The following morning, Pontis was reading the news paper about a man washing up on the shore and recognized him as the man they had picked up the night before. Reese wanted to go to the police, but Galliano had come into the office and stopped them before they had a chance to report it.

"I remember the first time we went to Ray's," Reese said, bringing Pontis back to the present. "We used to pool all our pocket change for a pitcher of beer."

Pontis grinned and said, "The good old days."

Reese nodded his head and slapped Pontis on the back. "Yup, the good old days; what I wouldn't give to go back and start over." Reese's face tightened.

Limboshia

Cameron watched as Damascus prepared for his return to Earth. He did not know how to feel after the incident with the Starling woman. It usually took him several days to get over Damascus raping women. Cameron had never met Starling, but he knew he liked her. Damascus' men had locked her in the root cellar at the edge of the compound at the Pasture House just across the valley. The boy knew she was important to Damascus because otherwise he would have thrown her to his men for their pleasure.

Damascus noticed that the boy was unusually quiet. "Cameron, you know that I have to go…" Cameron sat on the hearth swinging his feet, saying nothing.

"What's wrong with you this morning?" Damascus asked, looking up from his writing. "Has someone been giving you a hard time when I'm away?" Damascus propped his elbows on the desk top, waiting for an answer. Cameron glanced at the large man, remaining silent.

"I want to know what is upsetting you." Cameron's attention focused on his swinging feet.

Damascus walked over to the boy and placed his hands on his hips. "I asked you a question and I expect an answer!"

Cameron's feet went still. "No one's bothering me," he whispered. He was afraid to tell Damascus that some of the men hassled him, asking many questions about what went on in the cabin. The boy decided to lie. "I miss you when you're gone…that's all," he said, stealing a glance.

Damascus laid a hand on the boys shoulder. "I will return in three days."

"I know," Cameron replied.

Damascus returned to the desk and picked up a piece of paper. "I made a list of things I need you to deliver to Leman at the Pasture House." When he mentioned Leman's name, he noticed the boy cringe. "Is Leman giving you trouble?" He asked Cameron. The boy shook his head, denying any problem.

"When I get back, we will go pay Leman a visit, just to be sure. In the meantime give this list to him, and if he does anything to you, I want to hear about it. Do I make myself clear?"

"Yes." Cameron said softly.

"Good." He said, handing the paper to the boy.

* * *

The Elders Village

The sun was just coming over the mountains. Tom, Marti and Laura were already out in the garden.
Tom was cleaning up the remaining scrap from the new construction, his hat threatening to fall off as he bent his head .“I think we can burn a lot of this in the fireplace,” he said, going on about his task. Laura and Marti sat between rows of vegetables, weeding.

“It’s going to be a beautiful day,” Laura said, looking up at the sunrise.

Pinks and oranges washed over the sky above them. Marti glanced up with a smile, and then continued to dig harder at the weed that would not come out.

“Man, where does the root to this thing go?” Tom laughed at the dirt on Marti’s determined face.

“Hey Laura, maybe you can give Marti a hand with that.” Marti rolled her eyes at him, then grabbed hold of the stalk and pulled with all her might. The weed popped out, sending Marti flat on her back. Laura and Tom started laughing as Marti held the weed up in triumph. Laura glanced at the village. A figure dressed in white was running toward them, kicking up dust behind him. “Look!” Laura exclaimed pointing. Marti stood and, wiping herself off walked next to Tom and Laura.

As the figure grew nearer, they saw it was an attendant to the Elders. “I have news,” he said, out of breath. “Starling has been kidnapped from the Gateway.”

Marti grabbed Tom’s shoulder. “Oh my God!” she cried out.

The attendant, still trying to catch his breath, said, “The Elders have called an emergency meeting.” He pointed to the structure in the center of the village. “They are assembling now.”

The meeting hall was full of villagers when they arrived. Tom removed his hat and held it in his hands, looking for a seat with both women behind him. Silence fell over the crowd as the

Elders entered. After being seated, the head Elder, Samone, motioned for Tom. He approached the Council, leaning in toward Samone. "Those three seats in front are for you," Tom acknowledged, then sat with Marti and Laura in the chairs. The Elders were dressed in fine white silk robes with ornate embroidered stitching on the collars and with sleeves made of pure gold thread. All seven of them had flowing silver hair, flawless milk white skin and intense steel blue eyes. Laura stared at their beauty, finding it hard to break her gaze. She knew that these beings chose to remain in Limboshia, even after they had fulfilled their lives' destinies and were free to travel the universe with no responsibilities.

"We have called you all here today to bring you up to date on a situation," Samone said, her hands lying flat on the Council table before her. "Starling has been taken from the Gateway, by Damascus of the Dark Realm." The villagers gasped. Samone raised a hand. "Please remain calm." She looked over all the faces in the room, then to Tom, Marti and Laura. "We must send a rescue party to retrieve her."

The Elders talked for a moment among themselves, then sat back in their seats.

"We have chosen the three before you," she said pointing. Tom felt fearful and honored at the same time; he didn't want to let them down. "Tom, I know this is much responsibility," she said folding her hands in front of her. "We have chosen you three because of your faith and loyalty, not only toward one another, but your fellow villagers as well," Samone said, smiling.

"As you know, we Elders can travel from realm to realm," the head Elder continued. "We can protect the angels on Earth. We can do many things. But we cannot interfere in matters concerning the Territories." She rested her elbows on the table, steepling her hands.

"This is the law, and I believe it is a good law. Now I ask, will you three accept this mission?"

All the Elders were looking at the trio, waiting for their decision. Tom looked at Marti and Laura. They nodded. Tom stood, facing the Council. "We do."

Samone was very pleased. "Good. All the preparations will be made. You will leave in the morning."

After returning to their cabin, the three laid equipment out on the dining table. Marti checked the mountain climbing gear that she had come to Limboshia in, pulling on the lead ropes to check for damage. Tom packed flint, rope, and skins for shelter. Laura gathered water skins, dried meats and fish. Outside a storm was brewing, curious, they walked out onto the porch. Big, billowy, cotton ball clouds hung in the sky. A bolt of lightning shot across the horizon. Sudden darkness covered the land.

"Damascus," Tom whispered. The clouds above turned into giant balled fists, as if attached to enormous celestial beings. A crack of thunder. Another, and this one shook their bones. The three craned their heads watching a dense soup twist and twirl like water down a drain, clockwise into a pinhole. As fast as it had come, it was gone, leaving blue skies.

"There goes Damascus, that son of a bitch." Marti said. They went back to the cabin to pack.

"How many days till we get to the Pasture House, Marti?" Tom asked, loading the packs.

"Five…maybe six," she said, concentrating on what she was doing.

"Damascus will be gone three, then return for three, then go again…right?" Tom asked, knowing the answer.

"Right," Laura answered.

"We're going to have to time the rescue according to his next departure." Tom's voice sounded strained.

"It's going to be fine," Marti said, moving alongside him. He nodded.

Marti wiped the salt from the cured meats off her hands and walked the food pack over to the door. "How did Damascus get Starling away from the Gateway — that's what I would like to know," Laura said.

"Good question. Been thinking about that myself. I've known her for six years and she's never left the caves," Marti said, rubbing her temples. Tom finished packing, putting two more bundles next to Laura's.

"What kind of an animal *is* Damascus, that he causes such pain everywhere he goes?" asked Laura.

"The kind that we don't want to meet face to face," Tom murmured.

The Villa on the Bay

Rada Damitree sat leaning against a tree across from the villa she had followed her brother to. This was the third day of no movement. She peered through the binoculars again; nothing had changed. The drapes behind the French doors on the second story of the house were closed. She scanned the front of the villa with the glasses…nothing. She put the binoculars on the ground next to her and rubbed her tired eyes. She entertained the idea of a hot bath at the hotel; her mind sighed at the thought. As she relaxed against the tree, she felt a funny sensation on her skin. She sat erect, noticing the sunlight looked different. *I must be really tired,* she thought.

In the sky, colors formed around the sun. Rada squinted to take a closer look. The clouds also had tiny rainbow prisms in them. "Sun dogs," she said aloud. Rada picked up the binoculars and swept over the bay, to the villa. The drapes were open. She felt panicked. Continuing to look, she saw her brother walk out onto the deck overlooking the bay. He leaned on the railing, watching the boat bob in the water. He looked thinner. She felt her heart beat against her chest. Her brother stood for a long time looking at the ocean. Slowly he turned his head, then snapped his attention at her. She gasped. His eyes were staring at her. How could he see her from such a distance, she wondered as she dropped the glasses. With boneless legs, she made an attempt to run toward her rental car. Pins-and-needle feet carried her with so much speed that she almost overshot the vehicle. As she reached for the door handle, a dark shadow covered the car. Rada frantically looked up to see if a plane or bird was between her and the sun. Nothing there.

She yanked the door open and lunged inside, belly down on the seat. Rolling over, she shoved her hand in her jeans pocket, pulling out the keys. Her hands fumbled as she tried to get the key in the ignition. She managed to start the car and drop it in gear. Tromping on the gas peddle, she spun out, shooting two plumes of dirt from the back wheels. The car fishtailed down the road.

"Dear God, what the hell was that?" she said aloud, slamming the gas peddle to the floorboard. Rada held tight to the wheel as the car swerved back and forth across the road.

Do you think you can spy on me? A voice said in her mind. She shook her head, trying to quiet the words.

Run Rada, run...

"Shit! What the hell…" Rada white-knuckled the steering wheel the entire trip to the hotel.

Anusca and Jennifer jumped when Rada came crashing through the door of the room. Anusca's heart sank at the sight of the fear on her daughter's face. She ran to Rada, Jennifer on her heels. They eased Rada's shuddering body into a chair in the living room. " Rada!" Anusca's tone was firm. She could see that her daughter was detached. Anusca wrapped her arms around Rada.

"She is freezing," she said, looking at Jennifer. The reporter grabbed a shawl that was lying on the sofa and Anusca helped Jennifer put it around Rada's shoulders.

"Sun Dogs, Mama…" Rada whispered.

"Child, what Sun Dogs?" Anusca rubbed Rada's arms to warm her.

She looked with unfocused eyes at her mother. "Just before…he came," she said in a small voice.

"Who comes, child?" Anusca knew who *comes*, but she wanted Rada to keep talking so that she would not go into shock. Jennifer poured a cup of tea and put it between Rada's hands. She looked at the recorder; the tape was running out. She opened the briefcase and retrieved a fresh one,

"What are Sun Dogs?" she asked, putting a hand on Rada's arm. Rada looked at her mother over the rim of her tea cup.

Anusca smiled at her. "Have you seen color around the sun?" Anusca asked Jennifer.

"Yes," she said.

"This color is…how do you say…" Anusca looked at Rada. Her daughter set her cup in her lap.

"Portal, Mama, it's called a portal." Her teeth chattered the reply.

Anusca's eyes smiled. "Yes, port…hole, a way in from other realms." Damitree stood, smoothing her dress.

"A way in…from other realms, are you kidding me?" Jennifer said sarcastically.

Rada took another drink, still shaking slightly. "My mother is not kidding, but I know it's hard to believe."

Jennifer pulled herself up from the floor. "Your English is very good," she said to Rada. Rada nodded, grinning. Jennifer sat next to the tape recorder, glancing at it again. *I hope this is all being taped,* she thought.

"O.K," Jennifer said. "So what you're saying is that these colors around the sun are a portal into another realm, is that correct?" Jennifer felt a plastic smile on her face.

"Also…clouds," Anusca added, with an eyebrow raised.

Jennifer's pencil tapped the notepad. "Clouds…also," she repeated, looking at Rada and then to Anusca. She waited for them to laugh, or joke about it. Nothing.

Jennifer pinched the bridge of her nose, expelling a long breath. "How do you expect me to believe a story like this?" She stood, and began to pace the room. "Your son goes into a coma. He wakes and says, in perfect English, which, according to you, he doesn't speak, 'Leave me alone.' Rada follows him to some villa whose owner is unknown, where she stays three days watching." Jennifer looked at her notes. "Then out of nowhere, your son walks out and sees Rada, who by the way is so far away that no human could possibly see her. He gives her the evil eye, and then proceeds to attack her car and talk to her mind."

Jennifer glanced at Rada and Anusca. "Wait…there's more," she sounded as if she were selling not one, not two, but three free Ginzu knives. "A portal from another realm opened and this is how Stephane, no wait, Stephane's body came back…from wherever he was for three days." Jennifer plopped down in the chair, throwing her pad next to her.

Morgan Deveraux's Gallery

Morgan stooped and stared into the eyes of the Dark Angel sculpture. She was somehow familiar with his face, but where had she seen it? Her mind wondered if somehow the dream of Laura and the sculpture had something in common. As she contemplated him, she felt molten anger brewing just under the surface of her skin. Her chest was tight with emotion; she was being challenged by the clay face.

Morgan went up to the showroom and poured a cup of coffee. She collected the mail from inside the front door and took it to her desk. Sitting in her large armchair, she noticed the cell phone. *Crap! How did I leave this up here?* She picked it up and checked her voice mail. An artist friend, a salesman, and two from James. Guilt washed over her; James was probably feeling sad because of Laura's anniversary. She took a sip of coffee while his number rang. No answer. She decided to go back to Half Moon Bay and see her friend. She called an employee to run the gallery, grabbed her keys, and headed for James.

The Villa

John Malcolm had finally got himself calmed down after dropping Pontis and Reese off. He pulled into the drive of the villa; the night seemed darker there. A chill ran up his back as he contemplated the lights that dotted the walkway to the house. He always dreaded seeing Damascus. A figure stepped out of the shadows. Trying not to look startled, John got out of the car.

"Good evening, John, how did things go in Half Moon Bay?"

"Fine sir, just fine." Damascus looked in the back seat. Empty.

"Where is Mr. Peterson?" he asked. Malcolm shuffled his feet.

"I put him in the trunk," he said as he grabbed the keys to unlock it. Damascus jerked him by the arm.

"You did what?" his voice was angry. Malcolm opened the lid.

"I put him in the trunk," he repeated. James lay curled in a ball next to the spare tire and jumper cables.

"I thought I told you not to hurt him!" Damascus pushed Malcolm aside, staring at James.

"Look at his face!" he yelled. Obviously displeased, Damascus turned and walked toward the villa.

"Bring him in the house," he said, with his back to Malcolm.

John lifted the slender body over his shoulder, clasping his arms around James' legs. He followed the large man to the villa.

"Put him there." Damascus said, pointing to a large overstuffed chair. John Malcolm eased the body into the seat. James looked like a discarded toy, limp and lifeless. Damascus poured a Scotch and paced the floor. Malcolm said nothing, just watched and waited.

"For Christ's sake John, untie him and take that gag out of his mouth." With shaking hands, John Malcolm did as he was told.

"John," he said, his voice suddenly tempered. "I am concerned about your lack of self-control." Damascus took a long drink."I told you not to hurt this man, did I not?" Malcolm nodded.

Damascus put his face within inches of John's. His dark eyes narrowed into slits. A glow of red came from behind them, drilling a look into John.

Fear overtook John when he felt the pressure in his brain. He grabbed the sides of his head. "What are you doing to me?" he screamed. Damascus continued his dark-eyed, rage-filled drilling.

"Stop! You're going to kill me!" Malcolm fell to the floor, flopping, grabbing his head. The pressure became so great that Malcolm's eyes bulged from their sockets. He slapped his hands over them in an effort to keep them in his skull. John could feel his eyes pulsating against his palms. He vomited on the carpeting. "God…please…stop!" Blood oozed from between his fingers, down his forearms. Malcolm rolled around the floor, his hair now matted with puke, wet balls hammering against his blood-soaked hands. "Stop! For the love …of… God…"

Damascus released him. Malcolm's body went limp against the floor."I am guessing that you do not know with whom you are dealing…John." Laughing, he filled his glass with ice and poured another Scotch. Malcolm moaned, holding his face.

Damascus sat across from James silently sipping his drink. Finally he looked at Malcolm. "If you have done any permanent damage to this man, I will rip you limb from limb."

John pulled himself up on his knees. Slowly he dropped his hands from his face. He could not see much. "My eyes…my God…what have you done?" Malcolm held his hands out, barely making out the blood on them. He wiped them on his slacks. Damascus watched as John stumbled into the bathroom. He turned on the water and splashed his face several times; red ran down the drain. His hands gripped the edge of the sink. Lifting his head, he looked into the mirror. Blurred. He stood still, blinking, trying to focus on his reflection. All that he could make out was two white, hardboiled things staring back at him. Malcolm let out a cry.

Half Moon Bay

Morgan tried to shake off the repulsion that she felt from the sculpture on the way to James'. She found no one home at the cottage. She opened the door with her spare key.

"James?" she called as she entered. Walking into the kitchen she felt the coffee pot, still warm. On the refrigerator hung a post-it note: 'Client 9:00a.m. John M.' *I should have been a detective,* she thought to herself with a smile. Morgan checked her wristwatch: 9:30. She should have time to make it to James' office just as he was finishing up the session with John M. As she got there, she saw his purple Miata rounding the corner into the office parking lot.

The building itself was a handsome two-story structure. James wanted a southwestern flavor, and vegas and latias were used rather than beams and posts. The exterior was stucco, painted in Earth tones, much like the buildings James loved in Santa Fe. The upper deck off the office was constructed with peeler poles and lent itself well to the lush trees it was built around. The lower floor was mainly reception area with a small kitchenette, computer room and two storage closets. The interior was teal, turquoise, and rust with fuchsia accents.

When Morgan walked in, she immediately sensed something was off-kilter. She quickly passed the teal couches in the lobby and made her way to the banister rail leading to James' office. She was about to place her foot on the first riser when she noticed a dark stain. She bent over to take a closer look…blood.

"James!" she yelled, taking two steps at a time, until she reached the top. "James, where are you?" Frantically she scanned the room, and immediately the large smear on the glass door became apparent. She ran to the it. *Oh my God, more blood.* Her mind was racing. She looked out to the deck; a scream rose in her throat and she put her hand over her mouth. A dark gelatinous substance pooled on the deck; James' cell phone lay next to it. Morgan's body froze. She felt a tremor in her hands that spread up her arms and down her legs. She hung on to the door jamb, and her legs giving in to gravity, slid down onto the deck.

Morgan pulled her cell phone from her jacket and dialed detective Delgato's number. Ryan was on her way to her new office when the phone rang.

"Delgato," she answered, rolling up the car window.

"Ryan…"

"Hello, this is Delgato,"

"Ryan, this is Morgan." Her voice was clearly pained.

"Morgan, are you all right? What's going on?"

"I…I'm at James' office…" Her words trailed off.

"Morgan! What the hell is happening?" Ryan's tone was professional, commanding.

"There is blood…I can't find James," she whispered.

"Morgan, give me the address." Though thoroughly rattled, Morgan managed to give Ryan the information.

"I'm on my way and don't touch anything. Do you hear me?"

"Yes. Hurry." Morgan said, letting the phone drop in her lap.

Ryan tossed her phone onto the passenger seat and stomped on the gas peddle. The landscape passed by in a green and blue wash of color as the car flew down the highway.

Limboshia, the Scrimshaw Mountains

Tom, Marti and Laura were on their way to rescue Starling. Before they had left, the Elders told Laura that Morgan was being warned of the dangers that surrounded her, James and Ryan. She knew better than to ask how Morgan was being contacted, at the risk of disrespecting the Council. She would be content knowing that it had been taken care of.

The Scrimshaw Mountains towered vertically, like fingers of stone. Thousands of pillars stretched upward, completely covered in etched faces that represented every human who has ever carried a soul on Earth. Horse hooves echoed off the canyon walls as the three riders entered what the Elders called the fourth territory.

"Dear sweet Jesus," Laura whispered, pulling her horse to a halt. "They are so beautiful. Look at them."

Tom and Marti marveled at the sight. They had heard of the towers, but had never been allowed to enter the Territory.

"I've heard legend tell that if you see your etched reflection in the towers, you return to your first life," Tom said, pushing his hat back on his head and wiping the dust off his face with a gloved hand.

"Wonder what the odds of that would be?" Laura asked.

Marti smiled and said, "Probably the same as winning the lottery."

Laura dismounted. "I think we should set up camp here tonight," she said, brushing the dirt from her clothes.

They pulled the gear and saddles off the horses and let them run free.

"Yesss, ssstay."

Laura shot a look at Tom and Marti. "Did you hear that?" she asked. They simply smiled at her.

As daylight began to fade, Laura gathered rocks and wood for the fire. Marti and Tom quickly laced together the skins into a large tarp, making a tented structure for shelter.

"Wow!" Laura snorted, "Remind me to take you if I ever go on Survivor." Her two friends grinned at her. Laura went down to the stream, watched the horses drink for a while, then decided to wash up for dinner. She crouched by the water's edge and removed her blouse. The last rays of the sun felt good on her bare skin. She splashed the cool water on her arms and chest. The sound of the creek passing by was soothing. She dipped her hand in the water and let it run through her finger tips.

"Yesss…it is she."

Laura looked up at the cliffs. *That voice again.* She surveyed the towers. *There must be tens of thousands of faces,* she thought. Laura stood up, shook out her blouse and slipped back it back on.

"Yesss…" the towers snapped her attention back.

"Did you…say something?" she whispered, feeling foolish. She walked over to the horses, who stood with eyes closed, swatting their tails. Laura ran her hand over their large haunches as she passed by. Her eyes fixed on the stone pillars. As she neared them she asked a question.

"Were you talking to…me?" she laughed at herself, turning to go.

"You… are the chosen one…yesss."

Laura spun on her heel to face them. She let out a gasp when she saw that all the faces had their eyes open, looking at her. She held a hand to her chest. She felt faint; how could stone be talking to her? She took a step back.

"Chosen…one?" she asked. Chosen for *what* was the question.

"Yesss, you are she…"

"I think you have made a mistake," Laura said, thinking she was making her own mistakes at the very moment, talking to rocks.

"No mistakes…you are she."

Now that she was calming down, she noticed they whispered in unison, all of one voice. She saw their eyes were loving, like parents', or grandparent's eyes would be if they were talking to a child. Laura sat in the sand, looking up.

"Close your eyes…Laura."

She closed her eyes. It was not hard to do as they asked.

Behind her eyes, Laura saw a vision — a winged woman, looking much like herself. Colors radiated from behind her, blue, fuchsia and yellow. It was so bright that Laura could hardly make out the figure of the woman. Then, from behind her came a darkness. It looked to be a man, or shape of a man. He towered over her, his eyes red with hatred. She could feel the energy from both beings; it was a passion, both equal…but different. Laura understood that this was good and evil. It was a balance of power, and she knew that one could not exist without the other. When Laura opened her eyes, the faces were smiling and nodding at her.

"Chosen…you are."

"What do I do now?" Laura asked. She had many questions.

"You must remember that you are the light, Laura. The light that burns, for all souls to see."

"Am I the winged one that I saw in the vision?" she asked, not knowing if she wanted to hear the answer.

"Yes…you are the warrior of which the Star Scrolls speak." This statement caused the faces to become very excited. They looked at one another, smiling and nodding.

"Star Scrolls? I don't know what you're talking about. I'm sorry, but…"

Her words got lost in her throat.

"It will be revealed…Laura…in due time." They began to close their eyes.

"Wait!" Laura cried. "I need to know if that is what Damascus is after — I…"

"Yes, Laura, this is what he seeks; he will stop at nothing to get the Scrolls." Their voices started to fade. Laura's face twisted with frustration.

"All will be revealed…in due time." Their eyes closed. Laura stood in silence, looking at them. "Please come back! I…"

"Who are you talking to, Laura?" Marti had her arms folded over her chest, staring at her…waiting for an answer.

Laura's face was flushed. "I…was, talking to myself." Marti knew she was not telling the truth and raised an eyebrow.

"I thought…I…heard." Laura gave up, knowing it was futile.

"You hearing *those* voices again?" Marti asked, with tongue in cheek.

Laura nodded. She wasn't ready to tell Marti, or Tom, what had just happened. *All would be revealed…in due time,* she thought.

Ray's Bar

Oldies played on the jukebox as Ray drew beers from the tap. The bar was dark and smelled of yeast and cigarettes. Ray Watkins was an ex-Marine who had fought in the Korean War. During his tour, all he thought about was opening a neighborhood bar, a place where a guy could shoot pool and pound a few down. Ray, in his sixties, still had a muscular build, his now gray hair was still worn in a razor-cut. His friends came back from the war with mental issues, so he made it a point to be happy, telling jokes all the time.

"Hey Ray! Can a guy get a beer?" yelled one of the customers.

"Hold yer damn horses. Can't ya see I only got two hands?" Originally from Texas, Ray was what you might call a "good ol' boy." He finished pouring the beer that he worked on and sat them on a tray. "Hey, Fran! Yer order's up!" Ray grabbed another beer mug and poured the impatient man a beer. He slid it down the bar. "Stop yer caterwallin'," he said, watching the beer meet the man's hand.

The door opened, shooting a bolt of light across the bar. Everyone looked up out of curiosity, then returned to their conversations.

"Well, well…lookie here what the cat drug in." Ray threw the bar towel over his shoulder as he went to greet Pontis and Reese. "I wuz thinking the other day, that you two are too big for yer damn britches. Can't come and see ol' Ray anymore."

Pontis and Reese had sheepish grins on their faces, much like children at the doctor's office waiting for the nurse to return with a shot. "Hey, Ray," Pontis said, shaking Ray's hand. "It's not that we're too big for our britches…too busy for them, more like it." Reese reached over and slapped Ray on the shoulder.

"What can I get fer ya fellas?" Ray asked.

"How about a cold pitcher of Bud, like we used to have?" Reese said.

"Ya got it, partner." Ray walked back to the taps and began to pour.

"Pontis, I have to take a leak. I'll be right back," Reese announced. Pontis nodded. He watched as Reese walked past the row of barstools, his eyes stopping at the sixth one. That was where he had met his wife. He stared at the stool, trying to materialize her. If only he could. He longed to turn back the clock and be free of Damascus. He was afraid to go to the police, he was afraid to tell his wife; he was just plain afraid. He had seen too many things, things that were not normal, not human. The man, if that's what he was, had powers. Reese and he were in deep, too deep to get out, he figured.

Returning to the bar, Reese slid onto a stool next to Pontis, and said, "I wish we could go back to the way things use to be."

"Me too, but let's not talk about it now, O.K?" Reese nodded.

Ray yelled from the other end of the bar. "So ya say yer real busy nowadays, huh?"

"Yes, we're real busy all right," Pontis whispered. "Busy beating people up, kidnapping, your basic lawyer stuff." Reese elbowed him.

"Here ya go guys, ice cold beer and two frosty mugs," Ray said as he approached the two men.

"Thanks, Ray," they said in unison.

" You fellas are startin' to sound alike." Ray took a closer look at them. "Yer startin' to look alike, too." Ray gave a belly laugh. Pontis and Reese grinned at each other.

"Maybe you guys oughta take a vacation, go to one of those foreign countries." Ray wiped off the counter. "Think about it." He slapped the bar. "Ya could take them lil' fillies with ya." Voices called for beer down the counter, and Ray once again threw the towel over his shoulder. Pontis and Reese watched the bartender's broad back as he walked toward the other customers.

"I think Ray has a good idea," Pontis said.

"I know. How come we didn't think about a vacation?" Reese replied.

"Probably because we're too big for our britches," Pontis said, smiling.

The Villa

"James!" Damascus yelled, trying to revive the unconscious man. Malcolm sat in the corner pulling at his eyelids.

Damascus tried again. "James!"

This time a small movement came from the crumpled body. James tried to open his eyes but they snapped shut.

"James, I did not want you hurt — for that I am sorry." Damascus almost sounded civilized.

James made another attempt to open his swollen eyes. He tried to focus through narrow slits. He sat up. It felt like a steel rod were shooting through his temples, and he gave in to the pain, lying back against the chair.

"Malcolm, get this man a glass of water and a washcloth for his face."

John flinched at the sound of Damascus' voice. He was still having trouble seeing but felt his way to the kitchen cabinet for a glass. Slowly he filled it at the faucet. Fumbling through a drawer he found a dishcloth and wet it.

An urking sound came from deep inside James' throat when Malcolm handed him the glass and cloth. He turned his attention toward Damascus. "Who are you?" He croaked. James drank the glass of water looking over the rim at the large man in front of him.

"Would you like a drink?" Damascus asked, holding up the scotch bottle.

"Please." James said, looking at Malcolm, still pulling at his eyelids and rubbing his face.

Damascus filled a glass with ice and poured the liquor. "I did not intend for you to get hurt," he said, handing the drink to James.

"Who are you?" he asked Damascus again.

"We will get to that. All in good time. First, I want to ask you a question or two."

James held the wet cloth to his face. "What kind of questions?" James asked.

Damascus glared at him. "About Morgan Deveraux and Laura Saubert."

James winced at the sound of their names coming out of the man's mouth. "I don't understand. What could I possibly tell you?" James drank the rest of his cocktail, wiping his mouth with the bloodstained sleeve of his shirt.

"Let's not play cat and mouse James. It is very unbecoming."

Damascus poured more Scotch in their glasses. James looked like a deer caught in the headlights.

"You know who Morgan and Laura are, on the…other side, so save us some time and stop all this nonsense." Damascus said, smiling over the top of his drink.

"Yes…I do know…" James said softly. Damascus moved closer. "But…the other side?" James asked, feeling the terrible weight of Damascus' stare.

"Do not insult me with your games!" Damascus stood, glaring down at James. "You regress people, take them back to their past lives. Correct?" James looked at the ice in his drink.

"Yes," he said.

Damascus moved closer yet. "You are telling me that you do not know of the other side? Do you take me for a fool?" He pointed to John Malcolm. "That is what happens to people who play games!"

James stole a look at Malcolm. Blood still trickled from the corners of his eyes. James dropped his head.

"You are not…" Damascus said.

"Not what?" James asked, confused.

"Not betraying Morgan and Laura." Damascus grimaced.

"Who are you?" James asked a third time.

Damascus sat on the edge of the coffee table in front of James. "I am known as Damascus." His voice was arrogant.

James was well aware of the name. He also knew of course about Morgan and Laura. "I should know this name, *Damascus*?" James said, trying to play dumb.

"You should, James, and I think you do know my name."

"Why would I know?" James asked.

Damascus leaned within inches of James' bloody face. "Because I am your brother…James."

Half Moon Bay

The sun was going down in Half Moon Bay. Ryan had been at James' office for hours. She shot a roll of film out on the deck, stairs and parking lot. She also collected hair and blood samples, carefully placing them in plastic evidence bags. Morgan sat quietly on the couch, watching. Ryan walked around James' desk looking at his calendar for his last appointment. John M. at ten o'clock. No number, just the appointment. She played the answering machine, listening to messages as she continued to study the office. One of the voices sounded familiar, but she couldn't quite place it.

After the third time replaying the recorded message, Morgan wondered if she was on to something. She pulled herself up from the couch and stood next to Ryan.

"What is it?" Morgan asked. Ryan shook her head.

"I'm not sure. The voice… I feel as if I know it, from somewhere." Ryan slowly walked across the room. Morgan stood staring at the machine.

"Play it again," Ryan said. Morgan pushed the button. Ryan pulled the evidence bags from her jacket pocket and walked back over to James' desk. One by one she laid them out in front of her. "Does James smoke?" she asked, picking up a bag containing a cigar butt.

"God no, he's a health freak!" Morgan exclaimed.

Ryan, still holding the bag, scrutinized the other evidence. "Play the tape again…please." Morgan again pushed the button. Ryan's stomach tightened. "Malcolm." she whispered. Her eyes shot to the appointment book, then the bag…John M. "John Malcolm," she said.

Morgan didn't know the name. "Who's John Malcolm?" Ryan shoved the bags back in her pocket. He's the Chief of Detectives. He's also a crooked son of a bitch." Ryan took Morgan by the arm. "Listen, I was going to call a friend of mine over at the precinct, but I'm thinking that it's not such a good idea, considering…"

Morgan moved her head up and down in agreement. "Why do you think the Chief of Detectives would do a thing like this?" she asked, tears still in her eyes.

"I wish I had an answer for you Morgan, but I really can't imagine why he would be involved." Still holding onto Morgan's arm, Ryan led her down the stairs. "Look," Ryan began, "I have a friend over at the crime lab. If we can get some DNA off this cigar, we might have a chance to get a warrant for Malcolm's arrest." Ryan knew in theory that it sounded easy, but in reality it would be tough.

When they reached the bottom of the stairs, Ryan stopped and looked at Morgan. "I have something to tell you, Morgan." Morgan thought it was more bad news. She stiffened.

"I don't work for the Department anymore." Ryan said.

Morgan gave a silent sigh of relief. She had been worried about Ryan being an officer on the streets. "Did you quit?" she asked.

"In a way, I guess. My father is opening a private investigation firm and he asked me to be his partner," Ryan said with a slight grin.

Morgan sat on the teal couch. She was still in shock over what she'd seen upstairs. Ryan sat next to Morgan and placed a hand on hers. "I know this is really hard, but we will find out what's going on. And we will find James."

Morgan felt the pit of her stomach threatening to swallow her. "How are we going to find James…how?"

Ryan thought how small and sad Morgan looked. She wished she could snap her finger and bring him back. "I'm going to take you home…and…"

Morgan jumped to her feet. "I'm not going home as long as James is in danger!" she yelped.

"O.K," Ryan said, holding a hand up. "You and I will go to the crime lab, then we'll plan our next move." She raised her eyebrows. "O.K?"

Morgan nodded.

Jennifer Collins' Apartment

After the interview with Anusca and Rada Damitree, Jennifer drove home. She drew a bath, poured a glass of Chardonnay and set up the recorder next to the tub. Slipping out of her skirt and blouse, she let her bra and panties fall to the floor. Gently she eased her long legs into the fragrant hot water and lay back. For a few moments she sipped her wine and watched the steam rise above her. As much as she tried to relax, many questions ran through her mind. She reached over the edge of the tub and turned on the recorder. She listened with eyes closed. Anusca's words hung in the air, filling the room. Jennifer drifted off into a fantasy of mystical images conjured by the tape. She remained in the water until it was tepid, then stood and toweled her svelte body. She slipped into her robe, and with tape recorder in hand went to her computer. Jennifer worked for three hours on the story. It was straightforward, concise and conservative. It had no mention of shape-shifters, evil spirits, portals nor entities chasing young girls in cars. She faxed a copy over to Sam Mansfield's desk for the evening edition.

"Sam Mansfield knows not what he has done," Jennifer said out loud. She was thinking that if he knew what had transpired since their last conversation she would not be on the story. She poured herself another glass of wine, put on an over-sized sweatshirt and a pair of pajama bottoms. She sat back down at the computer and stared at the monitor. She reached over and played the last part of the interview.

Jennifer: "How am I to believe a story like this?"

Anusca: "Research."

Jennifer: "Excuse me?"

Anusca: "You are reporter, you have many streets to look."

Rada: “Avenues, Mama. She has many avenues to search.”
Jennifer: “Research what?”
Anusca: “Research times of Sun Dogs and world trouble.”
Jennifer: “World trouble?”

Rada: “What she’s trying to say is that Sun Dogs and world events, such as wars, major storms, and so on, do coincide with the portals.”

Jennifer shut off the tape. She booted up the computer and for hours surfed the internet. She decided to do an overlay graph between atmospheric phenomenon and major disturbances on the planet. Her findings were unnerving. Accessing meteorological charts from the weather services, she composed a chart. She further compiled data on any civil, political or religious unrest or confrontations. It looked as though Anusca Damitree’s theory had some validity. She went over the information several times, always coming to the same conclusion. Every time there was a Sun Dog, there was a major event on the planet. Could there really be spiritual battles fought in other dimensions and with these events on the physical plane as repercussions? Jennifer’s mind was bending like a sapling in a wind storm. The possibility shook the very core of her belief system. She wished that she could talk to Sam about all that had happened, but how could she expect him to believe something that she was having trouble believing herself? Somewhere inside her, all of the black magic and talk of gypsies felt right, deep inside. But on the more conscious level, she was afraid that this obsession was about to pull her through the doorway of the occult.

✡ ✡ ✡

Cameron's Trip to the Pasture House

After Damascus had left for Earth, Cameron had paced the cabin for hours; he did not want to go to the Pasture House and see Leman. Finally he shoved the list in his back pocket, saddled his horse and headed south. He kept thinking about Starling. He usually could forget about Damascus and what he did to women, but this time he was unable to. Cameron traveled half a day to reach Leman. When he arrived, he jumped off his horse and tied it to the post in front of the dwelling. He heard cheering and shouting inside. He snuck to the side of the building, climbed the wood pile and peeked through the window.

Inside, he saw a group of men gathered around a large table, in the middle of which sat a naked woman. Cameron was familiar with her; she was known as Candice, who gave sex in return for favors and goods. She was leaning back on her hands with her legs spread apart. The men were bidding a price for her. Leman stepped in to settle the arguing. He had decided that his foreman, Jones, had won. Leman grabbed half the items lying on the table and put aside the other half for Candice.

"You're mine, Sugar!" Jones shouted. He moved to the end of the table. Candice slid to the edge where he stood.

"Show me what ya got there, big boy," Candice said, imitating Mae West. The men roared with laughter. She put her feet up on the table and spread her legs wider. The men began to push and shove one another to catch a glimpse of her sex, as they slapped Jones on the back, hooting and hollering at him. He looked around the room, his eyes darted this way and that. He smiled and began to unbutton his fly. Then he pulled out his penis, grabbing it with both hands obviously proud to show Candice.

"Well, now," she said, "you are a big one, aren't you!" She glanced at the faces around the table. "In fact I would say that you're the biggest man here." They all laughed and pointed at one another, making jokes.

Leman grew bored and shot a look at Jones. "Either fuck her or let someone else do it," he said.

"I'll do it! I'll fuck her!" someone yelled from the back of the room. Jones looked in the direction of the voice. Quickly, he reached across the table, grabbed a leg in each hand and pulled Candice's buttocks to the edge. He positioned his body between her legs and thrust into her as the men cheered him on.

Leman was enjoying the sight. He was about to pleasure himself when he noticed Cameron's face in the window. "Why, you little bastard!" he snarled, gnashing the words from between clenched teeth. While buttoning his pants, Leman ran out the front door and around the side of the building. Cameron caught him in his peripheral and made a mad dash. He slid down the woodpile, hit the ground, picked up a log and threw it at him.

Leman held his hand up to his face to block the incoming missile. "If I get my hands on you…"

Another projectile shot toward him, cutting his words short. Cameron ran as fast as his little legs would carry him back to his horse. Quickly he untied it, mounted and kicked deep into its flanks. The horse reared back on its haunches.

Leman stopped at the sight of the two hooves. A piece of paper hit Leman in the face. He swatted at it. By the time he realized what it was, his mouth was full of the dirt kicked up by Cameron's getaway. Leman stood watching the plume of dust that rose against the sunset.

The Limboshia Mountains

Laura woke up refreshed. She could not remember the last time she had slept so peacefully…so sound. Tom and Marti were cooking breakfast, talking.

"Laura looks really good this morning," Marti said as she flipped hotcakes.

"I noticed that she's got a different energy around her; she's more confident," Tom replied. He poured coffee, setting it down where they would eat.

"Where is she, by the way?" Marti asked, looking up from the sizzling pan.

"I think she went down to the creek to fill the water bags."

As they were speaking, Laura knelt at the edge of the water, filling the last bag. She thought about the conversation with the stone faces; she knew she had to get Starling, no matter the cost. Damascus would stop at nothing to get the Star Scrolls. He not only wanted the Dark Territories to consume all of Limboshia, but to dominate Earth. Laura understood that she was one of the chosen souls, one of a select group that would battle Damascus to ensure the safety of humanity. When she was on Earth, her friend James had regressed her and revealed to her who she was. Laura never really believed him. She'd tried, but it seemed so far-fetched at the time. He had told her that her name, as well as Morgan's, was on a list, a scroll, and had been for thousands of years. He explained about Fire Angels and how they kept the balance on Earth between good and evil, that their souls had lived thousands of lives. It bothered Laura that she had laughed at James — he was so sincere when he had told her these things. She remembered the night well. Morgan and she had never discussed it seriously; so many things were happening back then. How she wished now that they would have — if only she had listened to James. Laura could only hope that Morgan knew what and who Damascus was.

"Laura! Breakfast is done. Come and eat it while it's hot!" Laura heard Marti calling, and turned to the stones.

"I won't let you down. I promise to get Starling back to the Gateway and make sure the Star Scrolls are safe." She got up and collected the filled water bags, slinging them over her shoulder.

"Remember…Laura, you are the light, we are counting on you…"

* * *

Tom, Marti and Laura rode quietly through the outskirts of the towers. "How many days to the Pasture House, Marti?" Laura asked.

"Three. Today we'll be out of the Fourth Territory," Marti replied, looking at the large mountain range ahead. "Once we get to those mountains," she continued, pointing, "we have to go on foot. It's too treacherous for the horses." Laura turned in her saddle and watched the towers disappear into the distance.

"We are going to have to stash the tack and go up and over, right into Damascus' territory." Marti's voice had hatred in it. Damascus had kidnapped her close friend, and she was sick of him and all his crap.

"It's going to be all right, Marti. We'll get Starling back." Tom tried to sound sure of himself. But he knew the odds were not in their favor.

As night crept in around the three riders, they found the perfect place to let the horses go and hide the tack. Marti spotted a small cave about a hundred feet up the mountain. They agreed it would be a good place to keep the gear from being found by Damascus' men.

The following morning, Tom pulled out the crossbows they had packed. "I thought we would do a little target practice this morning," he said, looking at the women with a bow in his hand. "Have you ever shot one of these Laura?"

She smiled at Tom. “I never had a use for one of those while I was a reporter.”

“Very funny this morning, aren’t we?” He handed a bow to her, as Marti came alongside.

“We’ll shoot in the sandy loam there at the base of the mountain,” he said, pointing. He began to explain the fundamentals of the weapon. “First, you want to pull this string over this piece here.” He butted the stock against his abdomen and cocked the bow. “Then, you place an arrow here.” He pointed to a groove carved in the stock of the bow. He placed the arrow where he had indicated and raised the weapon. “When you have your target in sight, slowly pull the trigger.” He released the aperture, allowing the arrow to rocket away from him. He turned to Laura, grinning. “Now you try, O Great Reporter.”

Laura struggled for a time, but managed to successfully get the bow cocked, arrow in place. Raising the weapon, she aimed at the arrow that Tom had shot and pulled the trigger. The projectile flew from the carriage into the hill next to Tom’s.

“I did it!” Laura exclaimed, looking at Tom.

He had a pleased expression. “Try it again,” he said. She shot several arrows, and with each one she became more confident.

“You’re a natural,” Marti chimed.

Laura gave a small grin. “I should be — my zodiac sign is Sagittarius, the archer.” She said, her face beaming with pride.

Tom collected the arrows and returned them to the great Sagittarian reporter. “From here on out, we have to keep our eyes open. Remember, we’re in the Dark Territories now,” he said, looking up at the top of the mountain range.

Marti took charge of the climbing equipment. She had all the rope neatly wound and hung over her left shoulder. Readjusting her gloves, she looked up. Slowly she grabbed a hold of a crevice with her hand, then found a foot hold. As she climbed she felt the rush she had known so many years ago. Her muscles ached as she went higher up the side of the mountain. It felt good to feel her arms and legs burn as she pushed on. Laura and Tom watched in awe. She climbed like a spider.

“She’s really something, isn’t she?” Laura said.

“I’ll say!” Tom was holding a gloved hand over his eyes to shield the sun. “She told me stories when she was a kid,” he said. “There was this huge tree in her parent’s back yard that she would climb, and one day I guess she decided to parachute down with a bed sheet.” Tom snorted. “She was rushed to the hospital with two sprained ankles.” Laura smiled, picturing Marti as a little girl.

Marti reached the top, swinging a leg over the stone ledge, rolling herself a safe distance from the edge. She lay there for a moment to catch her breath. “You all right?” Tom yelled up.

Marti stood and waved down to them. She tied the end of the rope to a large pine tree, put her foot against it and pulled on the rope. She did this twice, to prevent a repetition of her own fate when she had gone climbing with her husband Joe. Walking to the edge, Marti tossed the bundle of rope over the side. Laura grabbed the end and looked up.

“Laura,” Marti yelled down, “see the knots every four foot or so?” Laura nodded. “O.K, what you want to do is, grab a knot with your hands, then get your feet above one and push with your legs as you pull with your arms.” Marti lay down on her stomach, watching.

Laura took hold of the knot above her head, got her feet on one and did as Marti instructed. She did well the first sixty feet, and then she began to have a hard time keeping a firm grip. Her hands threatened to slip out of her gloves. Marti watched as Laura hung from the rope.

“Grab the next knot,” she yelled down to her. Laura tried, but Marti could see she was having problems with the gloves.

“Grab the damn knot!” she yelled again.

“I can’t reach it!” Laura called back to Marti. Sweat was running down her face, stinging her eyes. She could taste it as it passed her lips. Laura reached with all her might for the next knot. She climbed another twenty feet and hung. Marti could see that Laura was in big trouble — she had to keep moving or she was going to fall. She couldn’t pull her climbing cohort up because of the knots in the rope. They would get stuck on the ledge because of Laura’s weight on the rope.

"Laura, you have to grab the next freaking knot! Keep moving!" Marti was trying not to yell, but it was not looking good for her friend swinging below. Suddenly Marti saw the look on Laura's face as her hands slipped out of the gloves and she began to fall.

"No!" Marti screamed. Tom stood helplessly below. He heard his friend howl in pain as she got a grip on the rope and jolted to a stop, causing an involuntary grunt to escape. He covered his eyes.

Laura felt the blood run down her arms from her hands. She closed her eyes and pictured the towers, the stone faces. Like a madwoman she climbed, wet blood sticking to the rope. Hands throbbing and stinging, she climbed.

Marti shook her head. She had never seen anyone move up a rope so fast. Marti grabbed her wrists and pulled Laura up over the ledge. "Are…" Marti swallowed to reclaim her voice. "Are you trying to give me a fucking heart attack?" she asked, looking over the edge at Tom, who had fallen on his butt, and remained there. The two women lay on their backs looking at the sky, catching their breaths. After a few minutes, Laura turned her head toward Marti. "That wasn't so bad…was it?" Laura asked, laughing.

Marti hauled off and hit her. "Has anyone ever told you how insane you are?" Marti asked, having trouble concealing her smile. "Now, let's see those hands."

Laura sat up and held out the bloodstained palms. They were ripped and torn.

"That has got to freaking hurt!" Marti exclaimed. Picking up a water bag, she poured some of the contents over the wounds. Laura winced. Marti took a rag from the rope bag and tore in several strips and wrapped Laura's hands. "Better?" she asked.

Laura nodded, but her attention was on the rope. By the tension and movement, she knew Tom must be climbing up. Soon, Tom's leg swung up over the edge, where Marti helped him. "Are you all right Laura?" he asked, his face twisted with fear.

"I'm fine, don't worry. It looks worse than it is." She lied.

They set up camp against a small bluff of rock not far from the ledge. Marti pulled up the rope and neatly placed it in the bag.

"Are you sure you're all right?" Tom asked again, his face showing his concern.

"It hurts, but I'm fine." She looked at her hands. "That climbing thing
looks easier than it is," she said, smiling.

Tom raised any eyebrow. "I'm going to get some firewood. I want you to relax, O.K?" He stood with his arms crossed over his chest, waiting for an answer. Laura shot a look at him. "I mean it, Laura." She could tell by the tone of his voice that he was not playing around, and relented with a roll of her eyes. She watched as Marti collected rocks for the fire ring; she felt stupid just sitting there. *The great warrior…my butt,* she thought. She leaned against the cool rocks. Her hands were throbbing.

Suddenly, from above, pine needles rained down on her. She was about to yell up at Tom when she heard voices. It was not Tom…not Marti. The crossbows were almost within reach and she quietly crawled on her elbows over to the gear. Laura picked up one of the bows, her teeth gritting in pain. *How the hell am I going to cock this thing,* she wondered. Tom came from behind her and threw his hat at her.

She turned around, relief washing over her face. "Where is Marti?" she mouthed silently. He shrugged. They could hear two men above them, still not close enough to make out what they were saying. Laura sat up and saw Marti. She was crouched over, tight against the rocks, walking slowly toward them. Laura pointed above. Marti nodded, holding a finger to her lips. More pine needles came down on them, small rocks followed, and just overhead…footsteps.

Two shadows formed on the ground where they had just sat not more than two minutes ago, one tall, one very small. "What are we looking for?" The small shadow asked.

"I don't know." The tall shadow replied in a thick accent. "I hope to find city…" he said, when suddenly his words stopped. The small shadow nudged the bigger one, and they crouched down, the smaller one pointing. Tom, Laura and Marti all looked where in that direction. There, in the clearing, was a water bag. Marti grabbed her face with her hands and shook her head. She looked between her fingers at Tom. He shrugged with his palms facing up.

"What's that?" asked the little one.

"Shhhh!" the big one put his hand over the other's mouth. The bigger shadow jumped off the rock. As soon as he hit the ground, Tom was on top of him, trying to put a hold around his neck. It looked something like David and Goliath. The smaller man jumped behind his friend, picked up a rock and was about to hit Tom. Marti sprang forward and grabbed the cocked arm in midair as her other hand clawed his face. He dropped the rock. Marti had a full-body death grip on the little man.

"Who the hell are you?" she growled behind clenched teeth. He fell to the ground, yelping like a scared animal. Tom, on the other hand, was having a hell of a time trying to hang on to Goliath. The large man reached over his shoulder and threw him to the ground, putting a foot on Tom's chest.

Laura had somehow managed to cock the bow and was aiming at the big man's neck.

"Hold it right there, Mister!" she yelled. Tom was trying to get the boot off. He had both hands around it, but it would not budge. "If you don't get that damn foot off him, I'll shoot you!"

By the look in Laura's eye, she meant it. The man took the boot off Tom, bent over and offered a hand up.

Marti straddled the little one, both hand wrapped around his throat. "I asked you…who the hell are you?" she was hissing.

"Jimmy! My name is Jimmy!"

The big man laughed. The sound surprised everyone. "I am thinking…you should be…name…how do you say? Pip Squeak." He looked at Laura. "And you…you wish to shoot me?" He laughed again.

Tom was brushing himself off.

"Who are you?" Laura asked, still holding the bow on him.

"Allow me to introduce…I am...Damitree." Everyone's mouth fell open. They knew who he was. The Elders had told them who Damascus had as a host body. Laura lowered the weapon, and Marti got off the little guy named Jimmy Monroe.

Morgan and Ryan

The trip to the lab was quiet at first, but by the time they arrived Ryan had eased Morgan's fear about James. "So we can't go to the police," Morgan said. "What makes you think that this guy won't call Malcolm?"

Ryan smiled. "Because he can't stand the bastard. Malcolm's made a lot of enemies." Ryan opened the door and stepped out. "You coming?" she asked, looking through the cab, she then directed her attention across the parking lot. She could just make out the back door to the precinct. The two women walked the opposite direction, down a narrow alley to the lab. Ryan stopped at a metal door, and knocked.

"No secret knock?" Morgan queried.

"That's only in the movies," Ryan grinned. The door opened and a small ghostly face with large black-rimmed glassed poked out.

"Hey, Ryan." The man pushed his glasses back up his nose. "You can't stay away, huh?"

"Hey, Joey, how's it going?" He opened the door to let them in.

"Your timing is good; I'm on break," he said, walking down the hall. Ryan and Morgan followed the white lab coat.

"Welcome to the illustrious break room." He waved a hand, imitating Vanna White. Two long tables with chairs, a small sink, counter, coffee pot and a microwave filled the room. He grabbed three Styrofoam cups and the coffee pot, setting them on one of the tables.

"Joey Spencer, this is Morgan Deveraux." He extended his hand to greet her.

"Nice to meet you, Joey." Morgan couldn't help but think about her pet goldfish when she was a child as Joey blinked through his thick lenses. Joey's attention shifted to Ryan.

"What do you need?" he asked. She was going to defend herself, but what was the use? Joey knew that whenever she came to see him she needed something. She pulled out the evidence bags, laying them on the table.

"I need you to run DNA on these." Joey picked up a bag, looked at it and then tossed it back on the table. "Anyone I know?" he asked, knowing that if it had been a normal case she would not have come to the back door.

"John Malcolm."

"Why doesn't that surprise me?" he said, pouring coffee. He motioned with his hand for them to sit. Joey stared at Ryan from across the table.

"What?" she asked, smiling coyly.

"There is always more. It's never this easy, Ryan."

Morgan made a squeaking sound in her throat. Ryan nudged her, eyes still fixed on Joey. "O.K," Ryan allowed. "There is one more thing." Morgan and Joey held their hands over their grins. Ryan shot a look at the two of them. "I need to get a glass or a cigar, something from Malcolm's office."

Joey slid his glasses up on his head. Morgan was shocked to see how handsome he was.

"It's just a glass," Ryan said.

"Just a glass. That I have to sneak out of an office. Wait, not *just* an office; the Chief of Detective's office." He rubbed his face with both hands and blew out an exasperated breath. "Shit," he said, "I'll do it. I can't stand him anymore than you can."

Ryan's smile lit the room. "I appreciate it, Joey, I really do."

Joey rolled his eyes. "Listen," he said, standing up. "I got to get back to work. I'll call you as soon as I find anything out." He pulled his glasses down on his nose, gathered the evidence bags and put them in his large pocket. Ryan was about to thank him again when she saw the tail of his lab coat go through the door down the hall. When Ryan and Morgan got to the parking lot, a uniformed officer was running toward her SUV.

"Who's that?" Morgan asked, taking hold of Ryan's arm.

"I don't know. I can't see that far," Ryan said, opening the doors.

The two slid into the cab. The officer ran across the lot, calling out to Ryan. "It's Kenny Wilson, he's a rookie." Ryan rolled down the window. "I wonder what he wants?" she murmured.

Kenny came alongside the vehicle. "Delgato," he said, bending over to catch his breath. "There is a guy that called, like three times yesterday." He took a couple of deep breaths. "I told him that you didn't work for the Department anymore, but he was insistent that you get the message." Kenny was young and handsome, a poster child. "I saw your truck over here and thought it was important enough to run this over." He handed her a pink message slip: "Bill Cameron."

Ryan took the paper.

"He wouldn't leave his number. He said you had it." Kenny's eyes were filled with worry; he had tried to get the number.

"You did great, Kenny." She looked down at the message again. "Did anyone else see this?" she asked him.

"No ma'am," he smiled. "I was the only one."

Ryan nodded. "Kenny, can you do me a favor?"

His eyes lit up. He'd had a crush on Ryan since starting the job.

"Sure."

Ryan wrote down her home phone and cell numbers. "Can you call me if there are anymore messages?"

Kenny looked at the numbers, folded the paper carefully and slipped into his breast pocket.

"And Kenny, don't tell anyone that you saw me this evening, all right?"

He nodded his head. "You got it, Detective Delgato."

Morgan fought to keep from laughing.

"Call me Ryan," the detective said as she patted his hand. She started the engine and backed out of the parking lot.

"Ryan," Kenny whispered, watching the vehicle pull away.

After some bantering back and forth about how adorable Kenny was, Ryan and Morgan were on their way to Bill Cameron's home, located behind the Wild Side Club. It was dark in the parking lot. The club was still closed due to the current investigation. On the way, Ryan called to confirm that Bill was going to be home. As the two women walked into the alley leading to Bill's residence, the wind whipped discarded papers into tiny whirlwinds. The smell of garbage pierced their nostrils as they passed a large dumpster.

"That's the place." Ryan pointed to a small house with security bars on the windows.

"Not the best neighborhood to be running around at night in," Morgan said softly.

"Welcome to my world," Ryan said, as she knocked on the door.

"Who is it?" answered a muffled voice.

"It's Ryan Delgato, Mr. Cameron. We spoke earlier."

The curtain on the door pushed aside, exposing a face. "Who is that with you?" the man attached to the face asked nervously.

"It's a friend of mine, Mr. Cameron. Her name is Morgan Deveraux."

Several locks clicked, and the door opened slowly. "I don't mean to be rude, Detective. Please come in."

Ryan and Morgan slipped inside. The door was quickly shut and re-secured. The air in the room smelled of bourbon and smoke. A cigarette smoldered in the ashtray on the kitchen table. A desk sat on the opposite wall, stacked with newspapers. Ryan guessed a year's worth. One small lamp on an end table was lit but provided little light.

"Can I get you a drink?" Bill Cameron asked as he walked to the cabinet for glasses. "Please ladies…sit," he called over his shoulder. Bill brought the bottle and glasses back to the table, and looked at Ryan. “I don’t know where to start, Detective. I wasn’t completely honest with you about Jimmy Monroe’s death.”

Ryan didn’t even raise an eyebrow. She was used to being lied to. It came with the territory. She pulled out one of the new business cards. “Mr. Cameron, I no longer work for the Department. I’m a private investigator.” She said, handing him a card. He stole a quick look.

“So this is off the record?”

Ryan took a sip of her drink. “That depends on what you tell me.”

Bill looked at her with tired, sheepish eyes and began to tell her his story. He told of his involvement with John Malcolm, his son’s suicide and the cocaine abuse. Morgan flinched every so often at the mention of “the reporter” that left cards, and how he had tried to reach her. Ryan laid her hand on Morgan’s balled fist as a silent show of support. After Bill Cameron was finished with his story, he ran his fingers through his hair and poured another drink, waiting for a response from Ryan. She lifted her cocktail and took a long drink. The clinking of ice cubes was all the response Bill received. She sat back in her chair and studied him. He looked tired and beat to hell; she could see the man was blaming himself for his son’s suicide. She thought about John Malcolm and how he had betrayed his profession. She thought about Morgan and the pain she must be feeling, not only for Laura but for James. She thought about how desperately she wanted to kick John Malcolm’s ass. Ryan slid forward in her chair and set her drink down.

“Mr. Cameron, I think you have a couple of different issues here. The first one being the drug use in your establishment, not only of your clients, but your employees. I’m sure this will come out in the investigation.” Ryan stood up and paced the floor. She was trying not to show how angry she was about Malcolm.

“The second issue is *your* addiction and the blame you are laying on yourself about your son.” She stood in front of the towering newspapers on Bill’s desk.

“John Malcolm,” she said, behind slightly clenched teeth, “is to blame for your son’s suicide. I can help you with the legal problems; we can get you in a Federal Protection Program…if you testify against John." What she was really thinking was that it would be better for everyone if someone capped the son of a bitch.

"Witness Protection Program?" Bill looked scared to death, as he should have been. She turned away from the papers and walked back to her chair and sat down. Bill lit a cigarette and exhaled a plume of smoke. "Detective, I wanted you to come here so that I could get some justice…for my son's death," he said, shrugging his shoulders.

Morgan sat silent, but her insides were screaming. She understood about wanting justice. "How did you get involved with John Malcolm?" she asked.

Bill took another long pull from his cigarette and stubbed it out in the ashtray. "He came around not too long after I took over the club. I didn't know he was an officer until after my son's death." He put his face in his hands. "He was a nice guy at first. Everyone liked him." Bill shook his head. "First impressions," he said, holding his drink between his hands and looking into it. "He used to bring cocaine in every once in a while. As time went on he would bring it in more often, then every day." Bill blew out a laugh. "I see how calculated it all was. He got the whole fucking place hooked."

A scowl crossed Ryan's face. "I know were the drugs came from," she hissed under her breath.

"Some of the guys were talking about him not turning in *all* of the evidence, and there were drugs missing from the evidence locker."

She really wanted to kick Malcolm's ass, just for the hell of it.

"How does a guy like that look at himself in the mirror?" Bill asked.

"Obviously he doesn't," Ryan stated.

Bill nodded.

"Mr. Cameron, you mentioned that Laura Saubert had left cards on your door?"

He nodded his head. "I tried to call her. When I found out that she had died, that's when I called you."

Morgan white knuckled the chair arm at the mention of her name. She knew somehow that all of this was connected.

Bill pushed himself up from his chair and walked to the desk.

Morgan leaned toward Ryan. "Thanks, I really wanted to see those cards. Does that sound silly?" she whispered.

"Not at all," Ryan said quietly.

Bill returned with several cards in his grip, and handed them to Ryan. She took the stack and passed them to Morgan. It did not go unnoticed that Morgan's hand was shaking as the cards met her waiting palm. She carefully inspected each one.

"What do you think Laura Saubert wanted to talk to you about?" Ryan asked.

Bill poured another drink. "I think she had tied John to my son's suicide…or was fishing for information." He took a deep breath. "I guess we'll never know."

Ryan scribbled more notes on her pad. "Mr. Cameron, you also mentioned Jimmy Monroe's death…that you weren't completely honest. Do you want to tell what that's about?"

"There had been some trouble between John and Monroe." Bill leaned back in his chair. "In the beginning John didn't mess with the stage men, but with the use of cocaine, I guess he became more aggressive. He started pushing some of the guys around." He rubbed his face with his hands again.

Ryan looked up from her notes.

"What guys?" she asked, lighting a cigarette. She blew out the match and tossed it in the ashtray.

"I'm sure that you've figured out one of them was Jimmy Monroe." He took a drink. "The other man was Jimmy's best friend Arthur Leman." Ryan raised an eyebrow and continued to write on the notepad.

"I don't think that it's a coincidence that the two men that John was harassing are both dead." Bill said. Ryan took another pull off her cigarette.

"Did you call the police?" she asked.

Bill sat forward in his chair and put his elbow on the desk. "I wish I had, but John promised me that it wouldn't happen again."

Ryan blew out a stream of smoke. "But it did, didn't it?"

Bill nodded.

"Is it safe to assume that you owed him a lot of money for the cocaine?" Ryan queried.

Again he nodded, then dropped his head in his hands.

"I was into him for thousands of dollars. He pretty well ran the place when he came in. All the employees were scared of him."

Ryan took a last hit from her cigarette and stubbed it out. "Do you think that John killed Monroe and Leman?"

"I wish I knew for sure, but it sure looks that way to me." Bill took a long drink.

Morgan sat silent, listening and thinking about Laura wrapped up in all this. She must have been frightened as things began to unfold. She knew that Laura was protecting her, but maybe if she had confided in her Morgan could have helped.

After leaving Bill Cameron's house, Ryan dropped Morgan off. It was getting late and she still had to meet with her father at the new office to discuss some business matters. The brick structure was built in the nineteen twenties, and showed the pride the craftsmen took in their work. Ornate masonry details dressed the windows and parapets, giving the building a unique flavor. Ryan stood in the cool night air and looked at the wedge of light that spilled out on the brick wall. It comforted her to know her father was just on the other side.

Ed had worked the entire day buying office furniture, computers, and two executive desks for him and his partner.

As Ryan approached the door she saw a professional sign — Delgato and Delgato. She opened the door, stopping in the threshold at the sight of the filled space. "This is wonderful, Dad. I can't believe you did all of this in one day."

"So my partner approves?" Ed was thinking that the look on his daughter's face was worth all the effort. He would move heaven and Earth for her.

"I love everything that you've done. Did Mom help you?" she asked, grinning.

"Hey, how about a little faith in your old man, huh?" Ed walked over to her and folded her in an embrace.

"I think tomorrow I'll go down to the District and find some paintings to dress up the walls," Ryan said, wrapped in her father's arms.

Ed released her and went to sit at his desk. "Ry, will you take your mother along? I want her to feel like she is a part of this. After all it was her idea."

"Sure, Dad." Ryan assured her father, feeling her new leather chair. She ran her hands over the dark mahogany wood desktop. Ed could see she was deep in thought.

"Dad, the other night I wanted to talk to you, but when you asked me about being your partner…" Ed smiled.

"Do you remember the Saubert case, about two years ago?" Ed looked surprised.

"Sure I do, but it was a quick investigation." Ryan stood, and walked around the front of her desk and folded her arms.

"The other night, when I was in the District, I went into a gallery. The owner happened to be Laura Saubert's lover, Morgan Deveraux."

Ed leaned forward in his chair and rested his arms on the desk.

"She told me that the day she brought Laura to the hospital, they found poison in her system." Ed's eyebrows raised. "A nurse that had seen the tox report had told Morgan in confidence what was in it. The funny thing is that all the paper work disappeared." Ryan walked over to her father's desk and sat on the corner. "Morgan wanted a full investigation. Laura was working on a story that involved a lot of people in high places." Ryan smoothed the material of her slacks.

"Do you remember the call I got this morning?" Ed nodded. "It was Morgan. Her friend, who happens to be the best friend of Laura Saubert, was kidnapped today."

"The plot thickens," Ed said.

Ryan laughed sarcastically. "It gets better. I go to Half Moon Bay to check her friend's office where the kidnapping took place. I'm looking around and I find one of John's cigars in the guy's office."

Ed opened his mouth to speak, but Ryan held up a hand. "I know what you're going to say. That doesn't convict the man, right?" she asked, with palms raised. Ed smiled. She knew him well.

Ryan stood and began to pace in front of Ed's desk, much like a prosecutor in a trial. "I drop off the evidence to Joey down at the lab. I'm getting ready to leave and Kenny, the rookie, comes running over with a message from Bill Cameron, the owner of the club." Ed gestured that he knew who Bill was.

Ryan flipped open her notepad and glanced at a few pages. "I go to Cameron's and guess who's name keep coming up?" Ryan leaned palms down on her father's desk, looking into his eyes. "John Malcolm." She said. "I know this is a crazy question, Dad, but who was in charge of the Saubert case?" Ryan smirked.

"John Malcolm." Ed replied, sitting back in his chair.

"I found out that John brought a lot of cocaine into the club. Do you remember the rumors about John a couple years ago?"

"You mean about the missing evidence?" Ed asked.

"Yes, the guys were accusing him of siphoning evidence, then all the rumors got dropped when he became Chief of Detectives."

"I remember," Ed murmured, as he lit a cigarette.

"Funny how that worked out, huh?" Ryan said dryly.

"Bill told me a story. One night he and his son Billie were watching movies and John broke down his front door. Bill owed him a lot of money for drugs. John Malcolm raped his son…in front of him." Ryan looked down at her shoes, then back to her father.

Ed's face was unbelieving at first, then it hardened. He slammed the top of his desk with his fist. "That son of a bitch!" He got up and went to the window, his hands on his hips as he looked out. "That lowlife mother fucker!" Ed took a breath. "When

Rugger took over the precinct, we had a discussion about Malcolm." Ed's head dropped. "I had suspicions, but couldn't get them substantiated." He turned and looked at Ryan. "Makes me wonder where Rugger's loyalties lie."

Ryan agreed. "That explains how Malcolm got assigned to the Saubert case, doesn't it?" she asked, shoving her hands in her pockets. "This is a dangerous situation, Dad. Who are we going to trust at the Department?"

Ed looked at her with a furrowed brow. "I think we still have a couple of friends there," he said.

Ryan perched back on the corner of her father's desk. "John Malcolm is a sneaky bastard, and he's got his hand in a lot of different pots by the sound of it. Who's he working for is what I want to know."

Ryan had expressed Ed's exact thoughts. He sat back and stared down at his desk blotter. He would make some calls in the morning to some of the officers he thought he could trust. He looked up at his daughter. "You're a chip off the old block, aren't you?"

She leaned over and patted his hand. "We can only hope Dad. We can only hope." She hated to see her father so upset. The situation was bad, but they were out of the politics. They could actually do something about it. She noticed her father's hat hanging on the coat rack by the front door. It was the old style of detective's hat. Bogart wore one. Ryan walked over and grabbed it. When she was a little girl and her father came home in a bad mood, she would play *Joe Friday, P.I.*

She put the hat on her head and walked around her father, sitting at the desk. "So, Mr. Delgato, when was the last time you saw your wife?" Ed took his head out of his hands and looked across the room. Ryan tried again. "Sir, if you don't answer, we can and will detain you."

Ed looked up at her. He knew that she was trying to lighten the mood. After all, it was their first day in the new office. Ed sat up straight. "I saw her this morning," he said.

Ryan pulled the hat down tighter to her eyes. "Do you recall the time, sir?"

Ed grinned. “Seven o’clock…no, seven-thirty.”

Ryan stood in front of him and leaned over the desk. “Which one is it, seven? Or seven-thirty, sir?”

“Seven-thirty.”

“Mr. Delgato, what were you and your wife doing the last time you saw her?” she asked, raising an eyebrow.

“We were having breakfast.”

“Breakfast…and what did you eat, sir?”

“Coffee,” Ed said.

Ryan stood erect, crossing her arms. “Coffee” You ate coffee? Is that what you’re saying sir?”

“No…no, we had muffins and jam.”

“Now it’s muffins and jam! How do you expect me to believe that?”

Ed put on an exasperated expression, pretending to feel pressured. “It was muffins and jam, I remember,” he said.

Ryan walked around his desk, as if to scrutinize his body movements. “Sir, what was your wife wearing the last time you saw her?”

Ed leaned back in the chair, slipped a cigarette out of his pocket and lit it. He smiled, looked up at Ryan and repeated, “What was she wearing?” Ryan nodded her head.

"She was wearing *way* too much."

Ryan let out a groan. Once again her father had beaten her. She took off the hat she was wearing and smooshed it on his head.

* * *

After Ryan had dropped her off, Morgan had been wandering through the house. The loneliness was closing in on her. The evening paper and mail still lay on the kitchen table. Not knowing what to do about James, she thought she might as well look through the mail. She sorted the junk mail from the bills, then opened the newspaper. She flipped through the pages, not really reading, just looking at the pictures. She opened to the “Features” section and there was a picture of her Dark Angel sculpture. She stood and placed her hands on either side of article, bent over and read. The man's name under the picture was Stephane Damitree. She read the entire article, and when she got to the bottom she saw that it was written by a reporter named Jennifer Collins. Her body was shaking, but she felt no emotion. The day seemed to turn into a week. She wanted to call Ryan, but thought better of it. Ryan had done so much for her already. No, she would take matters into here own hands. First thing in the morning she would go see this reporter.

Jennifer Collins

Jennifer had decided to go to the villa that Rada had talked about; the computer search piqued her interest. She went to the hall closet and retrieved a duffle bag with her Minolta camera and tripod. High on the shelf were her father's old binoculars. Jennifer packed a tape recorder, tapes, and extra batteries. She changed into dark jeans, a sweatshirt and hooded jacket. She felt like a secret agent on a mission, and laughed to herself for being so excited over a story.

Jennifer found the location that Rada had described to her, and parked the car down the street. The small grove of trees on the property was a good cover for her to unpack her equipment. She watched the house. There had not been any movement. Slowly she crept up to the main house, and looked in the windows. No lights were on.

She noticed that a smaller bungalow in the back had the lights on. Carefully she made her way down the drive and under a side window. Heart pounding, she wiped the sweat from her forehead. *This is hard work. I wonder if Diane Sawyer had to go through this?* Jennifer raised her head just above the outside sill. She could see two men. One, with red hair, was hurt. The other man was large, with jet black hair; he appeared to be Anusca Damitree's son. She sat back down and took a breath. Slowly she eased the recorder's mic into the window sill. After a minute she checked to see if the tape had picked up anything. Nothing. She could see the men were talking. She crawled to the next window, which was half open. Again she eased the mic onto the sill.

"James, you know what I want. I came to give you one last chance before I leave." Jennifer could hear the voices and peeked in the window. The large man was talking.

"I told you that I don't know anything about the Star Scrolls. You tell me your name is Damascus, that somehow you are my brother." James shook his head. "You expect me to believe we have a soul connection?"

Jennifer checked the shutter speed of the camera; she wanted to make sure to expose the film correctly. She knew she would have to take the shot when they were talking. The last thing she needed was to be caught.

"If you tell me what I want to know," Damascus said, "I will not hurt your friend Morgan Deveraux."

James had an angry look on his face. "I'm supposed to trust you? You kidnapped me and had the crap beat out of me." James could not tell him anything. He knew he had to keep the Scrolls safe at any cost, even if it meant his life.

"You don't have a choice!" Damascus interrupted. James sat forward in his chair.

"You say you're my brother?" James spat. "How can you be any relation to me? You're evil!" Damascus stood and looked down at James.

"My patience is running thin — you leave me no choice but to visit your friend."

"You leave Morgan alone! She knows nothing!" James screamed. Damascus smiled.

"That means that you *do* know something, in order to have knowledge that she knows nothing." James dropped his throbbing head into his hands.

Jennifer saw another man come out of the bathroom and snapped a shot of him.

“Your friend Laura, she would do anything to protect you and Morgan, wouldn’t she?” Damascus questioned, with folded arms across his chest. He grimaced.

James jumped up. “You bastard!” he yelled, his fists raised in front of him. Damascus smacked James with the back of his hand. James fell back into the chair, holding his mouth. “I wouldn’t tell you anything, even if I did know.” James had defiance in his muffled voice.

“You will James. Trust me, you will.” Damascus laughed as he walked away from James. “I’ll be back in a few days, and we’ll talk again.” James lunged at the large man’s back. Damascus swung an arm, knocking him to the floor. He landed with a thud. Jennifer gave a silent gasp and closed her eyes. Malcolm sat the entire time rubbing his eyes, trying to focus, and to stop the trickles of blood that came from his tear ducks. Damascus looked at Malcolm and said, “Keep an eye on him, and if anything goes wrong, you will wish I had killed you earlier.” He grinned at the eye comment. The door slammed shut behind him as he left. James crawled to it. “Let me out of here, you oversized piece of shit!”

Jennifer ducked below the window. She quickly gathered her belongings and listened for a few moments until she felt it was safe to leave. As she ran across the greens to the grove of trees, she felt bad at having to leave the redheaded man. She wished she could go to the police. But would they believe her, she wondered. No, they probably would not. She would go to Anusca Damitree — surely she would know what to do. Jennifer had both hands wrapped tightly around the steering wheel on the way to the Penthouse. Her head was spinning with names she had heard at the villa. James, Laura, Morgan and Damascus. But most of all the Star Scrolls. What were they?

* * *

The Hilton Penthouse

Rada, Anusca, and Jennifer listened to the recording. Jennifer stole looks at Anusca while she listened. Anusca sat with knees together and hands folded in her lap, the corners of her mouth turned up in a knowing gesture.

She was familiar with the name Damascus. He had many other names as well — Genghis Khan, Saddam Hussein, Hitler, Ayatollah Khomeini, Osama Bin Laden, to mention a few. He was the evil in the universe, he was the dark that made the light even lighter. He was the very thing that kept the world balanced, the world that he hated so much. Damascus' soul had been in existence as long as time itself. His purpose was to seek the total destruction of all living things. Anusca's mother, and her mother's mother, had fought this entity. And now, at last it was her turn. So, she smiled.

Jennifer was confused at the sight of the small woman listening, smiling. Anusca had always known she would be called to fight. Many, many generations of her female ancestors had done so, even before her mother and grandmother. At last it was her turn to do battle, and so she smiled. She understood that the other side was in conflict, and the fallout would soon begin to affect their world. Anusca's dilemma over her son had changed. It was now the matter of saving the world that she knew, and loved. Many souls were at stake; the planet was in jeopardy. It was not a question of *her* saving it — she was only a part, as were Jennifer, Morgan, James, Laura and her daughter.

"Jennifer!" Anusca's voice startled the young reporter. She pushed the stop button on the recorder. "There are many things that I wish to tell you," she said, standing up and smoothing her dress. "By now, you know that we deal with more than just coma? You yourself sat outside of window and heard strange things, no?" The small woman stood with hands locked behind her back, facing Jennifer.

"Yes, I do think it's more than just a coma…but what, I don't know," Jennifer said, looking at the recorder, then to Anusca.

"Let me tell you this…" Anusca was trying to choose her words carefully. "There is war being fought, but not like man's war. This is spiritual war."

She knew that this was going to be hard for the reporter to grasp. "Laura is name you hear on tape. James is Laura's and Morgan's friend. Now you tell to me, who is Laura?"

Jennifer could see by the expression on the old woman's face that this was going somewhere. "Laura," Jennifer began, "was a reporter where I work. She died two years ago."

Anusca raised an eyebrow, then a hand. "O.K, you say she is dead, but this Damascus say he will go to hurt her."

Jennifer thought about that statement. "Yes, he did say that, but…"

"No buts. These things, all true." Anusca went and sat next to Jennifer on the sofa. "You come to me, I think for answers."

Jennifer threw her hands against her head, It felt like it was going to explode. "It's so hard to believe all this!" she exclaimed.

Anusca put her tiny hand on the reporter's leg. "I know these things are strange to you. When you were little girl, was not everything to you strange? Now they are not." Anusca smiled and patted her.

Jennifer looked at the woman and understood, she really understood. Anusca was telling her that the story, in time, would become believable. "Rada said the day that she was at the villa, Damascus knew she was there. Why didn't he know I was outside the window when I recorded this tape?"

Anusca looked at her daughter, then back to Jennifer. "You say that Damascus, he was drinking…no? Think on what I say. He may be evil entity, he may be strong, powerful, but he still has human body, with…human problems."

Rada sat up in her chair. "Do you mean human frailties, Mama?"

"Yes, this is what I say."

Jennifer blew out a nervous laugh. "So, he can't do what ever it is that evil entities do when he drinks too much?" she asked.

"This is correct," Anusca said, grinning.

"That's terrific! All we have to do is get the evil entity drunk!" Rada snorted. Anusca shot a look at her daughter.

"Sorry Mama, but it sounded so funny." Rada covered the grin just beneath the surface.

"Tomorrow, we go to talk to this Morgan Deveraux person," Anusca declared.

Jennifer knew that they should do as Anusca said. She also knew that she had a lot to do before then. Jennifer packed up the recorder. "I will find out where she lives, and also get this film developed. In the morning, I'll pick you two up about…eight?" Anusca and Rada nodded agreement.

At the front door as Jennifer was about to leave, she remembered the article. "In this evening's paper will be the article about your son." She laughed slightly. "I didn't put in that your son's body was taken over by an evil entity."

Rada snorted a little. Anusca wished she knew how to snort — it sounded like the thing to do at this point in time.

Morgan and Ryan

Thinking about the sculpture, Morgan had only slept a few hours. At daybreak she took a cab downtown to the gallery, the article at her side. After she arrived she put a call in to Ryan; then made a pot of coffee. The Fallen Angel sculpture sat on its pedestal. She thought about her dream involving the angel. She gently touched the statue, like a lover would touch the other. *What the hell is happening? How could you be in my dreams, and how did I finish the Dark Angel? Something is happening…*Morgan jumped at the sound of someone knocking on the glass entry doors.

It was Ryan. She ran to the door, yanked it open and grabbed the small detective.

"Well, good morning to you, too," Ryan said. She hoped that nothing else had happened.

"Ryan, you're not going to believe this," Morgan said, pulling the newspaper from her back pocket.

"Did something happen? Is everything all right?" Ryan asked, concerned. Morgan held the article up in front of Ryan.

"Look!" The detective had to back away from the paper slightly in order to focus in on it.

"What am I looking at?" her expression underlining the question.

"It's the face on my sculpture!" Morgan exclaimed. "The one I did the night before last!" Ryan placed her hand on her hip.

"I don't know what you're talking about." She took another look at the article, then at Morgan. "I swear, I really don't know what you're trying to show me." Ryan looked around the showroom. "Can a girl get a cup of coffee?"

Morgan felt heat crawl up her face. She was embarrassed. "Oh, my God, I'm sorry. Of course you can have a cup of coffee."

Ryan rubbed her eyes. She had not slept well either. She was thinking that maybe the lack of sleep was making her unaware of what Morgan was trying to show her.

Morgan brought two cups of coffee, and handed one to Ryan. "I'm sorry, it was rude to blast you with all this, so early in the morning," she said, sheepishly, looking in her cup.

Ryan took a sip of the steaming contents. "Try again. This time go slower," she said.

Morgan smiled, still red in the face. "The night before Laura's anniversary, I was downstairs working on a sculpture." She took a slow, deep breath. "I couldn't get the details of the face right, so I laid my head down for a minute and fell asleep. When I woke, it was finished." Morgan searched Ryan's face for a reaction.

"You don't remember finishing it?"

"I don't remember, because I didn't finish it," Morgan blew an exasperated breath. "Look, I started the sculpture weeks ago, way before the paper came out with this story." Morgan took Ryan by the arm and led her downstairs. Ryan kept both hands around her cup, trying to keep at least one drop in it. When they reached the bottom of the stairs, Morgan turned Ryan toward the sculpture. "Look!" she said.

Ryan looked at it, then at the newspaper. Last night's date. "I've heard about things like this before," Ryan stated.

"Really, have you?" she asked, eyes wide with surprise.

"Sure I have. Steven King, Dean Kootnz," Morgan slapped Ryan on the shoulder.

"Ryan! This is not funny! I'm not kidding!" Morgan snapped.

Ryan took Morgan in her arms, pulling her tightly against her. "I'm sorry, I don't mean to make fun of you. I just don't know what to make of it."

Morgan felt bad for yelling. "I'm sorry, too." She whispered.

* * *

Across town, Jennifer showed up promptly at eight. She had researched Morgan and found out that she was an artist and owned a gallery downtown. She also had had the film developed and brought the photos with her.

The three women got into Jennifer's car. As they traveled toward the Deveraux gallery, Anusca tried to explain in more detail about the many faces of Damascus, how he affected so many generations, how they all had fought him. Jennifer's head spun with all the mystic information. As they pulled up to the curb, Jennifer tried to center herself, to open her mind up to the possibilities that lay ahead. She was going to meet a woman whose name had been mentioned through a window the night before. The redhead named James was not only being held by force, but had been beaten badly. Jennifer blew out a breath, opened the car door and stepped out.

She wore blue jeans, a cable knit sweater and tennis shoes. It was not often that she was allowed the luxury of comfortable clothes. Anusca stepped out looking like some sort of foreign royalty. Her maroon pantsuit and black silk scarf flipped over her shoulder, trailing behind her. On her arm was Rada, white linen slacks, peach blouse, wearing a gold heirloom necklace. The three women walked up to the large glass doors of the gallery, cupped their hands around their eyes and pressed against the glass, trying to see in. Jennifer laughed quietly to herself, thinking how they looked like tourists.

Morgan and Ryan held one another, when suddenly the upstairs buzzer rang. They didn't want the closeness they were sharing to end.

"Are you expecting someone?" Ryan asked, her warm breath on Morgan's neck. Morgan shook her head. The two went upstairs. As they reached the top, they saw Anusca, Jennifer and Rada looking through the glass doors. Morgan flipped on the main showrooms lights. The three visitors quickly pulled their faces away from the glass.

Morgan walked over to the door and unlocked it, opening the door a crack. "May I help you, ladies?" she asked.

"Good morning, we're looking for Morgan Deveraux." Jennifer said.

"I'm she."

"My name is Jennifer Collins, and this is Anusca and Rada Damitree."

Morgan was shocked. This was the very person she was going to seek out about the article.

"May we have a minute of your time?" Jennifer asked.

"Please, come in." Morgan opened the door and ushered them into the showroom. "This is Ryan Delgato," she said, indicating the detective.

The threesome introduced themselves, and an awkward moment of silence followed. Jennifer cleared her throat. "Mor…, may I call you Morgan?" she asked.

"Of course," Morgan replied, dying to know why she was there.

"I know this is going to sound crazy," Jennifer began.

Morgan looked at Ryan. They smiled, each knowing what the other was thinking — that it couldn't be crazier than their conversation downstairs. They had no idea of the bombshell that was about to be dropped.

"Last night," Jennifer continued, "I was…well, let's just say I overheard a conversation that a friend of yours was having. His name is James." Jennifer waited for Morgan's reaction.

"James!" Ryan exclaimed, swapping looks with Morgan.

"James!" Morgan echoed. "Where is he? My God, we've been worried sick!" Ryan took Morgan's arm.

"You're Anusca Damitree, Stephane's mother?" Morgan asked.

"Yes, she is. And this is his sister, Rada." Jennifer said, pointing at the girl in the peach blouse.

Morgan looked at the article, then handed it to Jennifer. "You wrote this?" she asked. Jennifer nodded. Turning to Anusca and Rada, Morgan said, "And you're the family of the coma victim?" Slight nods of acknowledgement. Morgan looked back at Jennifer. "You really saw James?" When Jennifer looked back at her, in silent assent, all the color drained from Morgan's face. She quivered slightly.

Ryan steadied her friend. "What the hell is going on here?" she demanded. "Is this some sort of sick joke, because I don't think it's…"

Jennifer cut off her words. "I assure you, this is no joke. I wish it were, and when we're done explaining, you'll wish it were as well."

Ryan sat Morgan in the chair behind the desk. "O.K, let's everyone settle down," Ryan said. "Would you ladies like some coffee?"

The three nodded. Morgan started to push up from the chair, but Ryan held a hand up. "Stay there, I can manage." Always the detective, she knew the best way to get information was to get them to trust you. Coffee and cigarettes always worked at the precinct.

Anusca looked at all the sculptures, and she knew she was in the right place. Slowly she walked around, standing in front of each one, nodding as if having a conversation with them. Her heels echoed on the hardwood floor as she made her way through the room.

"Here we are," Ryan said, handing Jennifer and Rada a cup.

Anusca walked over to the desk where Morgan sat. She stood looking at the artist, her hands clutching her purse. She smiled at Morgan, but said nothing.

Ryan set a cup on the desktop next to Anusca. "Thank you, child," Anusca said as she turned to look at the detective.

Ryan stood next to Jennifer. "Where did you see James? He was kidnapped yesterday."

Jennifer's expression made it clear that she had suspected something of the sort. "I saw him on the bay, in a villa. He was with two other men." She reached in her purse and pulled out the photographs. "I took these last night through a window. I also have a tape recording." She handed the prints to Ryan, who went and perched next to Morgan on the desk.

Rada slid over next to her mother. They all watched as Morgan and Ryan went through the pictures. Ryan looked up every so often with the *I'm watching you* look.

"This is James," Morgan said to Ryan, pointing at the photo. "And *this*, is Mr. John Malcolm."

Ryan noticed that the man in the picture next to Malcolm was Anusca's son, and her face twisted. "Mrs. Damitree, is this your son?" She turned the print around and held it up.

"Yes…and…no," she said, setting her purse down. She picked up her cup and took a drink.

"What do you mean by yes and no, Mrs. Damitree?" Ryan asked. *I'm watching you.*

"Here we go," Jennifer said under her breath.

Anusca shot a look at the reporter. "His body is my son, insides not my son," she said dryly.

Rada could see this was not going well, and took the lead. "My mother thinks that my brother's body was taken by an evil entity named Damascus while Stephane was in a coma."

Rada looked at everyone and grinned ear to ear, "Oh, I forgot to say that if we want to get rid of him, we need to get him drunk." She smiled again.

Jennifer started to laugh uncontrollably. She tried to cover her mouth to stop it. I didn't work. When she could stop for a moment, she wiped away the tears running down her face. Clearing her throat, she said between giggles, "I know it sounds strange, but I'm beginning to believe her. I spent a lot of time on the computer researching information she gave me. Everything checked out…" Jennifer dabbed under her eyes. Her mascara was beginning to run.

Anusca stood by, sipping her coffee. Morgan and Ryan sat with mouths agape.

"When I was at the villa last night listening through the window, Morgan's name was brought up," Jennifer went on. She pulled out the tape recorder and set it on the desk. "This Damascus, a.k.a. Stephane, who also talked about Laura."

Morgan's eyes shot up at Jennifer. "Laura? Why would they be talking about Laura, she's…dead."

Jennifer put a hand on her hip, and cocked her head to one side. "Apparently not. They were talking about the *other side*. It seems there is another realm…"

Anusca set her cup down and said, "There are many realms — play tape and we listen." She smiled at Morgan. Only Anusca knew that Morgan was the key.

After they listened to the conversation that took place at the villa, a cold silence held the room hostage. Ryan was a detective. She dealt with the here and now, not other realms, not spirits. She dealt with bodies, usually dead ones, that stayed dead. Morgan remembered James and Laura talking about something like this, but could not recall the details. She spent most of her time staring at Laura thinking how beautiful she was. Rada was walking around the room admiring the Angel sculptures. She was nineteen, and as she looked at each statue she wondered if she was too old to take an art class. Jennifer watched Ryan and Morgan's faces. They looked like she felt when this whole story landed in her lap. Now that other people were involved she felt better.

Anusca was still sipping her coffee. She observed all the women in the room, giving each one of them a slow assessment with her wise old eyes.

Startling everyone, Ryan broke the silence. "I'm having a hard time with some of tape recording," she said, rubbing the back of her neck." Right now however, I can't worry about it. I have to think about James Peterson and how to get him out of the villa safely." She pulled out her notebook and scratched some notes in it.

Jennifer wondered if she was a cop. Ryan saw her looking at her. "I'm a detective…a private detective." Jennifer's eyebrows flew up in surprise. She didn't realize that Ryan had seen her staring.

*That's right, I'm still watching...*Ryan didn't know these people. For all she knew it could be an elaborate plan by John Malcolm to ambush her. She and John had a history of mutual distaste. He was a womanizer and she was everything that he wanted to stop, representing the freedom of women to choose their occupations and lives. Would he really go to this length? There was cocaine and a lot of money involved…the answer would be…yes, he would. The murders that she was investigating in the art district were connected to him. The conversation with Bill Cameron made that clear. Ryan needed to call her father and tell him what had transpired this morning. After all, he was her partner.

"Will you excuse me?" Ryan asked. She leaned over and whispered in Morgan's ear, telling her she was going to make a call to her father. Morgan nodded. Ryan stepped outside.

"Your friend doesn't trust us," Jennifer said, pointing at Ryan through the glass door.

"Goes with the territory of being a cop, I suppose," Morgan said, thinking that she didn't really trust them either. Her best friend had been kidnapped and these people could be involved. She scrutinized each woman in turn. She decided that Rada wasn't a part of the conspiracy. She was interested in everything but the conversation. She watched the young girl touch all the sculptures, and then get sidetracked by her reflection in the glass, stopping to smooth her hair. Morgan smiled inside at the innocence the young woman possessed, and for a moment felt jealous.

Morgan's attention moved to Ryan, speaking to her father. She felt grateful that she had Ryan in her life. The detective made her feel safe. Morgan's affection toward Ryan was growing; she thought about her more each day. Gazing across the room, Morgan's eyes were drawn to Anusca Damitree, standing in front of the Fallen Angel. She watched as she quietly talked to it. She slowly got up and went to stand next to Anusca.

Jennifer soon followed. Rada was adjusting her blouse in a reflection of the glass on a painting.

"This sculpture," Anusca said, gently touching it, "is a sign of spirit pulled between worlds." She smiled and walked to the next statue. "Ah. Yes, this one shows the force of three," she whispered, running her fingertips over it. "Rada, how do you say this thing…coming together?"

Rada tore herself from the image in the glass and walked over to her mother. She looked at the sculpture for a moment and said, "An alliance, Mama. It's called an alliance."

Anusca nodded. "Yes, an alliance, the force of three." She looked up at Morgan. "This is group of warriors, that are brought together…a." she said softly, then whispered something in her daughter's ear, a Romanian word.

"Reunion." Rada said.

Anusca smiled. "These souls…reunite to fight."

The sculpture was three Angels, two women and one man. They stood in a circle holding hands, their wings high above their shoulders, cascading down in a spiral around one another. The feathers formed a protective shield. In the center of them lay a single arrow.

"Mrs. Damitree," Morgan began.

"Anusca…you call me that."

"Anusca, you are telling a story about my sculptures. How…"

Anusca held a hand up in protest. "No story. This happens now, on the other side." Anusca took Morgan's hand. "Your Laura, she talks to you through statues. Cannot you see?"

Morgan's heart dropped to her stomach. Her body began to shake. Ryan, who had sneaked back inside, scooped her up in her arms, holding her steady. Everyone huddled around the statue, silently looking.

Anusca's attention fixed on Morgan. "Let us think of something. You start to make these sculptures after your Laura she die…no?"

"Yes," Morgan whispered.

"And you dream them, then you make them?" Anusca asked.

"Yes," Morgan whispered again. Ryan tightened her embrace.

"Anusca, how do you expect us to believe all of this?" Ryan asked. *I'm still watching you.*

"I ask to you, Detective, how can you not believe?" Anusca released Morgan's hand. "Let me prove one thing to you after we talk of next statue."

Everyone walked to the next sculpture. Rada started to drift and Anusca took her by the wrist, gently pulling her along. "This statue is two souls just crossing over to other side." Anusca pursed her lips, knowing one of them was her son. "Detective, who was last murder?"

"Jimmy Monroe," Ryan said, looking at the face of the smaller of the two men in the sculpture. She sucked in a sharp breath.

Morgan leaned into her and asked in a whisper, "Does it look like him? Ryan nodded.

Anusca turned to face the women that were gathered around her. She steepled her fingers. "This is not hard to understand. Our souls, they live many times. Some souls work together many lives. These three souls with the arrow work together before. Sometimes these souls work together across world, or worlds." Anusca raised her palms skyward. "This evil entity, called Damascus, he is after parchment called Star Scrolls. This is list of Earth Angels." She dropped her hands at her sides." He wants to kill these peoples, this way he cause big trouble for planet. He cause balance of good and evil to tip in favor of him" She walked over to the desk and sat down.

"I am old, need to sit," Anusca said, and folded her hands on the desktop. The group of woman shuffled to where she sat, as if hypnotized by her story.

"It used to be Scrolls were held by church, but over the years peoples sell them, they steal them, these peoples. They smuggled them to places all over world." She looked down at her hands. "These Earth Angels, they are angels in human form. They choose to come here from the realm of Limboshia. You call this place purgatory."

Morgan poured the old woman a fresh cup of coffee.

"Thank you, child," Anusca said, her voice weary. "If Damascus can kill many of these angels and humans, their families are sad to have lost them. These souls stay in Limboshia till family no longer sad. You see Damascus, he is wise. He knows he kills enough peoples, he upsets balance. The man called Hitler, he was Damascus. But you see he killed enough peoples during Holocaust to tip balance in his favor."

Anusca paused for a moment and took a shaky breath. "We still are sad for this Holocaust, no? This is a small thing compared to what will happen if he gets Star Scrolls."

Her words hung in the air like a guillotine over their heads. They were beginning to understand, even through the language barrier, what could happen. Morgan felt a wall of guilt hit her head-on. Grieving for Laura had prevented her from returning to Earth, keeping the balance.

Anusca took a sip of her coffee, then leaned back in the chair. "I must tell to you some more things. If you do not understand now, you will. I tell to my childrens and to the peoples, always do the right things. I know is not easy sometimes, no? But let me tell you one thing. For every promise broken, is payment due. For everything we say with mouth, or do with body, there is payment due."

She took a renewing breath. "Peoples they say, 'Payment? What payment?' Oh, there are many. Say maybe your family they pay for mistakes you make. I wonder then if man steal, does he know his mother must pay for the bad thing he do? Or, maybe this man he steals and he goes to jail. His mother she is sad. Is not this payment? Let me tell you one thing, sometimes it works like this. You see in the realm of Limboshia, souls they choose next life. These lives are the payments still due to universe. Do you understand what I tell to you?"

The women nodded.

"Anusca, am I the cause of Laura being trapped in Limboshia?" Morgan asked.

Anusca smiled.

"My dear child, let me tell you one thing. First, her death is still not solved. This must done. Then her mother and father, they are sad. This must be stopped. You sad for her, you must stop being sad. You can see is not just you, is many things. You can help by finding who killed this wonderful soul."

Morgan let tears of relief roll down her cheeks, like medals of honor. Ryan put her arm around her. She knew now more than ever that she had to solve the puzzle of Laura's death.

Jennifer had a question that she'd been hanging on to the entire time that Anusca had been telling the story. "Why did Damascus kidnap James?"

Morgan and Ryan fixed their attention on Anusca. Rada was still staring at the last sculpture, thinking that Jimmy was sort of cute.

"James is very special man, he is Damascus' soul brother. One good, one evil. They have known each other for all of time."

Ryan did not forget the promise that Anusca had made to her. She was to prove somehow that she had the insight into what was happening now in Limboshia. "Mrs. Damitree, you said that you could prove…"

"Yes, yes, Detective," Anusca interrupted. "I can show to you that I know what is happening," she said, smiling. "I can tell to you that last sculpture Morgan makes is of evil, a man, a Dark Angel. Am I correct?"

Ryan knew there was no way of her knowing about the statue downstairs. She also knew that they were going in a direction of no return.

Laura, Tom and Marti

After Laura lowered her crossbow aimed at Damitree's neck, Marti helped Jimmy off the ground. Tom rubbed his chest where the giant foot had been.

"How freaking much do you weigh?" he asked Damitree. Stephane was a handsome man with chiseled features, and dark skin. His hands, Tom thought, were the biggest he'd ever seen.

"I am over two hundred-fifty pounds," Damitree said in a heavy accent.

"No, shit…" Tom hissed. Laura couldn't help but blow out a laugh. Damitree looked out of place. He was still dressed in his concert clothes — formal tails, crisp white shirt with gold cufflinks. Jimmy stood looking at Marti as if she were from outer space.

"What the hell are you looking at?" she asked him. He looked quickly at the ground. "That's what I thought," she spat.

"Everyone needs to settle down," Laura said, ever the mediator. "These men are not the enemy!" She leaned the crossbow against the rocks and walked over to Damitree. "I'm sorry. My name is Laura." She extended her hand. "This is Marti," she said, pointing. "And this, is Tom."

Damitree bowed his head, then looked back at Laura. "Where is this place?" he asked. His eyes were sad and confused. Laura reached down and picked up the water bag, dusted it off and handed it to Damitree.

"This place is called Limboshia," Laura said.

Damitree's eyes lit up. "Is near Romania?" he asked, taking a drink.

Tom snorted, slapping a gloved hand over his mouth. Marti turned her back so Laura could not see that she was about to lose it as well.

"No, my friend," Laura said, "it's not near Romania." Her heart went out to the gentle giant. "Let's finish setting up camp, then we'll explain where you are," Laura continued, not knowing how they were going to tell these men they had departed Earth and now were in a different realm.

Five people sat crossed-legged around a roaring camp fire. They ate dried fish, bread, and fresh fruit they had picked along the trail. Jimmy tried to remember how he had gotten to this place. He could barely make out the face of Eleanor Himes in his mind. She was a friend, but beyond that he drew a blank. Laura chewed the fish carefully, finding a bone every so often, and studied Damitree. He ate and drank in silence, his eyes darting around the fire now and then. He had taken off his jacket, rolled his sleeves up to his elbows, which rested on his knees. His hands were beautifully strong. He was wearing a large emerald ring on his right ring finger; the flames danced off the stone's reflection.

Looking at Damitree, for a split second, Laura missed the Earth and its clothes, its jewelry. She felt an ache so deep that she thought her stomach might swallow her. Her attention slid over her friends, through the fire and to Jimmy, who was pushing his food around the bowl that contained it. He was wearing Levi's relaxed fit jeans, with a handsome navy blue pullover sweater. Peeking out of the collar and sleeves was a yellow button down shirt. She looked at his loafers with tassels. Her mind was swept from Jimmy to her bedroom in the house that she and Morgan lived in. They would try on several outfits, coquetting one another, behaving much as models in a fashion show. It was the ritual before going out on the town. They would sometimes find themselves dressing and re-dressing. Even after picking their outfits, passion would take control of their hands, minds, and bodies. They would lay and giggle, naked, sweating, looking into one another's eyes, arms and legs twisted together.

Tom's voice pulled Laura back to Limboshia. 'Laura…you all right?" he asked.

Laura nodded her head. “Fine, I was just daydreaming.” She’d lied. She was homesick.

Tom wiped his hands on his pants. The salt from the fish stuck to his fingers. “I was asking Damitree what he remembered before he ended up here,” he said, looking at Laura, who sat up straight, trying to pay attention.

Looking at Damitree, she asked “What do you remember?”

The large man unfolded his long legs. Pushing them straight in front of him, he massaged them as he spoke. “I was at concert, on last piece of music.” He closed his eyes, hearing the melody. “I had hurting in my head, then I was dreaming. I dream of my mother, she say not to go to States, I will never see you again.” He pulled the rubber band from his hair, combing it with his fingers, then banded it back. He flipped the ponytail over his collar. “I wake up in trees, one maybe two days ago.” Damitree cocked his head slightly, looking at Jimmy. “I find him in trees. He look at me like I monster.” Damitree crossed his legs, laying his large hands in his lap. “I tell him that I not monster, I lost. He say he lost, too. ‘We are lost together,’ I say to him. Jimmy he laughs, then we find you.” He took a drink from the water bag. “Are you lost, too?” he asked Laura.

She smiled. “No, we’re not lost. We’re going to get a friend of ours and bring her back to the valley where we live.”

Damitree nodded. “What is name of valley?” he asked, still trying to figure out where he was.

Laura’s gentle eyes sparkled. “It’s called the Valley of the Elders,” she said.

“This valley, you say in Limboshia?” He scratched his head and looked back at Laura.” What country, city…is this Limboshia?” he asked with a furrowed brow.

Laura took a deep breath and blew it out. “It’s not a country, and it’s not a city, Damitree.” She looked at Tom, then to Marti for assistance. They shrugged. “It’s a place,” she sighed. “It’s a place like Earth is a place.” She was trying to choose her words carefully. Damitree chewed his last piece of fish while he listened.

Laura favored him with a smile and said, "The Earth is a planet. Limboshia is like a planet…out in space…sort of." Laura was frustrated, trying to pluck the right words from her mind.

Jimmy jumped up, "What the hell are you talking about? Planets, are you nuts? Who are you people? Are you smoking crack or what?" He stood rigid as he ranted. "This has got to be Candid Camera!" He shook his head violently, his arms straight at his side, hands balled in fists. "Man, oh man, I must have got a hold of some bad shit," he said, talking to no one in particular, himself, perhaps.

Marti was sitting next to him and grabbed his ankle. Jimmy jerked from her grip. "Who the fuck are you people?" he asked sucking in a terrified breath. His eyes darted frantically around the faces that were lit by the firelight. He fell down, pulling his legs to his chest, and wrapping his arms around his legs. He shoved his face against his jeans. "I've got to wake up…Jesus…wake up!"

The fire popped and shot embers, along with the sound of Jimmy quietly sobbing. Marti wanted to comfort him, but knew that nothing could. She sat watching as the tightly balled man rocked like an infant. Tom and Laura were lost in quiet memories of their own arrivals, poking at them through the still night air.

Tom had had to be rescued from the Dark Territory by several attendants of the village. He had been wandering in the forest for weeks, mostly going in circles. When he came to the village, he was a filthy, clawing wretch of a man. Trusting no one, he did not dare speak a word for days. He couldn't remember anything but a gunshot. He thought that maybe he had killed his wife and son. This pushed him over the edge. Tom convinced himself that he had gone insane, and nothing mattered to him anymore. It was Samone who, in her wisdom, was able to contact Tom in the far reaches of his mind. Jimmy was a mirror image of what he had been like.

Damitree was rolling the concept of planets over in his mind, but as hard as he tried it would not congeal. "I do not know of planet called Limboshia…they not teach this in Romania," he said, rubbing his forehead.

Laura felt useless. "Damitree, I don't know how to explain Limboshia. Let me try this way," she closed her eyes for a minute gathering her thoughts. "During your concert, you passed out and went into a coma. Do you understand what a coma is?" He shook his head no.

"It's when a person can't wake up, no matter how he tries."

"Yes, I understand this," he said.

"Well, in the hospital, you couldn't wake up. Your mother came with your sister, brother and father from Romania." His eyebrows raised.

"I do not remember this," he said.

"They were by your bed side for maybe three days, and you would not wake up. Then one day you did."

"I do?"

"You did. But when you woke up, you were not…you."

"Not me? How can this be?"

"Well, they think, your mother thinks that your body was taken by an evil entity." Laura waited for the hysteria, the anger, all the emotions. Nothing. She stole a look at him. He was cool as a cucumber.

"This entity," she continued, "Tore out the tubes and IV's from your arms and mouth and walked out of the hospital."

Tom could not believe that he sat there accepting everything that Laura had just told him. Marti was surprised as well.

"Damascus," is all that Damitree said. He looked into the fire, pursing his lips.

"You know of Damascus?" Laura asked. He nodded.

"I have known of him all my life." His head dropped between his shrugged shoulders. He looked defeated. He started to murmur something in Romanian and crossed himself with his hand. A tear rolled down his chiseled cheek. Laura thought she would die, seeing this strong man cry. Marti came to his side, as did Tom and Laura. They just gathered around him silently. There were no words to speak. Overhead the clouds showed signs of Damascus' return. Quietly they sat and listened to the thunder rumble.

6

Cameron and Damascus

Damascus had left James with John Malcolm at the villa. Stephane's body was upstairs at the main house locked in the master bedroom. He traveled back to Limboshia to question Starling about the Star Scrolls. He had gotten nowhere with James, but would with the Starling woman, he thought to himself. He swung his legs off the edge of the bed and sat waiting for the vertigo to dissipate. He stood and walked out to the porch. Across the field he saw Cameron running as fast as his little legs would pump. The thunderous entry of Damascus had been heard by the boy while he was out hunting rabbits. Cameron waived a hand over his head when he saw Damascus on the porch. In the other hand was a sling shot that had been given to him by the large man after the last trip. Cameron hit the bottom step with a thud and ran to Damascus, grabbing him around the waist.

"Well, little man, I see you missed me. I was beginning to think not. I woke alone." Cameron looked up at Damascus, trying to catch his breath.

"I…was…hunting…rabbits…for…dinner," he puffed.

"How did you do? Is there rabbit for tonight's meal?" The boy hung his head.

"No. They're too fast." Damascus ruffled Cameron's hair.

"I was not in the mood for rabbit anyway," he said smiling. The boy's eyes lit up at the words.

"Yeah, me neither." He shuffled across the porch to a willow chair and sat down. He swung his legs, looking down at the sling shot, pulling on the elastic band.

"How did it go at the Pasture House?" Damascus asked, as he sat next to Cameron.

"All right," Cameron murmured.

"Did you give the list to Leman?" Cameron nodded. "Good, we leave in the morning. I have business with the Starling woman." Cameron cringed at the thought of him touching her. He was confused as to why; he just knew that he didn't want him to touch or hurt her in any way

The Pasture House sat in a deep canyon flanked by mountains. Trees crowded against the horizon, patchworks of groves peppered down the hillside, spilling into the pastures that surrounded the compound. The main house stood in the center of the property, an elaborate replica of a home from Tombstone, Arizona, that Doc Holiday lived in. It had a covered porch that ran around the entire house. Every post had hand carved corbels, and the tops of the railing were embellished with finials.

Damascus loved the old west on Earth. He had brought a picture of the home and had his men build it for his visits. To the east of the structure was a bunkhouse for all the hired hands. Across from the main house were the horse stables with a large tack room. Behind the main house was a root cellar, which was used to keep prisoners. Hitching posts had been built in the front of both buildings. As Damascus rode in with Cameron, he found his hired hands in the front of the bunkhouse, drinking whiskey and roughhousing. Candis was being passed around the group of men, she was wobbling, smiling with hair disheveled and blouse unbuttoned. She staggered this way and that way, laughing. Cameron thought she looked like an old Raggedy Ann doll.

Damascus pulled the reins and swung out of the saddle, tying his horse to the post, Cameron right beside him. Leman tore himself from the fun and went to greet him. "Hey, Boss, how was the trip?"

"Not as good as I had hoped."

Leman's smile disappeared behind his lips. "Sorry to hear that," he said, stealing a look at Cameron. The boy's eyes narrowed.

"So how's it going, Cameron?" Leman asked, his voice harboring a suspicious tone. He reached out to touch the boy. Cameron slapped his hand away, causing Damascus to look at the two of them. He didn't say anything about the incident, but instead walked to the main house. Leman ran ahead of him, trying to get the door open.

"Leman, get two glasses and my bottle. Bring them to the porch." Damascus demanded. Leman threw a hand up as he went through the door. He returned with the glasses and the bottle, as Damascus requested. His face showed unease in Damascus' presence. Leman bore a striking resemblance to Don Knots. His large lips sucked in and out when he spoke. That's what Cameron hated most about the man, those lips.

Leman wondered if Cameron had told Damascus about the escapades in the bunkhouse. He drew a breath and pressed forward toward Damascus. "Here you go. A glass of whiskey is just what a man needs after a long ride." Leman poured two shots and held one out to Damascus. He reached for the other, thinking it was for him.

"That is for Cameron," Damascus said, not giving even a look in Leman's direction.

"Of course…of course. Here you go, son." Leman passed the drink to the boy.

Cameron was perplexed and looked to Damascus. "This is for me?"

The large man nodded.

"I've never had a drink before." Cameron smelled the contents of the glass, scrunching up his nose. "Yuck!" He said, quickly pulling the glass from his nose." It smells awful!"

Damascus started laughing. "You say that I treat you like a child. This is what men do." He said, shooting down the whiskey. "It's up to you…are you a boy…or a man?" He raised an eyebrow in the boy's direction.

Cameron smelled the drink again; tears welled in his eyes. He pinched his nose closed and drank. The whiskey burned the insides of his mouth and throat, and gases burned up his nasal passage. "Ahhh, that hurts!"

Leman and Damascus laughed. Anger sparked inside the boy, bubbling just under the surface of his skin. He held the glass out to Leman, wiping his mouth with the back of his hand. With eyes like slits he watched as Leman poured another shot. Cameron looked into the glass and threw it down his throat. Damascus patted his leg with approval. Leman filled the two empty glasses.

Candis squealed with excitement as one of the men tore off what little of her blouse was left. She flung her head back, limp-necked as he grabbed her breasts. Her hands white-knuckled the man's shirt so she would not fall to the ground. Cameron watched as the men pawed and grabbed at Candis' half-nude body. He felt himself become hard, aroused in a way he had never experienced before drinking.

Damascus turned to the boy. "This is what men do as well," he said, pointing with the shot glass at the spectacle.

Cameron pushed his arm toward Leman once more. The boy drank several shots. He felt funny, yet good in a strange way. He watched alongside Damascus as the hired hands pushed and pulled Candis around the circle of men. Damascus had put his plan into motion. He would corrupt Cameron into loyalty, he would show him what it was like to rule and have authority, to have anything the boy wanted. He sat with a grimace on his face as he watched the boy growing into a man.

Starling had been watching the ordeal from the confines of the root cellar. She pressed her eye between the cracks of the wooden door. She had an idea of what Damascus up to. He would turn the boy into his protégé, to watch over things as he traveled from Earth to Limboshia. She hung her head as dread pressed in on her. She knew it was only a matter of time before Cameron would find that all the things that Damascus was showing him were necessities rather than atrocities. Starling also knew it was only a matter of time before Cameron would find out who she was. She looked down at her skin dress, soiled with the damp, moldy dirt she was forced to lie in. Her hands brushed off what little she could. This is what Dorothy must have felt while trapped in the castle of the evil witch in the Wizard of Oz, or so she thought.

Yelling and hollering brought Starling back to the crack in the door. She watched as Candis flung herself at Cameron, Damascus was encouraging her to pleasure the boy. Concern was quickly replaced by terror as Damascus' attention turned toward the cellar door.

Laura, Tom and Marti

The evening sky cleared the storm clouds that had announced the return of Damascus. Jimmy had rocked himself to slumber. Damitree told stories of his mother, and how as a child he had watched spirits come in and out of their home. His sister was not as exposed to the comings and goings of the apparitions; she was younger than he. When she grew older his parents had sent her to live with relatives and received her education in the States. He told of his mother's gypsy linage, how his grandmother had been called the fight the *spiritual war*.

"My mother she tell to me, she will be called to fight." He smiled, remembering how excited he was as a young boy when she had told him. He thought of his mother as if she were an American super hero, as in the comic books. Damitree shook his head.

"I did not know I would fight next to her in battle." Laura put her arm around his broad shoulder.

"We are proud to fight alongside you, Damitree." He looked at his new friends with fondness. He was not upset or fearful. He knew where he was now; he'd always known he would arrive at this place.

"I'm afraid that I wasn't totally honest with you earlier, Damitree," Laura said.

"I not understand…how not honest?" he asked.

"We are not just picking up a friend, we are going to rescue her. She was kidnapped by Damascus. He's trying to get the Star Scrolls."

Damitree knew about the Scrolls, and the importance of them. "This is a good thing you do…no?" His friends nodded. "I think I can help. Damascus, he take my shape in hospital. I take his shape here in Limboshia." He put his hands on his hips and smiled a toothy grin.

"I like the way you think." Tom said. Laura had thought of the same idea soon after meeting him, but wanted it to be *his* plan.

"What about the accent?" Tom asked. "How can we get rid of it before we arrive at Pasture House?" He had removed his hat and was wringing it in his hands. Tom had become preoccupied with the mystery of how to teach English in two days.

"Marti, how many days left?" Laura asked.

"Two, maybe three at the outside," she said, shooting a look at Jimmy. "What are we going to do with this one?" Marti asked, throwing her head in his direction. Laura threw her hands up. They decided to get a good night's sleep and discuss it in the morning. The mist from the mountains was creeping into camp and the air became crisp and damp. Marti tossed more logs on the fire. Tom covered Jimmy with a blanket and handed Damitree a large animal fur to lie under. Laura lay looking up at the stars through the tree boughs. She wondered if Earth was one of the shinning points of light that poked through the darkness. To keep out the cold, she pulled the skins up around her neck and slowly drifted off to sleep.

John Malcolm, James at the Villa

James was still asleep when he heard a voice early in the morning. It was not quite daylight. His arms were bound in front of him with duct tape, as were his legs. He opened his eyes, unsure of where he was. He felt the tape across his mouth; he had been kidnapped. Was this his second or was it the third day? He no longer was sure. James sat up and swung his legs over the edge of the bed. He hopped quietly to the door and reached up for the knob. He envisioned it opening; saw himself making his way down the hall and overpowering Malcolm. He positioned his fingertips around the knob and turned. Locked. He leaned against the door and listened.

Malcolm had been dialing numbers for over an hour; finally he reached Pontis.

"Hello?" The voice at the other end was distorted with sleep.

"Pontis? This is John." Silence. "Pontis!"

"What? Who is this?" John had little patience. He had not slept and his eyes were swollen and bruised.

"It's Malcolm!"

"What the hell do you want John? Do you know what time it is?" Pontis looked at the clock on his bedside table; the glowing red numbers said it was 4:24a.m.

"Pontis, I need your help at the villa…I…"

"You have got to be kidding me!" He was not yelling. It was a whispered shout.

"Man, I need your help. Damascus did something to my eyes. I can't see. I have the Peterson guy here and if I…"

Pontis cut off his words. "Malcolm! I have no intention of leaving my warm bed and wife to come and bail your fat ass out of trouble."

"Listen!" Malcolm screamed. The phone line went dead. Pontis unplugged the jack so he would not be disturbed again. He slid back under the sheets and lay there. He thought about the conversation that he and Reese had had at Ray's Bar. They had decided to go to Damascus and express their concerns about the undue attention that John had been stirring up. He rolled over on his side and put his arm around his wife. If he could not sleep, at least he could feel the warmth and the softness of her. As he lay there an uneasy feeling gripped him; that this could be the last time he would hold her.

* * *

Laura, Tom and Marti

Several hours had passed since breakfast, and the day was clear and bright. The blue sky had a few white cotton clouds that hung above them as they hiked over the last summit. Damitree and Tom practiced English, and every so often would laugh at Damitree's pronunciation of a word. Being a good sport he did not take offence, but rather laughed with Tom, half of the time not knowing what was funny. It felt good to laugh. Laura and Marti followed behind the two men, continually turning around to keep watch on Jimmy. He still had not said a word since the Candid Camera ordeal. He looked at them as if they were the enemy and followed out of need for survival. He knew he could not make it on his own.

Jimmy searched his mind for a clue as to how he had arrived in this place and what had happened. He remembered Eleanor Himes, and during the hours that he walked details came to him. He and Eleanor were going out on the town. He recalled getting dressed, and someone was in the apartment with him. He could not make out the face. Jimmy watched as the group ahead of him talked. Who were they, he wondered. Despite his reservations about them, he followed. Where else was he to go?

Two days had passed since Jimmy and Damitree had joined the others. Damitree had perfected several commands that Damascus was known to spew. The Pasture House was over the next rise, maybe half a day away. They had made good time, despite having to look repeatedly over their shoulders for Jimmy. At one point in the trip he had wandered off the trail in a zombie-like state. Laura and Marti found him standing in front of a tree, staring at it and mumbling. When they reached the rise leading to the valley below, Damitree staggered a few steps. They leaned him against a tree. Tom grabbed his arm,

"Are you all right, Big Guy?" he asked. He saw beads of sweat on Damitree's brow, and that his face was drained of color.

"I have funny feeling inside," he said, squeezing his eyes shut. Laura and Marti came up alongside him. Damitree held tight to the tree, he felt dizzy and sick to his stomach. He laid his forehead against the bark of the tree. "I hear rain, maybe wind…loud."

Marti leaned in toward Laura and said, "Do you think that he is having a reaction to Damascus, being so close?"

Laura was thinking about the possibility.

The statement landed on Damitree as if someone had spit on him. "He sick, too?" he asked.

Tom looked at him and smiled. "I'm sure he is," Tom replied, laughing out the words.

"Good, he not get away with taking Damitree's body, no?"

"No." Laura said, hugging him. "Marti, bring the water bag, he's burning up," she said, feeling his head with the palm of her hand. She poured some water on a cloth and held it on his forehead, then wiped the back of his neck. "I wish I could make it go away."

"Is O.K, I feel better if he sick, too," he said, trying to muster a smile. His face was pouring perspiration, his breathing labored.

"I don't think there is anything we can do. I'm afraid you're going to have to ride this out," Tom said to him.

Damitree slid down the tree and sat on the ground. "I good rider." They watched Damitree close his eyes and rest under a big pine.

"Where is Jimmy?" Marti asked. Tom and Laura looked around the area.

"He's here!" Tom yelled, pointing at the base of a bush. Jimmy was in bad shape. He clung to the root of the shrub as if his life depended on it, his eyes vacant.

Laura and Marti ran to where he was curled up around the bush. "What's going on with him? He couldn't be going to the Monolith so soon, could he?" Marti asked.

"I think he is. The grieving on Earth must be done already," Laura concluded. *What a pitiful life he must have led for people to mourn him only a few days.* It wasn't that she wanted anyone to be trapped in Limboshia, but a least it would be nice to have a couple weeks to readjust to the transition in such a beautiful place.

Jimmy was trying to say something, but nothing came from his mouth. He lay there screaming silently to them.

Laura reached into the bush and touched his hand. "Jimmy, you must listen to me," she said, shocked by the look of his body. He was beginning to blow up like a balloon. "Jimmy!" she screamed. "You must listen to me!" He slowly lifted his eyes and tried to focus on her, but his look was still vacant. Laura gripped his hand tight. "You are going on a journey. It's a wonderful thing that you are about to experience."

Grimacing, Laura turned her attention to Marti and Tom. They were shocked into silence. The shaking of the bush that Jimmy was hanging onto brought their eyes back to him. He was almost translucent. Laura felt her hand melt inside his skin. She recoiled, pulling it away.

The three backed away from the shrub, staring at Jimmy. A thousand tiny lines rippled across his flesh; he looked like a human puzzle. His skin began to glow, as if a light turned on inside his body, showing the details of the puzzle pieces. They let out a gasp, backing away even further.

Jimmy stood up. He appeared to be three times his normal size. They could see the forest through him. He was almost clear, like a light bulb. The pieces of his human puzzle form began to break apart. Light blasted through the cracks. Right in front them, a transformation was taking place. Jimmy became brighter and brighter. They shielded their eyes, looking through cracks in their fingers, trying to see the form in front of them. Jimmy's own eyes rolled back in his head. Then a smile crossed his face, a relaxed and beautiful smile. His whole body shook and trembled as it came apart at the seams. They watched in awe as the pieces splintered and swirled in a circle where he had just stood. The light was blinding as the pieces whooshed faster and faster past them. The noise, deafening. They took a few more steps backwards, trying to escape the wind and light blowing in their faces. It was now a small tornado that kicked dirt and debris at them. They turned their backs, bending over to shield their faces. Every so often they would try to look at the amazing sight and see a finger or leg of Jimmy shoot past them. Suddenly, out of nowhere, a whirlwind blasted straight up like a rocket, leaving a plume of dust, followed by complete silence.

They stood in the quiet or a long while, looking first at one another, then skyward, knowing that one day they too would experience what they had just witnessed.

"Wow!" Marti finally said, breaking the silence. Laura looked at them. She smiled. After what they had just witnessed there was nothing to say. She walked over to where Damitree sat and dropped next to him.

"This thing that Jimmy do…is good?" he asked, looking at the spot that Jimmy stood a moment earlier.

"It's a very good thing," she said, grinning.

"We will all do this thing?" he asked innocently.

"Yes, if we are lucky, we will all do this thing." Tom and Marti came to join them at the tree, sitting next to Laura and Damitree.

"That was the most incredible thing I have ever seen." Tom croaked. His mouth was dry from all the dust in the air. Marti handed him the water bag.

"I didn't think it would be like that," Marti murmured.

"Neither did I," Laura replied.

"Do you think it hurt?" Tom asked, wiping his mouth.

"Looked like it was more surprise than pain." Laura said.

"I hope so. I don't want to hurt," Marti said, with a shuddering breath.

* * *

The Pasture House

Just on the other side of the mountain, Starling sat in the dark in the corner of the root cellar. It had been two days since she saw Damascus look at the door from the porch where he had corrupted Cameron. She had expected him that day, but he never showed. She knew it was just a matter of time. The only sign of life was someone bringing a plate of food every day and sliding it under the door. When she tried to get their attention, they kicked the door and walked away. Not so much as a word spoken to her. The compound was unusually quiet. No one was outside. She wondered what was happening to cause the lockdown.

Damascus was given a gold lighter that was found twenty miles west of the valley. His riders, who combed the Territories, had brought it to him the previous night. He sat and studied it. The initials J.M. were engraved on it. They did not mean anything to him. He had put the compound on alert. The riders were assembling within the hour. They would scout the entire territory for the new arrival. Damascus was running out of time, he had to return to Earth before morning and still had to question Starling.

Leman and Jones had gathered the men on horseback and divided them up into teams. They would ride to the area where the lighter was found and the other men would ride the outside perimeters.

"Here's where I found the lighter," Jones said, pointing at the pine needled ground.

Leman had dreams of grandeur. If he could find the new arrival he would receive a sizeable reward. "Are you sure this is the spot?" he asked Jones.

"Of course! Christ, Leman, I'd like the reward just like the next guy. I'm not an idiot!"

Leman silently questioned the statement about being an idiot. As far as being in the right area, he only had Jones' word at this point. They rode through the trees, surveying the ground closely for foot prints or any other sign of someone passing through the area. They rode without conversation, with expectations they would find the new arrival off-guard, sitting amongst the trees or perhaps sleeping.

Laura, Tom and Marti

"What was that?" Tom said, looking up the summit they had just crossed over.

Laura crept next to him. "It sounds like horses," she whispered.

Tom crept up the small rock formation behind them and peeked over to see what was coming their way. He motioned for them to get down. His hands hardly were able to hold on to the smooth surface. Laura and Marti helped Damitree across the clearing against the rocks, where Tom was above them. He held up two fingers.

"There are two riders," Laura whispered, looking up. "Get some of that brush and pull it over us, Marti." She scurried across to where Jimmy had been and pulled up several dried bushes over to the rocks. "Damitree, lay down and be very quiet," Laura said in his ear. He lay down and Marti covered him with the dried branches. She and Laura climbed under with him.

Marti could see Tom pressed tightly to a jetted portion of rock. Then her eyes darted around to see if their gear was hidden. She did not see any visible sign that they had been there.

Two long shadows appeared on the ground and over the branches they were hidden under.

"Whoa!" a man's voice sounded. The horse hooves stopped just within earshot.

"I don't see a damn thing," the man who turned out to be Jones said.

"Me neither. I think we're chasing ghosts up here," Leman replied, looking around.

"If there were someone out here we would've seen some kind of broken branch or footprint by now," Jones replied.

"I think we should head back to the valley and open that bottle of whiskey in the bunk house," Leman said irritably, not wanting to search further.

"Damascus will have a piece of our ass if we don't bring some news." Jones' voice had an urgency to it.

"He's too busy with the woman in the root cellar. Besides, he's got to leave tonight…remember?" Leman sounded cocky and confident.

"That poor girl," Jones murmured.

"That poor girl," Leman mimicked. 'What the hell is wrong with you? You some kind of wimp?"

The two men started back down the mountain, bantering back and forth as they rode, until they could no longer be heard.

Tom was shaking so badly he was about to lose his grip on the sheer rock face. He watched as the horses made their way along the trail they would soon be following. He exhaled and jumped down next to the pile of branches. "They're gone," he said, pulling the debris off his friends. "Man that was scary!" he grinned.

Damitree sat up and took a deep breath. "Me better, I think." He was also grinning.

Tom started to laugh. Blinking, Laura, too, began to laugh, a sort of graveyard humor. Between what they had just witnessed with Jimmy and now the two riders, it was hard to digest all at once. Marti walked to the edge of the clearing. There were no signs of the two men. "It's all clear," she called back. They collected their gear and joined Marti.

Damitree looked at the horses' tracks. "We walk with these?" he asked. Some color had come back into his face.

"Yes, we walk with those," Tom replied.

As they reached the bottom of the mountain the clouds began to build. They knew it would not be long before Damascus had to leave. They took a trail around a small grove of trees. Just beyond the Pasture House, not more than two hundred yards across a field, they crouched together in a huddle, with the last of the forest as cover.

“”Do you see the cellar where they have Starling?" Marti asked.

"Behind the main house." Tom pointed to a log structure built low to the ground.

"Let's hide this gear and see if we can get a closer look," whispered Laura. Suddenly she felt nervous, wondering how it would play out. She thought about the faces in the Scrimshaw Mountains that spoke to her. It gave her strength. She took in a deep breath. There was no turning back.

Damascus had plotted a path to the root cellar; his step was heavy. He unlocked the hasp and pulled open the doors, spilling what was left of the day's light into the room. Starling winced, holding her hand in front of her face to block the sun's rays. She could see a man's figure coming toward her, but could not make out who it was with the light behind him.

"I am not playing with you any longer, Starling!" Damascus bellowed, his feet smashing a path toward her. "I want to know where the Star Scrolls are!" She backed against the log wall, pressing herself into it. He grabbed her by the throat and lifted her in the air. She expelled a deep guttural sound, gasping for breath, her windpipe was being crushed.

"Tell me where they are, bitch!" His face inches from hers, she looked in his eyes and mustered enough saliva to spit on him. He dropped her to the floor.

"Why you…self-righteous…piece of shit!" he gnashed, furious that only she could tell him where the Scrolls were being kept. "Tell me how to find those Scrolls!" She lay there, staring at him as he held her throat. He cocked his leg back and kicked her in the stomach. Her small body flew across the room. She tried to get up on all fours, but instead vomited. She began to crawl, her hair dragging through the contents of her belly, lying on the dirt floor.

Damascus knelt next to her, and in a calm voice said, "Why put yourself through this, Starling? Tell me how to get the Scrolls and I will let you live." He pressed his face closer. "Tell me!" He demanded. "Save yourself and your friends a lot of heartache." He grabbed her by the hair. "Give me those fucking Scrolls!"

She looked at him with defiant eyes. "I would rather die than to see you touch those Scrolls." Her voice hissed as it spit out the words. She closed her eyes, her fate sealed, and braced herself for his wrath. Damascus picked her up by her hair and slung her into the log wall. Blood spewed from her head as she slid to the floor. In a matter of seconds she lay in a crimson pool. Damascus kicked her one last time and walked out, slamming the doors and locking them. He kicked and kicked the wooden doors until his leg grew tired. He then bulldozed his way back to the main house to prepare for his return to Earth. He had to get the information out of James, no matter what the cost.

Tom and the group saw the clouds becoming darker, swirling and moving quickly across the horizon. Cracks of lightning followed by a rumble of thunder in the distance.

"That's our cue," Laura said. They began to prepare for the rescue of Starling.

Morgan and Ryan

Ryan had called her father earlier to advise him of the situation. Now she wanted to go evaluate the villa and get a layout of the area. Most of Morgan's questions about Laura were answered by Anusca Damitree. As the old woman stood in front of each sculpture, giving her rendition of the meaning, it became clear that since Laura's death Morgan had been in contact with her on the other side. It all made sense now, the obsession with angels. Night after night until the early hours of the morning, sculpting as if she were possessed. Morgan smiled, knowing that Laura saw her and stilled loved her even from another realm.

"Jennifer, can you remember the layout of the grounds around the villa?" Ryan asked, bringing a piece of paper and pencil to the desk.

"I don't think I can forget crawling around there too soon." She drew a map of the entire area, including the bay and grove of trees.

"We can go to where Rada sat and look at the villa through the binoculars as well," Jennifer offered.

"Good idea. The most important thing in making this successful is the element of surprise, and I'm not talking about *us* being surprised," Ryan said with a small smile. She looked at the drawing, then turned to the group of women. "First we need a diversion. I have a scenario in mind if you'd like to hear it." They were all eager to know what the detective had cooked up.

"What kind of diversion?" Jennifer asked.

Ryan smiled at her. "Funny you should ask, Jennifer, because *you* are the diversion."

Jennifer's expression was one of surprise. "Really…me?"

Ryan nodded. "Malcolm is one of the biggest womanizers I know, so the idea is that you, being an innocent female, needs him, the macho man, to help you."

Jennifer laughed. "A damsel in distress?" she asked, throwing her hand against her forehead. Everyone laughed at her showboating.

"You've got it," Ryan said. "He won't be able to resist you. I want to see some cleavage and a lot of leg." Ryan's face crawled with heat, slightly embarrassed at giving the suggestion.

Morgan thought it cute that Ryan, after all the things she had seen in her work, could still manage to have an innocence about her. Morgan was indeed developing some deep feeling for this woman who stood in front of her, skillfully formulating a plan to rescue her friend James. She watched as the detective pointed out locations, telling each person her part in the plan.

As Ryan showed Anusca how to work the hand held radio, she noticed Morgan staring at her. Morgan quickly looked away, suddenly interested in the map. Ryan smiled. She knew there was an attraction between them, but now was neither the time nor place. Ryan focused harder on the instructions she was giving Anusca. "Do you understand how it works?" she asked the old woman.

"Yes, child. I push here to tell to you someone is coming," she said, then looked to Ryan for confirmation.

Ryan patted her on the shoulder. "Perfect…that's right, you push the button and talk, *only* if someone is coming."

Anusca smiled and started pushing the button. Because the radios were so close together, Ryan's handset squealed loudly. Ryan jumped in surprise.

Morgan laughed, as did Jennifer and Rada. Seeing the shocked look on the old woman's face, they laughed harder.

Ryan held up her hands in futility and let them drop at her side; she could not help but grin at Anusca. Ryan stood and shook her head, then turned to Jennifer. "You are going to park the car down the hill." She pointed at the map. "You'll walk from there to the door of the villa." Jennifer was listening closely. "Once you ring the bell and he answers, you need to lure him out. When he steps out, I jam the gun in his face and take him down." Ryan felt a tickle in her stomach, much like a person feels on a roller coaster. She wanted John Malcolm. Nothing would please her more than to shove her .38 revolver up his ass and pull the trigger.

Rada had been listening to the conversation on and off, when finally she spoke. "I don't mean to put a damper on this plan, but has anyone thought about Damascus? Where are we going to hide afterward?"

They were shocked into silence. None of them had had a chance to think about the repercussions of the rescue.

"There is no place on planet safe from him, my dears," Anusca softly replied.

Without a resolution to the Damascus problem, they drove to the hill that Rada had perched on three days ago. Jennifer had been dropped at her location, with the car's hood open and a tire flattened. Rada had the binoculars and would keep an eye out for anyone approaching the villa. Anusca was to radio at the first sign of trouble. Both women would remain on the hill until Ryan signaled otherwise.

"Are you clear on what to do?" Ryan asked Rada and her mother.

"Yes, I watch, and if anyone comes up the street I tell Mom and she radios you."

Ryan looked at Jennifer standing at the car. She was all legs and cleavage. She pointed below. "Morgan and I are going down to the greens, and wait until Jennifer makes her way to the door," Ryan took a deep breath.

"You ready?" she asked Morgan.

"Ready as I'll ever be."

Rada and Anusca wrapped their arms around Morgan and Ryan. There was a closeness between the women that was hard to explain.

"The universe will watch over you. This is part of plan," Anusca said.

"Geez, no pressure here," Morgan quipped. She kissed the old woman's cheek and headed down the hill with Ryan.

Anusca and Rada watched their new friends go bravely into the unknown. The old Romanian crossed herself, then stared at the button on the radio, holding it tightly in her hands.

Once at the bottom of the hill, Ryan and Morgan ran across the street and up the rolling lawn toward the villa. Just as they reached the last hill of green, they stopped and lay down on their bellies. The lawn was like a plush carpet. Ryan raised her head and signaled for Jennifer to start her walk to the house. One cue, Jennifer swaggered her way up the road.

"As soon as she gets him outside, we run like hell up there. You take the back of the villa and try to get a location on James — I'll take the front." Ryan pulled her revolver out of its holster and checked the cylinder.

"Morgan, remember to keep your head down and be as quiet as possible. We don't know if anyone else is in there with John." Ryan watched as Jennifer got to the driveway, stopped and broke the heel off her stiletto.

"She's good. Maybe she's in the wrong line of work," Ryan whispered. Morgan was equally impressed with Jennifer's ingenuity. As they waited, the smell of fresh-cut grass and the sound of the bay took Morgan back to a picnic that she had had with Laura not too long before her death. They had packed brie, French bread, fruit, and a bottle of wine. They sat by the ocean in the grass and leisurely lunched the day away. She breathed in the smell of the grass as she waiting next to Ryan.

"Here we go," Ryan said, nudging Morgan. The two pushed off the grass and ran across the pavement to the west side of the house and crouched down as Jennifer rang the bell. Ryan motioned for Morgan to go around the back and look for James. Then she wrapped both hands around the revolver and waited. Morgan crept alongside the bungalow, looking carefully in each window. As she went up the east side, now almost completely around the house, she spotted James. Gently she tapped on the glass to get his attention. He was lying face up. His eyes were closed. Slowly, he turned his head turned in her direction. Morgan held her finger to her lips, warning him to be quiet. His eyes lit up when he saw her. Swinging his taped legs over the edge of the bed, he stood up, hopped over to the window and managed to open it with his shoulder. His mouth still taped, he tried to talk.

"Shhh," Morgan whispered. "We're here to get you out." She pressed her hand to the glass. James laid his head where her hand was, as if he could feel her touch. His face was still bruised, and dried blood had crusted in his nose and around the tape on his mouth.

"Did you hear the doorbell ring?" Morgan asked quietly. James nodded.

"Listen, I'm going to go," Panic crossed James' face.

"I have to go around to the front. When Ryan gets John, we'll come and get you out of here. O.K? Is the door to this room locked?" James once again nodded. "You need to lie on the bed. We're going to have to break the door down. I'll see you in two shakes. I love you."

James' eyes smiled back at her, then he turned and hopped back to the bed, lay down and waited.

Morgan continued up the east side of the villa, stopping at the corner. She peeked around the front and saw Ryan at the west corner and Jennifer at the door. Morgan pulled back to the side of the house.

Malcolm looked through the peephole. His eyes were still blurry, but he was able to see enough to know there was a beautiful woman at the door. "Who is it?" he asked.

Jennifer knew that everything rode on her performance. "I hate to bother you sir, but I had a flat just down the road. It seems that none of your neighbors are home…and…well, I was hoping that I could use your phone?"

John scrutinized the porch around Jennifer. He cautiously opened the door with the security chain attached. He looked through the crack and saw that no one was with her. "Just a minute," he said, and closed the door.

Jennifer's heart sank. She thought that she'd failed. Then she heard the chain being removed. The door opened. She was two or three feet from him, balancing on the broken heel. John stuck his head out the door, and by the expression on his face, she knew that she had him right where she wanted him. As John Malcolm stepped out over the threshold, Jennifer took at step toward him. The heel gave way and she fell against him. She grabbed his shoulders. "Oh, dear! Look what I've done now, my new high heels!" she squealed helplessly. Jennifer lifted her foot slightly as John reached toward her shoe.

"Let me help you with that, little lady," he said, hoping to get a peek up her skirt.

Ryan sprang from the side of the villa, hitting the porch in three strides. "Hold it right there, you son of a bitch!' she yelled.

Jennifer backed away quickly out of his reach. Ryan pushed John against the concrete slab with the gun to the back of his head. "Don't move or I'll blow your fucking head off!" she hissed through clenched teeth. "Is there anyone else here beside Peterson?" she asked. John shook his head. "If you're lying to me, you piece of shit, I'll kill you. Do you hear me?" John, lying face down, nodded.

Morgan looked around the corner. Ryan motioned with her head for her to go into the house. Morgan ran behind Ryan, yelling for James. Once she made it down the hall she took a left to the bedroom door and kicked it several times. Finally the jamb gave way. James swung his legs off the edge of the bed to greet her. Morgan pulled the tape from his mouth. "Oh God!" he exclaimed. "It's good to see you!" He laid his head on her chest. Morgan put a hand on his head. "I didn't know if I would see you again." she said. Tears ran down both their cheeks. "Are you all right?" she asked him, running her hand over his head.

James looked up at her, his face bruised, spots of blood dried at the corners of his mouth, streaks of tears running down his neck. She untied his wrists and feet, helping him to the bathroom to clean up.

Anusca and Rada waited on the hill. Rada had been giving her mother a blow-by-blow account of the action below.

Ryan held her gun with one hand and pulled the handcuffs from the waistband of her slacks with the other. She leaned down and snapped one of the metal bracelets around John's wrist. She pressed a foot into his back, and said to Jennifer, "Come around back here with me and secure the other cuff, will you?"

Jennifer kicked off the other high heel and did as she was told. Standing next to Ryan, she smiled. "Whew!" Jennifer said, "You can really be one mean bitch when you want to be."

Ryan laughed, not taking her eyes off John. "You know what they say comes in small packages," Ryan quipped. She held the gun steadily, aimed at the center of John's head. Morgan and James came out of the house and stood in the doorway. Rada told her mother as soon as they appeared. They smiled broadly.

James blinked at the brightness of the sun. With wet hair, bloodstained shirt and a bruised face, he glared at his captor.

"You're a sight," Ryan said, glancing quickly at him. Morgan was holding him around his waist. He had an arm over her shoulder.

Ryan lowered the revolver, and with one hand reached in her jacket, pulled out a cigarette and lit it. She leaned against a pillar and blew a puff of smoke. "I've been waiting for this for a long time," she said, pointing the barrel of the gun at John. "He's one sick fucker. I can't believe that he ever made Chief of Detectives." Ryan turned her attention toward Morgan and winked at her.

"James," Morgan said, "this is Ryan Delgato."

Ryan and James shook hands. "Nice to meet you, Detective, and thanks for coming to rescue me," James said, pushing a hand through his red hair. "I was getting worried. I didn't know what they were going to do to me." He pulled his arm from around Morgan's shoulder and hugged himself. "Damascus is coming back and I have a feeling he is going to be thirsty for blood," he said, his voice filled with trepidation.

Ryan took a long pull off her cigarette. "The main thing right now is that you're safe," she said. Ryan threw the butt on the concrete and crushed it out with her shoe. "We can't worry about Damascus. I need to get this lard ass to my father so that he can call the proper authorities. Then we can see what our next move is." Ryan looked at Jennifer and said, "Will you go down to get the car, so that we can load up this sorry piece of crap?"

"Sure. It will take a few minutes. Have to change that tire." Jennifer had never changed a tire before.

Ryan pulled her radio out and called up to Rada and Anusca. "This is Ryan, do you read me? Over."

Rada pointed to the button that enabled her mother to talk back. Anusca shooed her away from the device. "Yes, Detective, I hear."

"Will you and Rada meet Jennifer at the car? Over."

Anusca pushed the button and nodded her head yes, as if Ryan could hear her. Rada laughed, taking her mother's arm to help her to the car below. Anusca looked at her daughter, puzzled, not understanding the humor.

"Come on, Mama, Jennifer needs us to help her."

"Yes child, she needs us. The detective say so." Anusca's face beamed with purpose and pride. Rada had not seen her mother look so healthy and happy in many years. They held on to one another as they walked down the hill.

"Morgan, can you help me get him up?" Ryan asked, jerking her head toward Malcolm.

"You bet," James followed alongside her to offer what help he could. John had been quiet most of the time. With aching eyes closed, moaning was about the only sound he'd made.

Jennifer backed the car into the drive. Rada helped her mother out of the back seat of the car, then ran to Ryan. "You did it! You really did it!" she screamed, grabbing Ryan and hugging her. She looked at James and hugged him, too. Anusca stood at the bottom of the stairs leading up to the porch. Her hands were folded in front of her, she was smiling at Ryan.

Ryan smiled back at the old woman. "We need to get going. Who knows what might happen if we stick around," Ryan said. She and Morgan started to lift John.

"Let go of me, you stupid bitch!" he yelled.

"Shut the fuck up, asshole!" Ryan pulled with all her might, as did Morgan, to get John to his knees.

"You're going to pay for this!" Malcolm shouted. Ryan pressed her face within inches of his and laughed.

"Let me ask you, jerk off, just who the hell is going to make me pay? You?" Morgan and James helped Ryan get John off his knees and to the car.

"Jennifer, will you pop the trunk?" Ryan asked. Jennifer ran to the ignition and removed the keys, then opened the trunk.

"Get in!" Ryan said loudly.

Malcolm's look was more disbelief than hatred. "Fuck you!" He yelled back at her. Ryan smashed him in the back of the head with the butt of her revolver. Everyone winced at the sound of it as it made contact with his skull.

"Get in! I'm not going to tell you again, ass wipe!" John, dizzy, reluctantly put one foot in the trunk. Morgan and James helped him with the other. John laid down and quietly put his bloody head on the carpet floor. Ryan slammed the lid shut and holstered her weapon.

Anusca tried not to listen to the profanity. She did, however, understand that in Ryan's line of work they talked like that. She had seen enough movies to know. She shuffled over to James and introduced herself. "My name is Anusca Damitree, James. Is nice to meet you."

James knew her name because of the conversation with Damascus. He was aware that it was her son's body Damascus had taken. "I'm sorry about your son, Mrs. Damitree. I wish we were meeting under better circumstances, but I am truly honored to know you," he said, taking her hand and giving it a gentle kiss. Anusca's eyes had tiny lines around them as she smiled.

"I see why big fuss for you, so charming."

James helped her to the car. Jennifer got in the driver's seat, Morgan and Ryan with her in the front, and Anusca, James, and Rada in the back. "Jenn, take me to the office. We have a delivery for my father." Jennifer had a big smile on her face as she put the car in gear.

* * *

Laura, Tom and Marti

After the group had surveyed the area, they rendezvoused back at the grove of trees. Tom had been working feverishly on Damitree's accent so they could go get Starling. Tom was still not sure Damitree was ready, and conveyed his concern to everyone.

"Who are you to question me!" Damitree bellowed. Shocked, they all looked at him, blinking in silence.

"You dare ask me my reasons!" he bellowed again. He showed them he was ready.

"That's pretty damn convincing," Marti exclaimed. Laura and Tom had to agree.

"I guess that answered that, didn't it?" Tom replied.

"I think we should just get on with it. Get in, get her, get the hell out of here," Laura said impatiently.

Tom put his hand on Damitree's shoulder. "It's up to you, Big Guy. Are you ready?"

"I am ready. Damascus always ready," he said, wondering if he truly was.

Knowing that the real Damascus was gone, they decided that Damitree could go directly into the compound. He would take Marti with him. She would be his prisoner, the new arrival that they all were looking for. Tom and Laura would go around to the southwest side of the area, along the back to the root cellar. Once Damitree had convinced the men inside that he was Damascus, he would meet Laura and Tom with the key so they could get Starling.

Laura and Tom left first. When they made their way around the bunk house they signaled. Damitree and Marti began their walk straight across the compound. Marti was in front of Damitree, and told him that when they saw the hired hands, he had to push her to the ground and treat her roughly. He did not like the idea, but he knew he had to do his part.

"Listen," Marti whispered, "when we get to the light ahead of us, I am your enemy, do you understand?"

Damitree pursed his lips and furrowed his eyebrows. "Yes, I understand," he whispered back. He didn't like any of what he was about to do.

Just before they stepped into the light from the stables, he crossed himself with his hand. Marti yelled at Damitree, "You son of a bitch!" She pushed him. "Push me back," she said in a low voice.

Damitree pushed her to the ground. Marti screamed as she got back on her feet. Two faces appeared in the bunkhouse window. It was Jones and Leman. The other hands were over the ridge at Candis' house playing grab-ass. Marti saw them looking.

"You bastard! How can you treat me like this!" Marti yelled.

Damitree put his hands on his hips. "You will do as I command!" He bellowed. He had done so well, that Laura and Tom were frightened. Damitree grabbed Marti by the arm and pulled her around.

"Don't touch me, you pig!" she screamed. By this time Leman and Jones were running outside to see what the commotion was. Just as the two men approached, Marti slapped Damitree's face. He threw her against the stairs to the bunkhouse.

"What the hell are you looking at?" Damitree yelled at the men.

Leman and Jones didn't know what to say; they thought he'd left. "I…thought that you…" Leman's words were cut off.

"You thought what? You couldn't find your ass if you had a map!" Damitree spat. He looked at Marti. "I planned a fake exit to Earth to flush her out, you idiots!"

The hired hands had a new admiration for him, thinking that was the smartest thing they had ever heard.

Marti began to fake crying and laid her head on the stair tread.

"Shut up!" Damitree yelled at her. He turned to the men. "You," he said, leveling a finger at Jones, "Go get the key. I will lock her up with the other woman in the root cellar." Jones ran for the key as if his life depended on it. "You and your buddy had better get your asses on horseback and find whoever is traveling with this whore," Damitree said to Leman, narrowing his eyes and making the meanest face he could.

Laura and Tom could not believe that this was the kind and gentle man that they had been with for the past three days. Their mouths hung open in surprise and amazement.

Leman went to the stables and fetched the horses they had just ridden a few hours ago. Jones brought the key to Damitree and pushed it toward him. Damitree grabbed it. "You had better not come back without her companion. Do I make myself clear?" The two men nodded their heads as they mounted the horses.

"Go, assholes!" he shouted at them. The men kicked deep into the flanks of the animals and were out of sight in seconds.

"Don't drop your act, Damitree. Someone else may be here," Marti whispered.

"I won't," he whispered back. "Come with me, whore!" he yelled as he pulled her to her feet. He dragged her behind him as he stomped to the root cellar.

Tom and Laura waited at the corner of the bunkhouse until Damitree unlocked the cellar door. As soon as he did, they ran past him, into the dark room, with Marti joining them. Damitree stood guard.

Marti's hand trembled when she reached Starling. She lightly touched the matted blood in her hair. "Oh my God in heaven," Marti whispered. Laura and Tom formed a circle around Starling and joined hands with Marti.

Laura began the most sacred and beautiful song and mantra known in Limboshia. "Calling all Angels…Calling all Angels…" The others joined in. Outside, Damitree heard their voices chant over and over again. He could feel the power crawl up his body. The chant continued for a long period of time. He couldn't help but to say it along with them.

At last Starling moved. They continued until finally she sat up. "I think all the Angels are here." Starling said, with a crooked grin. Her face was covered in blood. Her dress and the floor were also soaked.

Laura took an arm, as did Marti, and they slowly raised her to her feet.

"Wait a minute…" she said. She swayed a bit and her head dropped between her shoulders. Then she lost consciousness.

"Damitree, can you come in here?" Laura asked. The large man moved quickly. "I need you to carry Starling. She's hurt, really bad." Damitree scooped Starling up as if she weighed nothing. She looked tiny in his arms.

"Wait, wait a minute…" Starling murmured again.

"We can't, honey," Marti said softly, "we've got to get you out of here."

Damitree whisked her out the cellar door, around the back of the bunkhouse and across the lit area to the stables, Marti and Laura on his tail. Tom locked the doors to the cellar, and threw the key into the darkness, then ran like the wind to catch up to his friends.

Safely inside the first stable they could reach, Damitree laid Starling on a blanket in the straw.

Looking down at Starling, Tom asked, panting, "Are we going to be able to move her?" His eyes were filled with fear. Being in the compound had brought back awful memories of his arrival.

"It *has* to be all right to move her." Hearing her own words, Marti's heart felt cold, but she knew they had to move her or be trapped.

"Marti's right. We have to move her whether she's ready or not," Laura said. Tom was making fast work of bridling three horses, while Laura and Marti started to clean up Starling, wrapping cloth around the wound on her head.

Damitree mounted a horse. "Tie her here," he said, pointing behind him. They put Starling in the saddle, tying her to Damitree with strips of horse blankets they had torn. She opened her eyes every so often, but they snapped shut before she could say anything.

When they were all mounted, Tom turned to the group. "I think we should take the flatlands around the mountain. We can collect our gear on the other side and head home." They all agreed for the sake of Starling it would be best not to go over the rough terrain. As they left down the main road out of the compound, Marti wondered how long the two men Damitree sent out would be gone.

After they had put some distance between the Pasture House and them, they talked.

"Man! You were unbelievable!" Tom said to Damitree.

"I'm so proud of you, Damitree!" Marti exclaimed. "Did you see the way he pushed me and pulled me around?"

Tom, Marti, Laura and Damitree laughed in unison. Damitree knew he had done well. He rode in silence with a big smile across his face, one arm behind him holding Starling. He thought to himself how proud his mother would be.

Morgan and Ryan

Jennifer pulled up to the curb of Ryan's new office. She told them the story of how her grandfather had bought the building after he'd retired and that as a little girl she had worked there. She didn't know why she felt comfortable enough to tell them that, but it had something to do with the camaraderie of the rescue. During the drive over the mood had been jubilant. Everyone was still in high spirits.

Ryan called her father from her cell phone and asked him to come down stairs. When Ed arrived, Ryan was leaning on the trunk, along with Anusca, James, Rada Jennifer, and Morgan. His face lit up when he saw the crowd. "Well now, what's all this?" he asked.

Jennifer handed Ryan the car keys. "We brought you a gift," Ryan said, looking at him. "But first let me introduce you to a few of my friends." Ryan made all the introductions, then opened the trunk. "And this is John Malcolm. I believe that you've met before?" she asked her father.

Ed's face froze in astonishment. He thought how bizarre the large man looked shoved in a trunk of a car. "Hello there, Detective Malcolm," Ed said, behind semi clenched teeth.

"Fuck you, Ed." John hissed. Ed pulled John out of the compartment with little trouble. Inside he was raging with anger. He let the man drop to the pavement with a thud, then shut the lid to the trunk.

Two of the men that Ed had contacted earlier at the precinct came down the stairs. After Ryan had called saying she was leaving for the villa, Ed thought it would be wise to have backup from his buddies.

The two men stood where John lay, not saying a word — they laughed at him. John hid his face in his hands. He could not believe that he had gotten himself into this predicament.

"Will you guy's take our friend up stairs? I'll be along in a minute."

The men nodded, and swiftly took John off the street and into the building.

"I wish you would have told me you were going on a raid," Ed said sternly.

"Sorry Dad, it's…you know how it is…the time was right and I had to take the chance, James was in danger."

Ed looked at James and nodded. "I would have done the same thing," he said, reaching out his hand to James. "I'm glad you're safe, son." They shook hands.

James glanced at Ryan , then back to Ed. "I sure can't thank your daughter enough sir, nor you."

Ed's face was puzzled. "Why me? Thank me for what?"

James put his hand on Ed's shoulder. "For giving birth to such a wonderful person."

Ed smiled. Ryan blushed. "Her mother and I are very proud of Ryan. A parent couldn't ask for a better daughter." He said. He walked over to Ryan and put his arm around her. "When she was six..." Ed began, "she was...a little..."

"Dad!" Ryan cut him off. "Please don't tell them the when I was six story," she said pleadingly. Everyone protested — they wanted Ed to tell the story.

"Ah, heck...I would never hear the end of it if I did. Remember, I have to work with her," Ed said, jerking a thumb in her direction. They all laughed, and Ryan, knowing it was at her expense, joined in.

* * *

Ryan returned to her office later in the day, after she had dropped James and Morgan in Half Moon Bay. Jennifer took Rada and Anusca back to the Hotel. Jennifer couldn't wait to get home to her computer and write. She didn't know where it would lead, but she had to document the events.

In the office of Delgato and Delgato sat John Malcolm, cuffed to a chair in the center of the room. Ed had been questioning him, but with few results. Ed's friends were out on the street, finding out what they could about the man who had apparently bought half of the police Department.

"Hey Dad, what's going on?" Ryan asked as she entered the room. She walked past Malcolm, throwing him a look somewhere between pity and loathing. Ed was sitting with his elbows on his desk, trying to keep his patience with the line of questioning directed at John.

"We've been having an interesting conversation since you left," Ed said to his daughter.

"I'll bet you have," she replied. Ryan thought that John looked a lot smaller now that he was in the chair, handcuffed. She shook her head at the sight of the corrupted detective. It was just not something that an officer did. Never compromise your power, or your duty to the public. "Did you find out anything about Laura Saubert's death?", Ryan asked her father.

Ed ran his hand over his face. "Not yet, honey, but I have faith that we will; it's a matter of time." Ed stood and stretched. Turning to the window, he stared out at the bay.

"Ed," Malcolm said, "I need a glass of water…we've been here for hours." Ryan wished she could watch him die of thirst. She would like nothing better than to see him suffer, slowly and painfully. "I'll get it," she said. She unlocked one of John's cuffs and handed him the glass of water. Ryan leaned against her father's desk, facing Malcolm.

Ed walked over and stood next to her. They both watched him drink. His hands trembled as the glass made its way to his mouth.

"John, why don't you make this easy on yourself and tell me everything. I'll get you into protective custody and you can live your life in the Witness Protection Program," Ed suggested.

John looked up at Ed and Ryan. "You know as well as I do, Ed, the chances of my surviving are slim to none." John held up the glass to Ryan. She took it and set it down on the desk.

"You should've thought about that before you hooked up with the scumbags that you did, John." Ed was not sympathetic toward the decisions that John had made.

"I needed money, Ed."

Ed cut him off. "Money? I had a wife and a child, John! I never compromised myself or the Department!"

Ryan put her hand on her father's arm, to show support and to remind him that he needed to keep his cool.

Ed closed his eyes and tried again. "John, we all make decisions in our life, some good, some bad," he said walking to his desk to get his bottle of bourbon. He poured two glasses and returned to his daughter's side, handing her one. Ed sipped his drink and looked at John.

Ryan was worn out. She had been on the go for three days. She wanted to know about Laura Saubert. She wanted to know how a man in John's position had gotten himself into such a predicament. She wanted to know it all. That's why she has become a police officer in the first place. She, like John, had found herself at the mercy of money and power. It was easy to lose sight of responsibilities when someone was flashing a stack of cash under your nose. When she had first moved out of her parents' house, money was tight. She lived in an empty apartment devoid of furniture and luxuries for the first two years of her career. Her parents had offered to furnish her place, but Ryan wanted to do it on her own. Not being able to pay a gas deposit, she would cook on a fifth burner, usually a casserole and eat it every day for an entire week. She had struggled to make Detective and it was a huge letdown once she understood that politics overrode justice. No wonder when her father had come to her with the offer of partner, she had jumped at the chance.

Ryan knew that the only way to make a difference was to be able to act on a situation without having to go through endless channels. How many times, she wondered, had she lost a collar, or failed to collect proper evidence because of all the red tape? It seemed to her that justice was on the side of the criminal. For eight years she stayed with the Department, only because she felt it was better to do something than nothing at all. Her head was filled with thoughts as she stared at John Malcolm, Chief of Detectives.

"John, tell me about the death of Laura Saubert two years ago," Ed asked. Ed poured a glass of bourbon for himself, and another for John, who drank his quickly. The pain in his head, where Ryan had hit him, was throbbing. "Ed, if I tell you what I know, I'm a dead man," he said.

"You're a dead man either way, pal. You did that to yourself," Ed said, filling John's glass again. He hoped that it would loosen the Chief's lips.

"Are you going to answer the question or not, John? Look, I haven't got all day here. I could hand you over to the Department now…"

"O.K, O.K., but I need some guarantees," John blurted out. The last thing he wanted was to be in hands of the Department. They knew by now what he'd done. The threat of him exposing all the other officers on the take would insure his immediate demise.

Ed Delgato was holding all the cards, and John knew it. "What guarantees, John?"

Ed was in no mood to make deals with a man who was a traitor, and a rapist to boot.

"I want immunity Ed. I need to get the hell out of California and start a new life." John drank his bourbon in one shot. He knew he was grasping at straws.

"If this man that you work for is so powerful, where do you think it is that you would be safe?" Ed raised an eyebrow waiting for an answer.

"I don't know Ed, but I have to try. If you want the information, you have to promise to get me out of here." Ed sighed heavily.

"O.K, John, you've got my word. I'll help you. But you'd better come clean about *everything*…do I make myself clear?"

John nodded.

Ryan slipped her hand in her pocket and turned on her tape recorder. Her father smile when he heard it engage. A chip off the old block, he thought. "Tell me about the Saubert case," Ed said.

John readjusted himself in the chair and took a deep breath. "Laura Saubert was doing an article on the Wild Side Club," he began. "She found out about the drug use, and that I was skimming the Department and some of my perps for cocaine." He shook his head, when he heard himself talking out loud about the things he had done. Things he wasn't proud of.

"She was approached by myself and a couple other officers to drop the article, but instead she pounded the streets harder. After the incident with Bill's son…"

Ed abruptly cut off his words. "Incident? You call the rape of a fourteen year old, an incident?" Ryan grabbed her father's arm. Ed pushed back the anger and poured another drink. His hands shook with rage.

John's head fell between his shrugged shoulders. "Look," he said, "I'm not proud of what I've done, I got caught up in drugs and money." His voice was soft, almost apologetic. "I don't know how it all got so out of hand. I've laid awake at night trying to figure it out, but I was so deep into it by that time there was no way out." Tears welled in John's eyes. "I wanted to be a cop for as long as I can remember. When I was a kid, that's all I thought about."

Ryan was having a hard time picturing John as a child. She only knew him as a womanizer. She tried to shake the thought out of her head and keep an open mind.

"I had been on the force ten years before I did anything under-handed," he said, "I tried to do everything by the book. Hell, Ed. You know how the system works. It's not easy to watch a criminal in court get away on a technicality." John's attention drifted toward the window. "I watched hundreds of cases fall apart." His voice was filled with emotion. "I would say to myself, the next case I'll do better, dot my i's and cross my t's. But it didn't matter how much time I spent, the case would fall apart. The bigger the crime, the bigger the attorney," he said, his face filled with futility.

Ed knew what John was talking about. Like his daughter, he had experienced the justice system's loop-holes.

John sat forward in his chair and started to talk again. "So, anyway, the Saubert woman was uncovering a lot of information that none of us wanted exposed. We had a tail on her for weeks. She was really good at what she did. She finally found someone to testify about the evidence room." John rubbed his eyes, which still looked and felt the worse for wear. "I was given the order to take her out, right after she had stumbled on the 'Brotherhood'."

Ed was not familiar with any gang named that. "Where is that gang located, what territory do they run?"

John laughed. "It's not a gang Ed. It's a cult of businessmen that banded together. Not only their finances, but their connections. It's been in existence for thousands of years."

Ed rubbed his temples with his finger tips. "Thousands of years? Come on, John. You're blowing smoke up my ass."

"It's the truth," John interrupted. "This is not a story that I'm making up. These guys have been around forever. Damascus is the ringleader. No one, and I mean no one, dares cross him. This man is not human. He's a devil. He almost blew my eyes out of their sockets."

Ed did notice that something was wrong with John's eyes, but a cult was a little hard to swallow for his taste.

"Dad, I know this is bizarre, but hear him out," Ryan said. Ed shot a look at his daughter, then back to John.

"This Damascus has been around; he can travel from Earth to other realms. I'm not joking!" John dropped his head in his hands. He knew that he sounded insane. "I didn't believe it at first, either," he continued. "This guy Damascus, in the beginning I knew him as Galliano. He looked completely different, he was Italian. Now he is a Romanian concert pianist."

"Stephane Damitree," Ryan said.

Ed looked at her, wondering how she knew.

"I know that Stephane Damitree woke from a coma, and when he did he spoke perfect English and didn't want anything to do with his family," she said. "Dad, this guy before the coma was very close with his family. He loved them, contacted them on a daily basis…" her words trailed off.

"This is nuts!" Ed said. "How do you expect me to believe all this shit?"

Ryan rubbed the back of her neck, her muscles getting tighter by the minute.

"Look, Ed," John said, "I don't care if you believe it or not, I'm telling you what happened. He put a hit on Saubert. He wanted her and the story shut down. He owns half of the town, including doctors, lawyers politicians, fucking Indian Chiefs. He had her poisoned at work, slowly and methodically. When the autopsy report came out, he had it squelched. He had Laura's notes, tapes…everything destroyed. This guy is not fucking around." John was in need of a lot of bourbon and held out his empty glass.

Ed thought it was worth drowning him in alcohol if it meant getting the whole story.

"He had me go and kidnap this Peterson fellow, because he knew Laura Saubert and Morgan Deveraux. James does past-life regressions. Damascus figured that James knew about him, the cult, and how he owned most of the damn city. James was becoming a bigger and bigger threat to him. The problem is his drinking is out of control. He may be an evil entity, but when he drinks, he's no more than a man." John snorted at the thought of Damascus drunk and him smashing his head in. "Now, Damascus is getting paranoid. It's a vicious cycle."

Ed stood and walked to the window again. He looked out at the water. He wondered how these things could exist. How in the name of God could any of what John said be real? He was an old fashioned man who was raised to believe you live, you die. There were no past lives, no evil spirits, and no evil entities getting drunk and paranoid. He tried to collect his thoughts. His stomach felt queasy.

"Let's get back to the Saubert case," Ryan said. "When she was in the hospital, what happened?"

John was growing tired of answering questions, but at this point had no other choice. "Damascus owns some of the staff over at Mercy General. Once they had her there, it was a matter of cutting off her air supply. She had been poisoned for six weeks, so I don't think she had much of a chance anyway." John said.

Ryan shook her head in disgust. "How, as an officer, could you go along with all of this?" she asked.

"Look," John said. "I was being threatened by Damascus. O.K, not in the beginning when I first skimmed the drugs, but it wasn't long before he caught wind of what I was doing and started to blackmail me. Then is when I saw his powers…" John fell silent. His face was flushed. He stared at the hardwood floor.

Ed went back to his desk, sat and leaned back in his chair. "I don't know if what you told me is true, but I'll keep my end of the bargain, I'll put a call in to the F.B.I. Being an officer, you know that they have jurisdiction anyway." John nodded. That he knew.

Ryan gazed at her father, how handsome he was she thought as she watched him make a telephone call. She could not shake a sinking in her stomach, a feeling that she would never see him again. Maybe it was because she was tired — she hoped. "Dad, I have to get going, there are still some things I have to get done. Are you going to be all right?"

Ed smiled, looked at his watch and said, "I've got back-up coming in about an hour."

Ryan walked over to him. He stood, and they embraced. "I love you Dad," she whispered.

Ed sensed something was wrong with her. "Is everything O.K, Sweet Pea?" hc asked, his eyes filled with concern.

Ryan chokcd back the emotion that had been building in her for the past few minutes. "Yes, I'm just tired, that's all. I'll see you in the morning, O.K?" she said, and quickly walked out the door.

* * *

Morgan and James had made a plan to meet at Ryan's father's cabin that was between the city and Half Moon Bay. Ryan had not told anyone, not knowing whom to trust and not knowing who might be listening. Ryan wanted to keep Morgan and James hidden and as safe as possible. She didn't know what Damascus would do when he found out that James had escaped.

They were on the way to the cabin. Morgan had her cell phone in her lap. Finally it rang. "Hello, is that you, Ryan?" James was in the passenger seat. He'd been staring out the windshield, and now turned his attention to the conversation.

"Yes, it's me. How are the two of you getting along?"

"Good," Morgan replied, "did you find anything out about Laura?"

"Sure did, but I don't want to talk over the phone. I'm just leaving for the location we talked about earlier. I should be there in a few hours."

"Please be careful," Morgan said.

"I will. I've got a lot to tell you, so hang tight and we'll talk. See you soon." Ryan said and hung up. The fog had moved in from the bay. Visibility extended just beyond the hood of the vehicle; it was getting harder to see by the minute. Ryan slowed to maneuver through intersections, barely missing sign posts and sidewalks. One more block and she would be at the freeway on-ramp. She hoped that the fog wouldn't be so bad up there. After a full stop Ryan stepped on the accelerator and began to cross the last intersection, when from out of nowhere she heard a blaring horn. She looked out the passenger side of the car to see a large delivery truck on a direct path into her SUV. Ryan grabbed the steering wheel as the truck slammed into her. Suddenly the grill of the truck sat on the seat beside her. Ryan could hear the engine winding as if it were going to explode. She looked up through the windshield of the monster that had invaded her cab. The truck driver's face was mortified. Everything was in slow motion. A scream rose in her throat; like a cotton ball it cut off her air. Ryan gasped for a breath as she continued to look into the driver's eyes. Silently he begged for forgiveness.

The two vehicles slid sideways for what seemed an eternity. She could feel the heat of the motor, inches from her leg. It was like a dream, sliding slowly, each movement exaggerated. She watched the man's mouth saying something, his eyes growing larger with terror. Then, as suddenly as it began, it stopped. They smashed into the side of a brick building. Ryan's small body ejected through the driver's window into the night. She was conscious when she hit the brick wall, slid to the ground and rolled to the street, stopping when she got wedged in the gutter.

* * *

Morgan and James paced the cabin floor. Three hours had passed without a word from Ryan. They had tried to call the cell, but there was no answer.

"Try again. Maybe she was out of range," James said.

Morgan was distraught with grief. She felt something was very wrong. She dialed the number again. "Still no answer. Oh God, I hope nothing's happened. Do you think Damascus already knows? Do you think he found her?" Morgan asked James.

"Try to stay calm. We can't speculate on what's happened. I don't think he could have tracked her down that quick." James was trying to sound upbeat. Inside he was terrified.

"Why is all this happening?" Morgan asked.

"Do you remember when I regressed Laura three years ago?", James asked.

"Yes," Morgan said softly.

“I told you that you two had special connection between you, a bonding of sorts,” he said. Morgan thought that he had meant a special connection in their relationship. She had no idea — until now — that he was talking about a soul connection.

“I remember,” she said.

“You are both very old souls that have spent many lifetimes together. I know it sounds like a sci-fi movie,” James smiled wryly. “Morgan, what’s happening is a battle, and it’s always been fought since the beginning of time. Laura and you are warriors. She’s fighting on the other side, you on this side. You’ve always fought together. The Creator, God, the Powers that be, whatever you want to call it, they make it easier by taking the memories from us. If you were to remember all your lives together, it would be hard to stay focused on the here and now. Do you understand?” James sat by the fire they had built when they had arrived.

Morgan looked at him. “I hear what you’re saying, and I believe you. I know for a fact that Laura has been contacting me through the Angel sculptures.”

James rubbed his legs, they were still sore from being in the trunk and being tied up. “I’ve been with both of you as well.” He said to her. Morgan figured that was a part of the equation. She nodded. “You, Laura, and I have been around a long, long time.” The people that don’t believe in reincarnation are in for a big surprise at the end of their lives,” he said, shaking his head. He looked at the phone in Morgan’s hand, and was about to open his mouth to tell her to call, when she dialed the number. After three rings, a man’s voice answered, “Hello?”

“Hello, who is this please?” Morgan asked, her face suddenly filled with fear. James ran to her side.

“My name is Kevin,” the voice at the other end said. Morgan recited Ryan’s phone number, in hopes she had misdialed.

“I’m sorry miss, I don’t know the number. I found this phone on the street. There has been a terrible wreck, and I was taking it to the police here on the scene when it rang.

Someone had pulled the bones out of Morgan’s legs while she listened. James held her arm to steady her.

“You say there has been a wreck?

"Yes, I'm afraid so, miss."

"Is one of the cars a silver SUV?"

"Yes, it looks like that's one of the vehicles involved. Is this a friend of yours?"

"Yes, Can you give the phone to an officer, so that I can talk to him?" Morgan's voice shook the words out.

"Sure. Hang on," the man said.

Morgan waited for someone to answer, but the line went dead. She and James stood in silence and looked at one another.

Laura, Tom and Marti

"How's Starling?" Laura asked Damitree as she rode alongside.

"She sleeps," he whispered. Laura smiled at him. She'd grown very fond of the man in a short time. Laura drifted back with Tom and Marti. "What are we going to do now?" Marti asked Tom.

"I don't know, Marti. We're going to have to play it by ear. Once we're back in the valley we should be all right."

"How's it going back here?" Laura asked.

"Fine…what's up with the smile?" Marti asked her.

"I had a vision that the Earth rescue was successful, too," she replied.

"That's great!" Marti exclaimed. She quickly slapped her hand over her mouth, afraid that she would awaken Starling. Shooting a look ahead, she saw that Starling was still asleep, swaying gently with the movement of the horse. The knot of frustration left her brow.

Tom was concerned about the wrath of Damascus, as they all were. He turned to Laura. "How long do you think it will be until he comes for us?"

"Well, we know we have three days until he returns, and that will be enough time to get to the valley. I suppose he will lie in wait for us to cross outside the territory," she said. Tom and Marti agreed.

"I'm just glad that we got Starling back in one piece," Marti said.

"Me, too," Tom added quickly.

"I'll bet you that Damascus is raising some kind of hell through the city," Laura said. "I'm worried for Morgan, James, and Ryan. I hope they're safe." She said, blowing out a shaky breath. Knowing that James was with Morgan made her feel better. At least he knew the in's and out's of the other realms. Laura smiled, thinking James was probably having fun at Morgan's expense about now. She remembered three years earlier when James had tried to tell her about Limboshia. Her being a reporter did not help. She worked on facts and evidence, not something related to believing in other realms and the like.

After two days of travel, they had made their way around the mountain, reclaimed their gear and were closing in on the Valley of the Elders. Starling was propped against a majestic pine tree. Tom had crafted a slant board from tree limbs and had cushioned the structure with pine needles and blankets. Her head was bandaged with cloth strips. Marti had taken herbs and made a poultice. She rested comfortably, watching her friends move about the camp.

"I'd like for all of you to gather around me. I have a story to tell," Starling said. Everyone came to her side. Starling stretched her legs out in front of her. "The Star Scrolls, as you know," she began, "are what I chose to protect here in Limboshia. I could leave here at anytime I choose, but I wanted to stay. Damascus and I go way back, and needless to say, he doesn't like me," she laughed. "This battle between us has gone on for thousands of years. He is constantly trying to find ways to get his hands on the Scrolls." She spoke with defiance, her lips pressed tightly together.

"Damascus is from the era in which the bible was written. The bible called him Satan." They all gasped at what she revealed. "In the beginning we all had wings," she continued, smiling with unfocused eyes, as if she were back in time. "It was called the Angelic Era. Damascus, wanting more power, started a war among the Angels, turning one against the other. These wondrous beings were lied to and tricked into causing trouble throughout the universes. The Creator decided to take the Winged Ones and cast them down to a planet that was created for them. This planet was called Earth. They were to have their wings removed and work their differences out on the planet. The Creator had hoped they would learn what it was to be humble.

"Damascus insisted that he rule the planet Earth, but instead he was cast down as a mortal as well. He grew angry, full of rage, and began to terrorize the planet. He formed armies of men that stole, raped, and killed. His name became known over the entire Earth, Damascus gathered riches beyond belief. He promised his men that they, too, could possess such bounty. As time went on they did indeed begin to join in the wealth. And the richer they became, the more they worshiped him. And so a cult was born." Starling took a drink of water, looking over the rim at the faces around her. She could see they were mesmerized by her tale.

"The Creator was very upset. It was hard to take one's own children in the first place, and remove their wings. Then to cast them in a far away galaxy —I can't imagine the grief. Damascus was finally killed at fifty earth years old. His followers mourned him, and their lasting grief pulled at his spirit, trapping him here, in Limboshia. He could not return to Earth, and after a thousand years he became truly hateful. But he also learned many secrets. He learned about shape-shifting, telekinesis. He travels at will from realm to realm." Starling was visibly upset as she recounted the story of Damascus.

"Why doesn't the Creator just stop him from all the evil he does?" Marti asked, she seemed to express the group's thought exactly.

"Because the Creator," Starling said, "wants us to learn the lesson we were put here to understand. We all know that good can't exist without evil. The balance between them keeps us from perishing forever. It's the law, always has been and always will be." Starling touched the dressing on her head and winced.

"So," Laura said, "you are saying that when the Creator took our wings and gave us bodies, that was a prison? And being on Earth to fight evil is another?"

"Yes," Starling said.

"That's terrible, horrible — and how are we ever going to go home?" Marti asked.

Starling smiled with her beautiful brown eyes. "We have more chances. That's why we live all the lives — to learn. Remember, I have earned my wings, I can leave — travel wherever and whenever I wish. This is the reward for doing the right things — we get to go home. All the Elders chose to stay, to help. We only want good for humanity, we are all brothers and sisters. Damascus is cunning. He puts things in our way on Earth, like drugs, alcohol, abuse, stealing. He uses these addictions to keep us bound to the planet, and in doing so has everyone trapped, right where he wants us. If we progress, he loses ground." Starling was growing weary. Her head still hurt and her body was sore. Tom had crushed his hat in his hands while listening to the story. Laura gently took it from him. She pushed it back to shape as Starling continued.

"Only the Creator and the universe know how it all turns out. But now you know your part and what you need to do," she said, closing her eyes. Damitree had been silent the entire conversation. His thoughts were with his mother on Earth. He knew she was going to have to deal with Damascus and his wrath.

"How can we help?" Tom asked.

"Right now it's up to our friends on Earth. Maybe they can trap Damascus in the host body," Starling said. Everyone's attention shot to Damitree. He knew that meant he would never see his family again — or Earth.

* * *

The Villa

When Damascus returned, he found an empty house. He rampaged through, tearing it apart as if it were made of cardboard. After acouple stiff drinks, he sat amid the broken furniture and glass. He dialed Pontis' phone number.

"Hello?" Pontis answered.

"Pontis! This is Damascus." Terror swept through the lawyer's body when he heard the voice.

"Yes?" he said.

"I'm at the villa. I left John here with James. Where the hell are they?"

"I don't know. John called me earlier, but I couldn't understand what he was saying." He knew if Damascus found out that he had hung up on John that there would be hell to pay.

"I want you to go get Reese and find them!" Damascus slammed the phone down.

Pontis pulled the ear piece from his head, wiping the sweat from his brow. "Shit," he whispered, replacing the headset on the cradle.

Mercy General Hospital

Across town at the hospital, Ryan laid on a gurney in the intensive care unit. Ed had already been relieved by his buddies when the call came in. He was scared to death to have his child there, after the information that John Malcolm had given him. He called in a Department marker and had an officer standing guard at all times with Ryan. He picked up Marion and they sat in the visitors' lounge, waiting for news about their daughter. Finally, Ed saw a man dressed in green scrubs coming toward them. He helped his wife to her feet and held her around the waist.

"Mr. and Mrs. Delgato?", the doctor asked.

Marion began to shake instantly. "Yes Doctor, we're the Delgato's. How's our daughter?" Ed's voice sounded detached in his head. He felt as though he was dreaming.

"I'm afraid that she is still unconscious. It's hard to tell about head trauma. She could come out tomorrow, next week or next year…maybe never. There is no way of knowing. I'm sorry."

"No!" screamed Marion, her knees went out from under her.

Ed held tightly. "Oh my God," he whispered. His wife looked at him as if he could change what the doctor had just told them, her eyes pleading with him to make their daughter wake up. He felt helpless. His little girl was lying on a hospital bed and there was nothing he could do. Was this a part of a conspiracy? Was it the hand of Damascus? Ed's head spun along with his stomach.

* * *

After the phone went dead, Morgan and James got in the Miata and raced into the city, Morgan making calls to every hospital she could think of along the way. When she found Ryan at the hospital, needless to say it brought back a storm of emotion. She wanted to charge through the doors and beat anyone she could find…for Laura…for Ryan…for herself.

On arrival, Morgan and James flung open the emergency doors, turning heads in the waiting room. They didn't notice the people looking at them and pointing, whispering. Morgan zeroed in on the admissions desk. Halfway there, Ed intercepted her. He grabbed her arm and spun her around facing him. He could see that she was angry and upset. Laura had died there. "Morgan," Ed said. James was standing beside her, his attention still on the admissions desk. "Mr. Delgato, where is Ryan?" she asked.

"She's resting…" Ed didn't know how to tell her the news. He put his arms around her and whispered. "Ryan is in…a coma. They don't know…if…"

Morgan tried to pull away, but Ed pulled her tighter. "No!" Morgan cried out. James shot a look at Ed, who gave him a firm nod to indicate what he had just said was true. James cupped his hands over his face. He couldn't believe everything that had happened in just a few days. The woman who lay in a bed somewhere in one of the emergency rooms had saved his life. Now he was praying for hers. He looked between his fingers at the waxed floor for answers. There were none.

Morgan took a shaky breath. "How did this happen?" she asked, still with her face against Ed's jacket.

"The police said that they think the truck driver couldn't see Ryan through the heavy fog." Ed loosened his hold, took her by the shoulders and fixed his eyes on hers. "The truck driver's being questioned, but they think it was just an accident…a stupid accident."

Morgan's face was tear stained. She took James' hand, then they hugged.

Ed moved back over to where his wife sat and crouched in front of her. "It's going to be all right, Mar. We have to show some faith." He took her hands in his.

She looked down at him. "That's our only child, Ed. If something should happen to her, I don't know if I could take it."

She was crying out the words. Ed dropped his head against his chest.

James and Morgan joined the Delgato's in the waiting room. Morgan placed her hand on Marion's. "I'm so sorry, Mrs. Delgato. We just want you to know that we love her too, and we're here if you need us." Morgan's voice was gentle and sincere. Marion never looked up; she simply nodded. Morgan leaned back into the sofa and stared at the admissions desk. That was where she had last seen Laura alive. This was the first time that she'd been back since that day. She scrutinized each doctor and nurse as they walked by. Were they there when Laura died, she wondered.

"I've called for security," Ed said. "I don't want Ryan alone after everything that's happened. He looked at his wife for approval. Marion squeezed his hand, letting him know that she agreed.

"I'm worried," Morgan said. "Damascus is not going to take it lightly that James escaped." Ed held his finger to his lips and cast his eyes toward Marion, making it clear that he did not want to upset her further.

James patted Morgan's leg. Together they stared down the hall, wondering about their friend.

Ryan Delgato

Ryan regained consciousness under a fragrant umbrella of pine trees. Sitting up, she surveyed her surroundings. Nothing looked familiar. She didn't remember how she had gotten to the forest. Did she meet James and Morgan at her parents' cabin? Ryan patted herself down, checking her body; no missing parts, no broken bones…good. None of the trees or terrain looked like the foliage around the cabin that she knew so well. As a child she and her mother and father would take holiday trips to the mountains. With exploring fingertips Ryan felt the cool metal revolver inside her jacket and relief washed over her. She stood, brushed herself off and slowly turned one hundred and eighty degrees. Still nothing was familiar. Pulling out her gun, she started down a trail that looked to be well used by horseback riders. After several hours, she knew that she was nowhere near the cabin. The fruit trees, nuts, berries and waterfalls did not exist that she was aware of. She came upon a campsite and, bending down, she felt the charred timbers…still warm. Ryan was not far behind a group of people, but what sort of people were they? She then noticed two parallel drag marks. They reminded her of the Native American sling, used to carry their wounded. She scratched her head. Ryan decided to walk through the night and catch up to the people, whoever they were. Perhaps they could shed some light on where she was.

Laura, Tom and Marti

Waking to a crisp sunrise, Damitree sat and watched the sun come over the horizon. Starling, not wanting to disturb him, let some time pass before she went to his side and said, "I want to thank you for rescuing me the other day."

"It was nothing," he said softly.

"You, my friend are much too modest," Starling said, putting her head on his shoulder. "If it were not for you, Damitree, I don't think I would be sitting here right now." He stared straight ahead at the sunrise, blushing slightly.

When Laura rose to greet the day, something was amiss. She wondered if it was because they were just a day from home. She helped Marti prepare coffee and breakfast for the others. After eating and washing the dishes in the nearby stream, they began to pack the bedrolls and gear.

"One more day," Tom said with excitement.

"I can't wait to take a hot bath," Marti chimed as she mounted her horse. Laura was the last to swing into the saddle. Just as she shoved a foot in the stirrup, she heard something behind her. She pulled her boot out and turned in the direction of the rustling bushes.

Tom saw that Laura's attention was suddenly in the trees. "Hey, did you hear something?" he whispered. She looked at him and nodded. Carefully he dismounted along with Marti, Damitree, and Starling. They stood looking into the forest. Marti saw a flash, or a reflection, come from the grove of pines. She pointed to the area. Tom cautiously walked in the direction Marti's finger pointed to.

Out of the tree line came Ryan, both hands gripping her revolver. With gun aimed right at them, she came into the clearing. "Where are we?" Ryan asked. Laura recognized her right away. She knew that Ryan probably had no idea where she was nor what was going on.

"It's Delgato," Laura whispered.

Marti walked alongside Tom and Laura. "No need for the firearm," Tom said, his eye fixed on Ryan's gun. "My name is Tom. This is Marti, Damitree, Starling and Laura." Tom spoke slowly and pointed to each person as he introduced them. "Now, could you please lower the gun?" he asked.

Ryan did but with reservation. She held it in her right hand pointing down at the ground. "Laura, that sounds familiar," Ryan said, with lines across her forehead. She knew the name, but felt confused. As hard as she tried to search her mind nothing came. She dared not get any closer to the group and held her position.

"Where are we?" she asked again. Tom stepped closer to her.

"Limboshia, we are in Limboshia. A day outside the Elders Valley."

"Limboshia," Ryan repeated. This, too, was something that was familiar, but why couldn't she remember. She tired to shake off the dream-like state she was in, "I don't know of any town called Limboshia…I…" Her voice caught in her throat.

"It's not a town, it's a place. Look, why don't we sit for a minute and we'll explain." Laura said.

"What's to explain? I just want to know how to get back to San Francisco." Ryan's voice sounded irritated.

"Your name is Delgato, isn't it?" Laura asked the gun-toting stranger.

"How do you know…my…" she couldn't force herself to form the rest of the sentence.

"You know my name, Delgato. I'm Morgan's lover. You're disorientated, and I haven't got time to explain everything. We need to get the hell out of here and back to our territory." Laura said, hoping that she didn't sound too cold.

"Morgan's lover…oh God, I remember. I was on my way to meet Morgan and James. I got in a wreck. The next thing I recall was waking up in the trees." Ryan's body was shaking, not from fear, but from shock. This is what Anusca Damitree was talking about. Ryan dropped to the ground against her will. Gravity pulled relentlessly until she succumbed.

"Delgato," Laura said, "we've been watching you. We know that you've been working with Damitree's mother, his sister, Jennifer Collins, James, and Morgan…right?"

Ryan nodded. Her hand lay limp in her lap, barely holding the gun. She looked down at it. "I remember," she said, staring at the revolver. "I left the office. My Dad had John Malcolm cuffed to the chair, waiting for his friends to show up." Ryan shot a look at Laura. "I can't believe all that Anusca told us is true." She shook her head.

"We need to keep moving — we're in danger here." Laura said. "You can ride with me." Laura pointed to her horse. Ryan knew she had to go with them. Laura mounted and then reached for Ryan's hand. Ryan stood and walked over to the horse. She shoved a foot in the stirrup and grabbed Laura's hand, swinging up into the saddle. As they rode, Laura explained what happened in Limboshia. She also told her about Damitree and how he was a hero in their eyes. "Damitree's mother saw one of Morgan's sculptures and knew that he was going to help. She called you the force of three." Laura smiled, knowing that Morgan had received all the messages through the statues. Laura looked at Ryan. "Morgan is something, isn't she?"

"She sure is," Ryan said, smiling. "I know how much she loves you. Morgan is trying to let go, since Anusca told her about Limboshia. She advised Morgan to let you move on and go do what you were destined to do."

Ryan felt strange talking to Laura. It was just a day ago she had been with Morgan. Just then, Laura felt Ryan's hands tighten around her waist. She pulled the reins and stopped the horse. She turned to face Ryan. "As Anusca told you, on earth, until the grieving is over, a death is solved, or in your case, you were in an accident, and your body is in a coma, it has not been decided whether you live or die. Your soul is here until…it's decided whether you continue on Earth or go on to another life. I'm sorry, Delgato, There is no easy way to say it. You're a strong woman and I thought you would appreciate the truth." Laura turned back around and kicked gently into the horse's flanks.

Ryan was trying to wrap her mind around what Laura had just told her. "My body is in a coma, laying in the hospital?" Ryan asked pulling a trembled breath.

"Yes," Laura replied.

"My poor parents," Ryan said. She pictured them standing over her bed and her heart dropped.

"It's going to be all right, we adapt quickly here, and in a day or two the emotional pain changes. It becomes more concern for the people we left behind," Laura said sincerely.

As the cool night air crept into the valley, the riders stopped to set up camp. Ryan watched as each person did their job. It amazed her how quickly everything fell in place. She sat between Laura and Damitree. "Your mother is very special, Damitree," Ryan said.

His eyes lit up thinking of her. "Yes, Damitree knows. Thank you for saying to me," he said, smiling.

"That's fantastic!" Tom snorted. "How do you go from a no accent Damascus, to Damitree?"

"Me like accent. Remind me of homeland."

Everyone was in high spirits, knowing that the following day they would be back in the valley

Ryan was trying to deal with her new surroundings. She had been schooled by Anusca. What a rare situation she was in — talking to Laura, the woman Morgan loved. She was also looking at Anusca's son.

Laura took Ryan's hand. "Do you want to see what's happening on Earth?" she asked her.

"You can do that?" Ryan asked in wide-eyed surprise.

"There are a lot of things you can do here that you can't do on Earth," Laura said.

"I don't know if I want to," Ryan said with apprehension. Did she want to see the suffering of her friends and family? On the other hand, of she didn't, not knowing would drive her crazy. Laura held out her hand to Ryan. She took it and they faced one another.

"Now close your eyes, Delgato, and clear your mind. It will come to you like a dream." Laura's voice was soothing and gentle.

Ryan saw a light slowly come from behind her eyes, fuzzy silhouettes of people. They became clearer. They stood in a room with shiny floors. It was a hospital waiting room.

Mercy General Hospital

A tall, slender man in his late fifties walked, eyes straight ahead, down hall of the Intensive Care Unit. His slightly graying temples gave him a distinguished appearance. He acknowledged nurses with a nod as his gentle green eyes focused on the waiting room ahead. His job was not easy, not glamorous. As he neared the Delgato's, his arrival was announced by his squeaky rubber-soled shoes.

"How's our daughter?" Ed asked. Marion held tight to his arm, looking frail and distraught.

The doctor looked at the chart he carried. "I've been in medicine a long time, and I will never understand comas. As much as medicine has progressed, I'm afraid we still know nothing about them. They are too unpredictable." Continuing to turn pages, he said, "I wish I could tell you that she will wake up, but the truth of the matter is that we don't know…if, or when, she will. All we can do is monitor the situation and pray." He closed the chart and put his arm to his side. A heavy sigh escaped him as he ran his hand over his stubble chin. "I'm sorry. I wish I could tell you more," he concluded, unable to look at the Delgato's emotional faces. Morgan and James blinked in shock, silently. As the doctor turned toward the admissions desk, a gurney crashed through the emergency doors with E.M.T.'s on either side. They ran past the Delgato's, James, and Morgan, who looked up and watched as the gurney
shot past them.

Pontis and Reese

Pontis called Reese after he had received the call from Damascus, and they agreed to meet at the Law Office, which was closed for a few days. Pontis paced across the indoor-outdoor carpet as he waited for his friend to arrive. He feared for their lives. How were they going to get out of this mess? He had no idea. What could have gone wrong at the villa between John and James, he wondered. He couldn't get the vision of James lying in the pool of blood out of his mind. He wanted to go to the police.

Just as the notion crossed his mind, Reese walked in out of breath. "Sorry it took me so long. I had to park down the hill," he said. He was wearing a cotton T-shirt, jeans and sneakers, unlike the usual suit and tie he wore to the office.

"What did Damascus say when he called you?" Reese asked, still trying to catch his breath as he sat in one of the lobby chairs.

"He wanted to know where the hell James and John were, like I had the faintest idea," Pontis said with an annoyed tone. Reese wiped the sweat off his forehead with the hem of his shirt. "And you told him that?" he asked.

Pontis shot a look at Reese. "I told him that I didn't know where they were. I sure as hell didn't tell him that I hung up on John when he called for help," Pontis said, biting his lower lip.

"I can't blame you for that," Reese said, fanning himself with a magazine off the lobby table.

"We need to go to the police," Pontis said.

"John Malcolm *is* the police!" Reese exclaimed.

"I know, I know. But we have to do something. I can't live like this any longer. I'm tired of looking over my shoulder," Pontis said, with his head in his hands. He felt helpless and worn out. He was tired of fighting.

Reese stood and walked over to his friend. "What if John killed James Peterson?" Reese's face had a frightened expression. His attention turned suddenly to a car passing on the street. The motor was loud enough to catch him off guard. He watched it drive past, then threw the magazine he'd been fanning himself with back on the table. "Pontis, we have to come up with a plan," he said, sitting back in the chair.

Pontis raised his hands in futility. The car that Reese had seen earlier was back — the driver slowed the car and gunned the engine as it stood in neutral. Then through the open window an arm extended; attached to it was a .45 pistol. Pontis stood frozen, staring at the vehicle.

Reese was about to get up from the chair when the first round was fired. The plate glass window blew into the office, showering Reese's back as he dove to the floor. Pontis shielded his face with his arms, as the second round hit him in the left shoulder, throwing him on the desk.

"Pontis! Get down on the floor!" Reese yelled. The third shot hit Pontis in the right leg and knocked him off the desk. Glass and gunpowder filled the air. Reese tried to crawl to where Pontis was lying, when the other two windows were blown in. The next round ricocheted off the floor, hitting Reese in the hip. "Fuck!" he yelled, grabbing the place where the bullet hit. "Pontis!" he screamed again.

There was no answer. His friend lay in a puddle of blood and glass. Reese continued to crawl through the shards, hands and clothes shredded. When he reached the desk, he pulled the phone line until the cradle fell in front of him. He dialed 911, then reached out to his friend. "Pontis?" Again no answer. He grabbed the back of his friend's shirt and rolled him over. Still breathing. He laid his head on Pontis' chest to listen for a heart beat. There was a ringing in his ears. Or was it sirens, he wondered.

* * *

The Villa

After returning, Damascus had made several calls. The Brotherhood had been instructed to kill Pontis and Reese, and so they believed they had. Damascus had been drinking too much, as he usually did when first taking a new host body. He had little discipline and had to switch often to a new host; it seemed he had a weakness for alcohol, drugs, women, and gambling. Even in Limboshia he would forget the 72-hour deadline to make contact with the host body and lose it. In the case of the coma victim, he or she would survive, and could never be taken by Damascus again. This is where the Fire Angels were created centuries ago. In Damascus' lack of self-control, he was building an army against himself. The victim would wake with special powers, or physic abilities, such as being able to contact and talk to the other side. This is why the Star Scrolls were so important to Damascus — the list of angels was contained there. When Damascus received word that Pontis and Reese were dead, he laughed and poured another drink at the villa.

* * *

Mercy General Hospital

Ed and Marion held one another while Morgan and James watched the gurneys pass. "Oh, my God!" James yelled. "Those are the two men that were with John Malcolm when he kidnapped me!" His face was flushed.

Ed looked over at the beds being wheeled through the hall, then to James."Are you sure those are the men?"

"Those are the guys. I'll never forget those faces," James' body shook at the sight of Pontis and Reese.

* * *

Laura, Tom and Marti

The night air carried the smell of pine, and the moonlight glimmered through the trees, casting shadows on the ground. Everyone sat enjoying the fire. Ryan thought about her parents and Morgan.

"How are you doing, Delgato?" Laura asked.

"I'm all right. I was thinking about my folks," she sighed.

"That's the hardest thing about being here, we all feel so helpless."

"How do you deal with it?" Ryan asked.

"Once you start making friends and start a life, it gets easier. We're all waiting for our next life, so we make the best of it."

"You mentioned that earlier, the next life thing," Ryan said, not knowing what to think.

"Delgato, you've heard of reincarnation, right?" Laura queried.

"Of course, but to tell you the truth…I never put much stock in it." She laughed nervously. Laura knew that Ryan was questioning a lot of her beliefs, just as she did when she had arrived. The others talked amongst themselves about the trip in the morning. They would be back in the valley…home. Starling was anxious to return to the Gateway, located east of the valley in the mountains. The Gateway was a portal, hidden inside the caverns and caves deep inside the mountains. She missed the security of the caves. All the Elders traveled through the Gateway, and many times she watched them go to Earth and other faraway destinations. The Elders had no need for host bodies, they had fulfilled their karmic debt and could travel freely about the universe. On Earth they were seen as ghosts or apparitions. The Elders would relocate the Star Scrolls within the caverns to ensure their safety. After talking with Laura for hours, Ryan drifted off to sleep. Laura covered her with a blanket and returned to her friends.

"How's Delgato doing?" Marti asked.

"She's going to be all right. She's worried about her parents, and the other people who love her. I think she'll be fine tomorrow," Laura replied.

"Delgato and her people performed beautifully on Earth with the rescue," Starling said.

Laura was proud of Morgan and James, but she knew they had put themselves in danger. "We didn't do bad ourselves," Laura said.

"We do great!" Damitree said, fist in the air.

"Yes, my friend…we do great. I think we should get some sleep. We still have a full day of travel tomorrow," Starling said, as she straightened out her bedroll.

"How's your head?" Laura asked her. Starling touched the dressing lightly.

"I'm all right, but I'll be better once we're home."

"We all will." Laura smiled. Marti threw a couple logs on the fire so that they would sleep in warmth during the night. She was happy. Her friend was safe and soon, very soon, they would be home.

Delgato and Delgato Investigations

Frank O'Malley, a retired friend of Ed's, and Eric Delani, Ryan's old partner, were watching John Malcolm while Ed went to the hospital. Before Ed left he had called the F.B.I, who were to send an agent to take custody of John. After some time had passed, a call indeed came in. An agent was on the way up to take John to F.B.I. headquarters.

"Well, John, your ride is here," Frank said. He was relieved to finally get John into the hands of the proper authorities. Frank decided to call Ed and let him know that John would soon be leaving. "Ed, this is Frank over at your office. How's it going with Ryan?" Everyone loved Ryan, and Frank was no exception.

"There's no change at this point," Ed said. His voice was soft and filled with emotion.

"I'm sorry to hear that, buddy. Our thoughts are with you. Listen, while I have you on the line, the F.B.I. is here to pick up John."

"That's great news," Ed replied. "Make sure all the proper paperwork is filled out, and make sure we have the agent's badge number, will you?"

"Sure thing, Ed. Hang in there. Things will work themselves out." Frank hung up the receiver. Eric Delani could tell by the look on Frank's face things were not good. His heart went out to Ryan. John Malcolm flinched when the knock on the door came.

"Agent White, F.B.I.," the voice said from behind the door. Frank opened the door to find a good looking African-American man standing with his billfold open exposing his badge.

"Hello Agent White. My name is Frank O'Malley, and this is Detective Delani," Agent White's attention turned toward John.

"This is the prisoner I presume?" Frank nodded. He pulled out his set of keys and unlocked John from the chair. Agent White cuffed himself and John together, handed Frank the necessary paperwork and escorted John down the stairs. As John made his way down the long stairwell his mind thought about Damascus; he knew there was nowhere on Earth to hide.

Once Agent White and John reached the car, the second agent opened the back door. John lunged for White's gun, put the revolver to his own head and pulled the trigger. Brain matter sprayed the car and the second agent. They stood in amazement — it had happened so quickly. John's body fell to the sidewalk, pulling Agent White behind him. Frank heard the gunshot and ran to the window.

"My God," he whispered. Agent White pulled himself off of Malcolm's dead body. His eyes could not help but stare at the remaining part of John's head. The smell of gunpowder, and car exhaust burned White's nostrils. His ears filled with an eerie silence.

The Villa

Damascus had been drinking all day at the villa. He wondered how everything had gotten so out of hand, and blamed himself for the miniscule amount of faith he'd placed in the people he had around him. As he searched the bar for another bottle of Scotch, the phone rang.

"Damascus?" the female voice asked.

"Speaking," he replied, but his thoughts were of Scotch.

"This is nurse Whittingham, at Mercy General,"

"What the hell do you want, Nancy?" he interrupted.

"I'm sorry to disturb you, sir, but Pontis and Reese were just brought in to the emergency ward."

Damascus stood. "They're still alive?" he asked.

"I'm not sure. They are shot up pretty bad."

"Call me when you find anything out," Damascus said, and hung the phone up. Finally he found the bottle he was looking for. "Fucking idiots!" he bellowed. He unscrewed the cap and threw it across the room. "They can't even kill two lousy men!" He fell in the chair and passed out.

Mercy General Hospital

Ed had still not heard about Malcolm. As far as he knew, John was in the custody of the F.B.I. Foremost on his mind was his daughter. He needed to figure out what to do about the men that James had recognized. Marion was asleep on the sofa in the waiting room. James and Morgan were huddled together talking about the two men that had aided in his kidnapping. Ed walked over to them. "James, I think you and Morgan should go back to the cabin. It's not safe here."

Morgan's head snapped in Ed's direction. "Mr. Delgato, as long as Ryan is here I'm not going anywhere." Her voice was stern. James agreed with her. Ed was fighting a losing battle.

"O.K," he said, rubbing the back of his neck. "Let me make a few calls and get some more backup over here. But you two don't leave my sight, understood?" He pulled out his cell and started to dial. His next move was to find out the name of the men that kidnapped James. Ed walked over to the admissions desk to find a gray haired nurse with glasses perched at the end of her nose.

"Can I help you sir?" she asked in a monotone voice.

"Yes, I would like to see Dr. Lang if I might," Ed said, his eyes searching the log for the names of the men just admitted.

"I'm sorry, but Dr. Lang is in the E.R," she said. Then returned to her paperwork. Ed saw the log: William Reese and Robert Pontis. "Thank you, nurse." Ed walked with some satisfaction back to the waiting room. He pulled out his notepad and wrote the names down. Then he called to his buddy at the Department and gave the names for him to run. In the meantime his two officers showed for duty. He met them at the door and filled them in. James was amazed at how quickly Ryan's father had put the word out. Ed called his old friend Lieutenant Thompson at the downtown precinct.

"Thompson here."

"Hey Lieutenant, Ed Delgato here. How're things at the station?" Ed tried to sound his usual self, even though his little girl was lying in a coma down the hall.

"Ed! Nice to hear your voice. How's the P.I. business?" Thompson's thick New York accent made Ed smile. "Can't complain, Lieutenant. The reason I'm calling is I need some info on a couple guys that were brought into the hospital. First name is William Reese, and the second name is Robert Pontis. See what you can scrape up for me, will you?" Thompson mumbled the names as he wrote them down.

"Ed, I'll give you a call as soon as I know something." The phone went dead.

Morgan and James were outside. Morgan was smoking a cigarette. Ed fished one out of his own pack. "My friend downtown will call us as soon as he finds anything out about our two kidnappers." Ed slumped against the wall — he was showing signs of fatigue. He lit his cigarette and took a long pull.

"What happens after we find out who they are?" James asked.

Ed rubbed his eyes; they felt like sandpaper. He knew he'd have to go home soon and get some sleep. "Well, son, we turn them over to the proper authorities and let the justice system decide." Ed realized he was too tired to smoke and stubbed his cigarette out. They returned to the waiting room and sat down.

"James, I want you and Morgan to go to her house, I'm sending two officers with you...clear?" Ed asked. James nodded his head yes. An officer came into the waiting room and headed straight for Ed.

"Chief Delgato?" the young rookie asked.

"I'm retired, son," he said smiling.

"I know you are, sir. The Lieutenant sent me down with this. Said it was important." The officer handed a packet to Ed, turned and left.

Ed glanced through the papers and grinned. "Well, it looks like we've got ourselves a couple a lawyers." He said, turning the folder toward James. "Are these the men that kidnapped you?"

James turned white and nodded. "Morgan I need you and James to go to your house now. We'll talk in the morning." Ed's emotions were spent. He needed to take his wife home and get a good night's sleep.

Morgan took James by the arm. "O.K, Mr. Delgato, we'll see you in the morning. It's going to all right, I just know it will." Morgan nodded at motioned to the officers that they were ready to go. They followed Morgan and James to the parking lot and into the night.

Ed closed the folder, took a deep breath and went to collect his wife. He reached out his hand to her. "Come dear, let's go home. There's nothing we can do tonight. We can come back first thing in the morning." Marion didn't argue. She got up and they walked arm in arm out of the hospital.

* * *

As the sun rose over Morgan's house, the telephone rang. "Hello?" Morgan's voice still had sleep in it.

"Morgan? This is Rada Damitree, how's Ryan doing?"

Morgan sighed. "Not too good I'm afraid, she's in a coma."

Rada gasped at the other end. "Oh my God, that's terrible! How's James?"

"He's all right," Morgan said, as she watched him shuffle to the coffee pot. Last night we were at the hospital, James and I were standing in the waiting room when two men were rushed by on gurneys. It turned out that they were with Malcolm when he kidnapped James." Morgan took a sip of coffee.

"That's crazy!"

"So Ed Delgato is checking them out. We should know something today."

"Listen if you need my mother or me, you call us…O.K?"

"I'll call. You say hello to your mom for James and me, O.K?"

"I will. Talk to you later." Rada said and hung up the phone.

James sat at the breakfast table heavy eyed.

"What time is it?" he asked, trying to bring the clock into focus.

"Seven forty-five," Morgan replied.

"Do you think it's too early to call the Delgato's?" he asked, yawning.

"Yes, I think so," Morgan said, "I want to know who those guys are too. We're going to have to wait until they call us." Morgan said, rubbing her eyes.

Ed and Marion

The Delgato's were having coffee on the deck. Marion had already put a call into the hospital. No change. Ed was reading the paper. "Hey Mar, listen to this: 'Yesterday in the 1000 block of Raymond Street, at the law office of Pontis and Reese, a drive-by shooting was reported.'" Ed looked at his wife. "I still can't believe these guys are lawyers!" He continued to read: "'William Reese and Robert Pontis were rushed to Mercy General with multiple gunshot wounds where they are listed in guarded condition.'" Ed threw the paper down and looked at Marion. "What the hell is going on around here? Lawyers, kidnapping?" Ed's voice was disgusted. Marion flinched when the phone rang. Ed put his hand on her shoulder and picked up the phone. "Hello?"

"Ed? This is Lt. Thompson. I guess you've already seen the morning paper. I have some interesting news. It seems that when these two guys first started out in the law firm, they had second jobs. Then out of nowhere they ran into a lot of money. I checked some leads, and by the looks of it, they got involved with a guy named Galliano, who had them doing some pretty shady contracts.

I'll bet if we dig a little deeper we'll find that this Galliano is behind the shooter."

Ed had as close to a smile on his face as he had had in days. "Thanks Lieutenant, I owe you one." Ed hung up the receiver and told Marion what he had learned. They got dressed and headed for the hospital. When Ed and Marion arrived, Ed's cell phone rang. It was Frank O'Malley.

"Ed?" Frank asked.

"Yeah, Frank, what's going on?" Ed could tell by the tone in Frank's voice that something was wrong.

"Ed, when Agent White picked up John late yesterday, there was an incident. As they approached the car, John grabbed one of the officer's guns and blew his head all over the street."

There was a long silence. Ed didn't know what to say. "My God, Frank, he must have really been afraid of this Damascus fellow." Marion looked at her husband. She could tell by his voice that something was terribly wrong. She pulled on his shirt sleeve. Ed looked at her and closed his eyes. He hung up the phone and shoved it in his coat pocket. "John Malcolm committed suicide late last night."

Marion grabbed tightly to his arm. "How awful," she said softly. She didn't even know how to feel anymore, so much had happened. She held tight to Ed. He looked so tired. She couldn't remember the last time he looked so worn out. Ed put a call in to James and Morgan.

Laura, Tom and Marti

Laura awoke to the sounds of birds singing in the trees she'd slept beneath. She lay looking at the majestic pines, watching the breeze blow the branches. Sweet grass filled the air. She wished she could lie there forever, enjoying the bliss of nature and its sounds. She finally raised up on one elbow, to see Ryan standing at the edge of camp overlooking the valley. She wondered what was going through Ryan's mind. Filling a large wooden bowl with water Laura washed her face. She came alongside Ryan quietly and drank in the beauty of the valley below with her. "Good morning, Delgato," she whispered.

Ryan turned her head. "Good morning. I don't think I have ever seen anything as beautiful in all my life." Ryan's attention turned back to the valley. She thought about all the time she had wasted in the precinct, closed up in rooms. She was feeling regrets about the choices she had made in her life.

"I should have done things differently in my life," she said in a whisper. Laura took her hand.

"Delgato, you chose to be a warrior, to stand for what is just in the world. That is an honorable life that you chose. Where would we be without people like you?"

Ryan considered this. "But Laura, I didn't take time out to enjoy nature, my parents…" Her words fell short. The chill in the air bit at her, and she pulled her jacket tighter to her body.

"Delgato, you have time to enjoy nature right now. Your parents are where they are supposed to be, just as you are. There are no mistakes in the universe." Laura wrapped her arms around Ryan. "Soon we will be home. You can live with Tom, Marti, and myself. Now let's go make some coffee and get these lazy bums up."

The Villa

Damascus woke to the drink he had had in his hand the previous night. It spilled on his chest. "Son of a bitch!" he yelled. His head was pounding. He smashed the glass against the wall, stood and walked across the room with the sound of splintered furniture crunching under his feet. He had destroyed the villa. Pontis and Reese were still alive, James and John were missing, and to top it off he hadn't heard from the brotherhood. He found the phone on the floor with the receiver off the hook. "Shit!" he hissed. He called one of the men from the Brotherhood. "What the fuck happened? Pontis and Reese are still alive!" Damascus' yelling only made his head pound harder.

"I fired a whole clip into the office!" the man yelled back. "What the hell do you want from all of us, Damascus? Your phone was off the hook all night. We tried to call. John Malcolm blew his brains out last night!" The man's voice was exasperated.

"Saves me the trouble of taking him out myself! Where the hell is James Peterson?" Damascus demanded.

"I don't know where he is. Fuck, I'm tired of this shit!" the man slammed down the phone. Damascus knew that he was losing control of the cult. He had to go back to Limboshia. How long had he been on Earth? He had to clear his mind. Could his 72-hour limit have expired?

Mercy General Hospital

Ed and Marion arrived at the hospital at 10:30 in the morning. The Delgato's went to the admissions desk. "Good morning," he greeted the duty nurse. "How's our daughter?"

Looking up from her paper work with an irritated expression, the nurse answered, "Dr. Lang is on his rounds. As soon as he's done I will have him speak with you." She quickly turned her attention back to the desk.

Just then Ed saw the doctor coming down the hall, and grabbed him by the arm. "Doctor, how's our girl? Can we see her?"

The doctor looked at Ed and his jaw tightened. "I'm afraid that there has not been a lot of change. Although she is off life support, which is good. Of course you can see her. Come with me." The Delgato's followed him down the hall to Ryan's room. They stopped in the doorway, afraid of what they might see.

Dr Lang turned to them. "I want to warn you, she looks pretty bad. When she was ejected from the car, she hit a building." He looked down at his chart. "She has a broken leg, several lacerations on her face and upper torso. The stitches in the facial area are superficial. She's lucky to be alive."

Marion covered her face with her hands and began to weep. Ed pulled her close to him. "It's going to be all right Mar."

The doctor walked to Ryan's bedside, checking her vitals. The Delgato's slowly walked to the side of the bed. Marion gasped and covered her mouth, seeing the extent of the damage to Ryan's face. Tears rolled down Ed's cheeks. He stood and looked at his daughter in disbelief.

"Talk to her," Dr Lang said. "They say that coma victims can hear what's going on around them."

Ed took Ryan's hand in his. "Hey, Sweet Pea, your mom and I are here. You're going to be just fine." Ed motioned with his head for Marion to say something. She walked closer to her daughter's bed. "Hey, sweetie, your dad I are here. Will you wake up for us?" The couple looked at one another. Their daughter was in bad shape. Ed pulled a chair up for his wife to sit in. He stood behind her, thinking about the two lawyers down the hall. "I'll go and get us some coffee, Mar." She patted his hand. Ed left the room. Marion laid her head on the bed, holding her daughter's hand.

Ed moved down the hall quickly, looking in each room as he walked. In the fifth room he saw one of the lawyers. William Reese was staring at the wall in front of him. Ed knocked on the door. No response. Reese's head, arms, and hands were bandaged.

"Mr. Reese, my name is Ed Delgato. I'm a retired Chief of Police." He stepped in and stood next to the bed. Reese looked at Ed. "Mr. Reese, I know this is not a good time for you, but my friend is James Peterson." Reese's eyes darted around the room. "He said that he recognized you as one of the men that kidnapped him from is office." Ed took out a notepad and pencil, pulling up a chair after hanging his jacket on the back of the seat.

Reese nodded. "I was one of the men."

"Was the other man Robert Pontis?" Reese nodded his head yes.

"John Malcolm was also involved, I know that much. How's your friend, Mr. Reese. Have you heard?"

"No, they haven't told me anything. The police came in last night, said we were victims of a drive-by."

Ed smiled. "Do you believe that?"

"No."

"What do you think the shooting was all about?" Just as Ed asked the question his cell phone rang. "Delgato, can I help you?"

"Mr. Delgato, this is Agent White. I was trying to call you all last evening."

Ed looked sheepish. "I had the phone off. My daughter is in the hospital and I didn't want to be disturbed."

"Mr. Delgato, I wanted to make sure that you were informed about John Malcolm," Agent White said.

Ed went into the hall to continue the conversation. "Yes, I was. It's a shame…"

"Yes it is sir. We've got a messy situation on our hands."

Ed leaned against the wall. "I should have had my phone on," Ed said softly.

"There was nothing that you could have done. I just wanted to call and make sure that you were informed, sir. I have to go now." Agent White hung up the phone.

Ed looked at the cell phone, walked back in the room and slipped the receiver back in his pants pocket. "That was Agent White from the F.B.I. He wanted to let me know that John Malcolm committed suicide last night." Ed waited for a response.

Reese turned a shade of green. "Are you kidding me?"

"I'm afraid not," Ed said. "Looks like you two are on your own." Reese fumbled for the glass of water on the bedside table.

"I can't believe that John would kill himself. He was such an egotistical bastard."

Ed raised an eyebrow. "Tell me, Mr. Reese, how is it that two lawyers got involved in a kidnapping?"

Reese set the glass down. "It's very complicated, Mr. Delgato," he whispered. "When Pontis and I first got out of school, we opened the law firm. We had night jobs as security officers on the docks; we had to pay the rent on the office." Reese's head hung to his chest. "We had new wives and we were stretched as far as we could go. One night we met a man coming off a yacht." Reese said, squinting at the window.

"Is the light hurting your eyes?" Ed asked. He nodded. Ed got up and closed the drapes. "You were saying Mr. Reese, that you met a man."

"Yes. He introduced himself as Mr. Galliano," Reese hissed. "I really don't know how to explain it all. The guy's name is Damascus now, and I have a suspicion that it always was. His latest name, however, is Stephane Damitree." Reese grabbed his head. "I know it sounds crazy, but he is some kind of a monster. He is a shape-shifter and runs a cult called 'The Brotherhood.'" Ed was writing as fast as he could, and did not look up. "It sounds like a movie," Reese said. "But I assure you it's not. I was there to witness a lot of strange things."

Ed finally looked up at Reese. "If it makes you feel any better, I got the same story from John."

Reese was trembling. "I'm sure that's why he committed suicide. Damascus is going to have us all killed."

Ed stood and stretched. "My daughter is down the hall. She was in a car accident. I don't know if it was coincidental or not, but she helped rescue James from Damascus' villa." Ed flipped the pages of his notepad. "I've been around a few years, and seen some pretty strange things…I don't know what to make of all this, but I keep hearing the same story." Ed rubbed his forehead. "I know that this Damascus is a very dangerous man. Mr. Reese, would you mind if I stop by later and talk to you a little more?"

"Sure, Mr. Delgato, it feels good to get this off my chest."

Ed closed the notepad and slipped it back in his jacket. He walked down the hall to the waiting room and bought two cups of coffee from the vending machine. He slowly returned to his daughter's room. "Here's your coffee, Mar," he whispered. She didn't respond.

James and Morgan

On the way to the hospital, James read the article about Pontis and Reese as Morgan drove. "I don't think these guys were victims of a drive-by shooting," James said.

"I don't either. I think they were in trouble along with John because you escaped. That's more likely." James agreed. He folded the paper and rested it in his lap. "What about Ryan? Do you think Damascus tried to kill her?" he asked in a small voice.

"I just don't know, James." Morgan said, pulling the car to a stop at a light, she laid her head on the steering wheel. "I don't know what to think…"

James put his hand on her shoulder. "I know, honey, I don't either." He tapped her. "The light's green."

Morgan pushed the accelerator, blowing out a heavy sigh. As they continued to drive toward the hospital, Morgan's cell phone rang, startling them. Morgan flipped it open and said, "Hello?"

"Morgan? Jennifer Collins here. How are you?"

Morgan navigated the car around the corner into the hospital parking lot. "I'm all right. James and I just got to the hospital to check on Ryan," she said, her voiced choked.

"Poor thing," Jennifer said. "Her parents must be beside themselves."

Morgan put the car in park and shut off the engine. "Her mom is taking it really hard, and her dad is trying to be strong."

"Morgan, I was at the office late last night and something came across the A.P. wire…"

Morgan cut her off. "A.P. wire?"

"Associated Press," Jennifer said. "It was about John Malcolm. He killed himself."

There was silence on both ends of the line. Morgan looked over to James and covered the phone. "John Malcolm's dead," she whispered. James' mouth hung agape.

"I'm sure you and James heard about the drive-by shooting," Jennifer said.

"Yes, we did. James and I were at the hospital when they brought them in. James recognized the two men — they were the ones who were with John the day he was kidnapped," Morgan said, her voice excited.

"Are you pulling my leg? What are the chances of you two being there at that exact moment?"

"Ed Delgato ran the names of the two guys through the station, and it turns out they're lawyers. I don't know what else he found out. He sent us home with two officers last night, so I'm a little scared. All these things are connected to Damascus." Her voice trembled.

"Listen," Jennifer said. "I'm going to pick up Anusca and Rada right now. We'll meet you at the hospital."

"O.K, see you then," Morgan replied.

"John killed himself?" James asked.

"Yes."

"That doesn't make me feel too safe. John dead, the other two shot at, Ryan in a car wreck…" James said, fumbling the newspaper.

"Let's go talk to Ed about it, and check on Ryan," Morgan replied. She stepped out of the car. Seeing the patrol car parked behind them made her feel a little better.

Laura, Tom and Marti

Laughter filled the camp as everyone finished breakfast. Marti was teasing Damitree about the way he pushed her in front of the hired hands at the Pasture House.

"You didn't really push me — I had to show you how," she snorted, as she acted it out to everyone.

Damitree blushed again. "I just push a little, I not want to break you."

Ryan smiled. She saw that these people were family. It was the first time she'd smiled since her arrival. This did not go unnoticed by Tom.

"Delgato, were you scared when you rescued James?" he asked.

"Sure! I'd be a fool not to be, but it sure felt good to shove that gun in Malcolm's head." She said, grinning.

"I'm glad you're on our team," Laura said.

"From what I'm hearing, you had quite the rescue here," Ryan said.

"Sure did!" Tom exclaimed.

"That bastard Damascus is really going to be pissed when he finds out everyone has escaped," Ryan stated. Everyone agreed.

"Delgato, will you help me fold these tarps?" Laura asked. She was glad to. "We need to get a move on. In a few hours we'll be home!" Marti yelped gleefully. The pace of the camp quickened.

As they made their way across the valley, they saw the caverns where Starling lived. "Starling, this time if someone comes and asks you to come out of the caverns to help them…" Marti said.

"I'm not going to fall for that one again," Starling said sheepishly.

She was new to the Gateway post and, being a compassionate soul, she trusted too easily. Ryan listened to the conversation and had many questions. The detective inside was crying out for answers, but she knew that when the time was right she would be told everything. The change inside surprised her; things felt so different in Limboshia. Laura was right when she had told her she would adapt quickly. The realm agreed with her. She felt no need to push; she felt calm and confident. Laura was riding next to her on horseback.

"You sure don't ask many questions for a detective," she said, smiling. "You know Delgato, when I first arrived I was a reporter. Now I can't even imagine that life. Things change here, your perspective is completely different." Ryan understood. Laura continued smiling as they rode. She knew that something wonderful was about to take place.

"There're the caverns!" Starling yelled, standing in the stirrups.

An Elder named Samone came out of the opening. "Starling!" she chimed. "My sweet Starling!"

Starling jumped down from her horse and ran to the waiting arms. "Samone! It's so good to see you!" Starling buried her face in Samone's chest. Ryan was in awe of how beautiful Samone was; she thought she looked a lot like Rita Hayworth. The breeze from the canyon gently blew the white gown and the silver hair of Samone as she embraced Starling. "I've missed you so much," Starling whispered in her ear.

Samone released her to greet the other riders. "You all have done so well. Because of your bravery we've prepared a feast in honor of your return." She led them down a small hill into the trees, where several attendants waited, to take the horses and gear.

"There is a hot spring just over there," Samone said, pointing. "You can clean up before we eat." She walked with them and sat at the edge of the spring, watching clothes come off as each one jumped into the steaming water.

Ryan sat next to her. "You are Delgato, our newest member?" Samone asked.

"Yes," Ryan answered softly.

"Delgato, you must try not to worry about your parents. Everything is as it should be," she said, as she watched everyone play in the water like school children.

Ryan couldn't help but stare at her. "You're so beautiful….just like I thought an Angel would look."

Samone smiled. "And you Delgato, are just what *I* thought an Angel would look like," She took Ryan by the hand. "You are with family here, my dear. These people whom you have been traveling with are special…they have earned their wings. They are the future Elders."

Ryan looked at them in the hot spring. Marti was holding Tom's head under the water. Ryan started laughing.

Samone joined her. "I know it's hard to believe, looking at them now, but…" Samone began to laugh harder, causing her words to trail off. She and Ryan watched as Damitree cannon-balled into the water, grinning ear to ear like a Cheshire cat. Marti finally let Tom up for air.

"Jeez Marti…you could have…" Marti slapped him on the back.

"Could have what? Killed you? Someone already beat me to it!" she yelped. They both started splashing one another. Ryan was a little shocked that they joked about dying.

"Delgato," Starling said, "you should take a quick dip so that you can put on a clean robe." Ryan did as she was told. The attendants brought fresh white gowns for everyone. Samone announced dinner. The table was filled with pig, chicken, beef, moral and coral mushrooms, fruits, and homemade breads.

"My gosh!" Marti exclaimed, "This is wondrous!"

After the group was seated, Samone sat at the head of the table. "When I sent you all on the journey to rescue Starling, I knew that you were the finest warriors. You have made me proud." From behind Samone arched the most magnificent wings. She was beautiful. Everyone gasped at how fantastic the sight was. She raised a glass of wine.

"You have earned your wings. With this comes much responsibility. But we will speak of this later. Now we will celebrate the return of my children." She sat and watched them talk amongst themselves.

"You are about to make a very important decision, my dear," she said to Ryan, sipping her wine. "Damascus is trapped on Earth right this minute. He missed his 72-hour deadline to return to Limboshia. He needs a body to host his soul." Samone set her glass down. Suddenly it grew quiet around the table.

"Delgato, it was written long ago that this day would come, that you would come. Damascus will try to take your body from the hospital until he can find a more suitable one." The group gasped with fear.

"You are a brave soul and the universe needs warriors like you to protect the people of Earth." Ryan's face showed Samone that she understood what was coming.

"Delgato, you have choices. You can return to Earth and continue life as it was. Or you can choose to stay here and allow another to take your place."

Ryan knew there was only one choice that she could make.

Mercy General Hospital

Anusca, Rada, and Jennifer arrived at the hospital. They sat with Morgan and James in the waiting room. Anusca sat twisting her handkerchief in her hands.

"Mama, why are you so nervous?" Rada asked, concerned.

"Something bad coming," she said.

"Bad?" James asked.

"Evil…is near," Anusca replied. Just then Marion and Ed walked into the room. Morgan stood and took Marion's arm, leading her to the sofa.

"Ryan's condition hasn't changed," Ed stated.

"Can we go see her?" Morgan questioned.

"The doctor said two at a time," Ed replied. Morgan looked at James.

"How about you and I go first?" He nodded and followed her down the hall. Morgan was afraid to enter the room. James held tight to her arm. As they slowly approached the bed, both held even tighter to one another at the sight of Ryan's face.

"She looks so small and fragile," Morgan whispered, as she sat in the chair next to the bed. James stood behind her.

Ed greeted everyone on the waiting room. Then his attention turned toward the emergency room doors as they opened.

Anusca covered her mouth with her small hands. "It's Damascus," she said in a muffled voice.

Rada spun around to look and gasped. "Oh my God, it is him." She backed away from the doorway.

"That's him?" Ed asked Anusca.

"Yes, he is here to claim body….look, he very sick,"

"He's here to take Ryan!" Jennifer screamed.

"Over my dead body!" Ed shouted. He called on his cell phone to the officers outside. "I need you boys in here. Now!" He shoved the phone back in his pocket. Damascus stood swaying in the entry way, his shoulders slumped. Ed could see the two officers coming up behind Damascus and held his hand up for them to stop.

"Ed, what are you doing?" Marion asked.

"Let me handle this, Marion." He started to walk toward the large man. Damascus grabbed a hold of the doorjamb.

"You cannot stop me. Step aside." His voice lacked its usual commanding tone.

"His body is dying," Anusca said with tears in her voice. That was her son, and she knew that she would never see him again. Rada also began to cry at the sight of her bother's worn-out body.

"What will happen to Damascus when your son's body dies?" Jennifer asked. She felt a need to be direct. It was obvious what was happening.

"He will return to Limboshia for a period of time, until he is able to shape-shift into a new host," Anusca said, standing. Rada took her mother's arm, Jennifer joined them. Damascus took a hesitant step toward Ed. His legs went weak. Ed motioned for the officers to come in.

* * *

Morgan had her hand on Ryan's. She felt it move. "James! Her hand moved!" James came alongside her. Ryan's eyelids began to flutter.

"Did you see that?!" Morgan yelled.

"Yes!" James exclaimed.

"Ryan! Ryan! Wake up!" Morgan screamed. She touched her face. Ryan's eyes slowly opened.

"Oh, my God!" Morgan said, her hand flying over her mouth.

Ryan's eyes darted around the hospital room. She looked confused.

"You're in the hospital. You had an accident," Morgan said.

"Morgan?" she asked.

"Yes, it's me…"

"Morgan is that really you? Am I really here?" she asked again.

"Yes, you're here."

* * *

Ed ran toward Damascus, tackled him and wrestled him to the ground. The two officers grabbed him and handcuffed his arms behind his back.

"Let me go you S.O.B.'s!" Damascus yelled.

Anusca walked over to where he lie, she knelt beside him. "You animal! You kill my son!"

Damascus turned his head to look at her. “I’ll be back, for you, you old crone!” His eyes suddenly went black. His head thumped to the floor.

Anusca wept over the body that once was her beloved son. The others joined her.

* * *

A new cascade of tears, tears of joy, rolled down Morgan’s cheeks, as it sank in that Ryan was going to recover. “Our kind of love comes but once in a lifetime.” she said to Morgan.

Morgan looked shocked. She turned to James, then back to Ryan.

“What did you say?”

“Our kind of love comes but once in a lifetime,” Ryan repeated.

“Laura?” James asked.

“Yes, James, it’s me.” She said with tears in her eyes. James looked at Morgan, who was in a state of disbelief.

“It’s Laura!” James yelled, grabbing her and starting to laugh.

“How can this be?” Morgan questioned, wiping the tears from her face.

“Ryan gave me her body, so that I could come back and finish what it is that I must do. Morgan, you, James and I have things to do.” Morgan and James clung tightly to Laura. They were all together again. As they fixed their eyes on one another, they knew the battle had just begun.

www.ingramcontent.com/pod-product-compliance
Lightning Source LLC
Chambersburg PA
CBHW030426310726
48979CB00009B/1634/J
9780981919300